The flush Hop
do with the s

The engine growl
slowed. Bear put hi
Her foot was off the peg and reaching for the
ground before she realized what she was doing.
It was instinct—to help balance and connect
with the sweet, sustaining earth.

"Feet up." His deep voice rolled like thunder
through his back and kept going, reverberating
through hers.

"Right. Sorry," she squeaked. They were at the
stop sign corner of King's Highway and Foxen
Canyon Road.

"You're not smiling."

Her lips *were* pulled back from her teeth, but it
wasn't quite a smile. "I'll try."

"Look at it this way. You wanted to push the
envelope, right?"

"Yeah, but I didn't want to fall off it."

"I won't let you fall, Hope." He took a hand from
the grip and patted the arm that was locked
around his waist. "Nothing bad will happen to
you when you're with me. I'll see to it."

Dear Reader,

I never dreamed when I wrote my first book that I'd ever see it in print—much less that it would become a four-book series!

Widow's Grove has become so real to me (and, I hope, to you) that I feel like I could walk downtown to Hollister Drugs and order one of those great shakes that Sin makes. Or run out to The Tippling Widow Winery. And while I'm out there, I could visit Sam in that beautiful Victorian on the hill...

But this story belongs to Bear. I gave him his very own Angel, as you'll see when you turn the page.

Now that the last book has been written, I can tell you that you can visit Widow's Grove! Well, not exactly, but pretty close. I based Widow's Grove on the central California town of Los Olivos. Sadly, you won't find the Bar None or The Farmhouse Café, but you *will* see the Victorians lining the road into town and the flagpole that graces the intersection at the center.

And somewhere, out in those rolling golden hills, is the run-down graying Victorian that began all this so many years ago. I saw it from the back of my husband's motorcycle in the '90s. I wouldn't even know how to find it now, but maybe someday I'll go back, on my own motorcycle, and cruise the back roads until I do.

I'd like that very much.

Laura Drake

PS: I enjoy hearing from readers. You can contact me and sign up for my newsletter through my website, www.lauradrakebooks.com.

LAURA DRAKE

Against the Odds

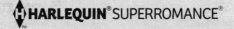
HARLEQUIN®SUPERROMANCE®

Recycling programs
for this product may
not exist in your area.

ISBN-13: 978-0-373-60961-1

Against the Odds

This edition published by arrangement with Harlequin Books S.A.

For questions and comments about the quality of this book, please contact us at CustomerService@Harlequin.com.

® and TM are trademarks of Harlequin Enterprises Limited or its corporate affiliates. Trademarks indicated with ® are registered in the United States Patent and Trademark Office, the Canadian Intellectual Property Office and in other countries.

Printed in U.S.A.

Laura Drake is a RITA® Award–winning author of romance and women's fiction. She's put a hundred thousand miles on her motorcycles, riding the back roads, getting to know the small Western towns that are her books' settings. She gave up the corporate CFO gig to retire in Texas and is currently working on her accent. In the remaining waking hours, she's a wife, grandmother and motorcycle chick.

Books by Laura Drake

HARLEQUIN SUPERROMANCE

Her Road Home
The Reasons to Stay
Twice in a Blue Moon

Visit the Author Profile page
at Harlequin.com for more titles.

CHAPTER ONE

HOPE SANDERSON WOKE to her worst nightmare.

The hand clamped over her mouth smelled of garlic and sweat. She gagged, struggling to get away. A cold circle at her temple made no sense until fetid breath washed over her. "Stop. I have a gun."

She froze, trying to see through the dark, her heart throwing panicky rabbit beats. Her breath, whistling through her nose, was the only sound in the room. If her body hadn't screamed for oxygen, she'd have held it, to hear better. A lone intruder? That rustling in the corner, was that another?

What do they want?

Her muscles were strung so tight she thrummed with their vibration. Clamped knees wouldn't stop them for long, if they intended rape. Her stomach roiled. She locked her jaws tight and swallowed. What would he do if she threw up on him? "Please, no." It came out muffled by his sausage fingers.

"You promise not to scream, I'll let go." A deep scratchy whisper abraded her face.

Her head jerked up and down in a spasm that once started, wouldn't stop.

The offensive hand withdrew, but the cold circle pressed harder. How did it stay cold, held against a head superheated with speeding thoughts?

Menace emanated from corners unlit by the weak moonlight spilling over the sill. A scuff of carpet in one corner, a wheezing breath from the foot of her bed.

Three of them?

Rape wouldn't be the worst they could do. Her throat worked, trying to swallow the drought in her mouth.

"Get up."

When the gunman pushed a finger into the soft underside of her breast, Hope fought the tangle of covers and leaped out of bed. She pulled at her nightgown, trying to cover everything at once, thanking God she wore a floor-length gown. Wishing it covered more.

"Get dressed."

"Wh-what do you want?"

"You're taking us to the bank to make a withdrawal. A very large withdrawal."

A bronchial chuckle from the shadow at the foot of the bed.

They only want money. Of all the scenarios pinging against her skull, that hadn't been one of them.

Her brain shifted from personal torture to bank manager mode. Procedures outlined what to do in the case of a bank robbery, but were woefully silent on home invasion and kidnapping.

"I can't get in." She jumped when the cold circle touched her breast.

"Do you think I'm stupid? You're the manager. You telling me you don't have keys?"

"I mean the vault. It's on time-release. No one can open it until seven." She snuck a look at the red digital display clock. One ten.

He turned to the shadows. "Fuck. You idiot! How could you not have known that?"

"The guy I talked to didn't—"

"Shut up, you fool. Jesus, if there was a brain between the two of you…"

The room fell silent enough to hear the spring wind outside the window, whipping the trees to a frenzy. It was nothing compared to the wind that whipped around the corners of her mind. She lived so carefully, tiptoeing around her own life… to have it end like this? "I—I'm sorry."

"Then we wait. Sit."

The menace in the corner spoke. "I can think of a way to entertain ourselves for a few hours."

Hope's heart convulsed, then throttled up, just short of fibrillation.

The gunman growled, "That is not happening. Now shut the hell up."

"C-can I put on my clothes?"

"Do it here."

She pushed down a whimper that scrabbled at her throat, knowing that if it escaped, it wouldn't be the last, or the loudest. And that would get her killed.

For the first time grateful for the shadows, she fumbled, hands shaking, doing the junior high school gym class quick-change, putting on clothes under her gown, praying all the while that the man with the cold circle could keep his dogs under control. *The power that cold circle could have over my life. Or death.*

When she was dressed, he led the way to her neat living room. He demanded darkness, docility and dead silence. Silence that made her thoughts scratch and skitter like manic rats in an unsolvable maze.

As it turned out, it was possible to be pee-her-pants terrified for five straight hours.

At six thirty, he stood, and with a gun prod, informed her she was driving them to the bank. She led the way to the carport, and her Camry. Black velvet overhead, but a strip of deep charcoal at the eastern edge of the sky was proof this night wouldn't be interminable after all.

Hands in a death grip on the wheel, she drove to Santa Maria precisely, conscious that rather than a rescue, a traffic cop's stop would mean death. His, hers, someone's.

In the shifting spotlights of the streetlamps, she saw her captors for the first time. The gunman beside her was swarthy with a three-day beard, broad nose, narrow eyes topped by a watch cap. In the rearview mirror the bronchial one was extremely thin, his hollow cheeks gray with straggly stubble. The one who'd wanted to be entertained in the bedroom was large, bald and mean-looking—a mug shot poster child.

They're not worried about you identifying them. Hysteria ricocheted through her, looking for a way out.

"Park around back. We'll go in there." He held the gun in his lap, the deadly cold circle at the end pointed at her.

Hands clenched white on the wheel, Hope pulled into the rear parking lot of her Community Bank building sitting cockeyed on the corner, a strip mall at its back.

"Unlock the door and shut off the alarm. I'll be right behind you. With the gun."

The air in the car was laced with nervous tension and the smell of fear. Most of it hers.

"Do not turn on any lights, and don't even think about pushing a silent alarm." The gun barrel prodded her side. "The first cop that shows, you're dead. Got it?" The cold glint in his dirty-green eyes would have evaporated doubt, if she'd had any.

"Got it." Her screechy voice echoed in the confined space. She clamped her throat shut to keep further sounds from escaping. They only frightened her more.

Once inside, she keyed in the code for the alarm, her fingers moving by rote—a routine task on a very nonroutine day. Her normally familiar workplace environs loomed spooky and strange in the dim security lights.

What is my plan? She could care less about the money. They were insured. But her first employee would be here in an hour. And her captors hadn't worn masks, so handing over the money and hoping for the best wasn't an option. She did have one advantage. She knew this place, knew it for six years running. They didn't. She had to do something. But what? She'd colored between the lines as a child, and lived by the rules ever since. It wasn't fair that she'd wind up here, where there were no rules. No lines.

"Give me the car keys." The leader stepped in and waved the gun at her.

She dropped them in his hand.

"Now, the safe."

Guts jumping, she walked through the hall of glass-walled offices to the bull pen of teller windows. She angled to the huge metal door on the left wall, weighing actions and possible results. None of them ended well. She worked the combination, and with a loud snick, the lock disengaged.

She grasped the handle and swung the ten-inch-thick door.

The mug shot dude muscled her aside, and they all rushed into the money-lined room. "Woo-fucking-hoo." The skinny one wheezed.

Hope stood in the breech of the door, one hand on the jamb. She'd lock them in, if the vault hadn't been equipped with safety releases inside.

"Use those canvas bags. Hurry." The leader stood tall, his gun trained on her, but his gaze held captive by all that cash.

She inched her fingers along the metal doorjamb, hoping in all the shuffling, he couldn't hear her heart, pounding out an SOS.

The minions worked fast but loud, laughing and chattering like agitated squirrels.

When the pads of her fingers found the alarm button, they hovered, and she wondered if she had the guts to push it...wondered if she did, if those guts would end up splattered red ribbons on the marble floor.

Straining her brain for hours in search of a solution hadn't helped. She could either die a good little girl or die trying. There was no way out.

She pressed the button.

"YOU'VE KNOWN THIS was a condition of your parole since the day you were released, Doug."

That his parole officer would be the first since his mother to use his given name was an insult. The injury was this ridiculous "trauma group" the state dictated he attend. "Look. I paid my debt. I don't need a stupid—"

"Let's see here." The officer flipped open a cardboard file folder with Douglas Steele on the tab. "An army scout sniper for four years, your last mission in Iraq." He pushed the heavy glasses up his paper-pusher nose. "When you got back in the States…well, you know. You were there." He looked over his glasses. "I'd say you have an anger issue or two. Wouldn't you?"

"How can you say that, with all the money California dumped into criminal rehabilitation?" He raised his hands. "I'm cured."

The officer shook his head. "You can argue all day, Doug. I'm just the messenger. I have no authority to change this, and you know it." He dropped the folder full of societal sins on the desk. "Look, this is the last hoop you have to jump through and the state will be out of your face. Why not just get it over with?"

Because it's a flaming hoop, asshole. Bear had always been a private person. The thought of talking to a bunch of whiny losers about his "issues"? It went against his upbringing. It went against his nature. It went against his guts like a punch from a heavyweight. All he'd wanted since he got stateside was to be left alone. There were lonely people everywhere. Why wouldn't they just let him be one of them? "Give me the damn address."

"I mean it, Doug." He scribbled on a sticky pad. "Don't blow this off. You're never getting off parole if you don't. I have a huge caseload, and I don't have time for this."

"You're breaking my heart here, dude, really." Bear took the fluorescent bit of paper, stood, snatched his leather jacket from the back of the chair and headed out. Ignoring the startled look of the guy approaching the door when Bear barreled through, he held his breath until he hit the parking lot.

The sun reflected off the chrome of his badass Harley-Davidson in a blinding laser that made him squint. And smile.

He pulled his skullcap helmet from the leather side bag and slapped it on. He'd sit through their wimpy-ass class, then he'd be free. Forever.

Two HOURS POST button-push, Hope stood with the gun to her head, the leader's arm squeezing her neck, facing down the local SWAT team on the other side of the glass doors.

"Do you want her dead?" the robber yelled.

She'd stopped wincing at the screaming beside her ear ten minutes ago. When her knees threatened to buckle, she sent the last of her energy to stiffen them. "I have to go to the bathroom." She'd made up her mind. Time to finish what she'd started. The gunman's face appeared in her peripheral vision. "Do you think I give a flying spider's asshole what you *need*?" His breath hadn't improved overnight. His arm cinched even tighter around her throat. "You may not have noticed, but we have a situation here. Hold it."

"If you let the hostage go, we'll talk," the bull-horn-distorted voice said.

She had serious doubts about the negotiating skills of the small-town cop. *Surely this can't go on much longer. Maybe the FBI will show up with a negotiator that isn't a relative of Barney Fife.*

"We're gonna die," the skinny one wheezed from behind the desk.

"I'd rather die than go back to jail," the bald one replied from behind another.

"Shutthefuckup. We've got us a hostage. They're not gonna—"

Ssssst...whap!

It sounded like a missile hitting a watermelon. Hope whipped her head around in time to see the bald guy, sans forehead, drop behind the desk. Brain and blood sheeted the wall.

She heaved a breath to scream.

Ssssst...splat!

The hollow-cheeked one clutched his throat as if to stem the blood. It didn't work. He fell, face-down on the desk.

Two neat holes marred the bank's floor-to-ceiling window.

That's going to be expensive to replace. Her brain worked in slow looping sweeps. The ringing in her ears surged, then retreated.

"She's gonna die! You're killing her!"

The gun barrel ground into her collarbone, loosing the screams that had built in her since she'd been awakened—it seemed a hundred years ago. "Eiiiieeeee!"

When her captor jerked in surprise, she unlocked her knees and dropped.

He'd held her in a tight grip, but it was with only one hand. She hung choking, his arm around her neck as time distorted, stretching and compressing.

Sssssst...

Squid's ink bloomed at the edge of her vision and spread, filling the world with black.

CHAPTER TWO

HOPE SANDERSON WOKE to her second worst nightmare.

A gray-haired woman in a scrub cap so pink it hurt, leaned over her, calling her name.

"Hope, how are you feeling? It's good to have you back. You've been shot. You've just come out of surgery."

Dopey and disoriented, Hope battled the cotton in her head. "Wah?"

"You're going to be fine." Her eyes crinkled in a mask-covered smile. "Sleep now."

When the cotton expanded, Hope sunk into its soft embrace.

Until, sometime later, a piercing siren stabbed her brain.

She's crashing! Bring the cart!

There was nothing for her to do, so Hope floated away again.

The cotton released her to the sound of squeaky shoes on waxed floors. She didn't know how much time had passed, but the window in the corner was a blacked-out rectangle. Monitors hovered over the bed, their snaking wires and tubes disappearing into several of her body parts. She shifted her arms, legs. All there, thank God. When she lifted her head, her guts bellowed, Stop—stop—stop!

With the pain came the memories, rushing at her: her finger on the alarm button, the evil black eye at the end of the gun barrel, blood and brains trickling down a cream-colored wall. *Who shot me? The cops or the robber?* She moaned. Did it matter?

The squeaking shoes got closer, and a nurse's face appeared over her. "Try not to move. You had a bullet nick your stomach and take out your spleen. You gave us a scare, but you're going to be okay." She turned over Hope's palm and put something in it. "The doctors repaired the damage, but it's going to hurt like a mama bear for a while. Just push the button on the end of that, and it'll dispense pain medication."

Right now Hope didn't feel strong enough to stand up to the pain—in her body or her mind. She pushed the button and the cotton came rushing to envelop her again.

When she woke, it was daylight. There were fewer machines, fewer tubes than before. She found if she didn't move, her stomach only felt as though a smoking coal was burning its way through her gut. Her throat felt as if she'd inhaled desiccant.

"Well, look who's awake."

She carefully turned her head. Her boss, Andrew Horner, rose from the guest chair and stepped to her bedside. And here she lay in a too short, too skimpy hospital gown. Imagining what her mother would have said, she pulled the covers over her in spite of the knife in her guts. Nothing she could do about her bare face, or lack of suitable underwear.

His tie fell across her when he leaned in. "How do you feel?" His bushy eyebrows drew together, at odds with his thin, receding hairline. "We've been so worried."

"W-water," she croaked.

He lifted a cup from the tray hovering over her legs. "They say you can only have ice chips." He fumbled with the spoon, managed to snag a few chips and dropped them in her mouth.

"Hmm." The cold seeped into her parched tissues and down her raw throat. She wanted more, but asking her boss for personal maintenance was embarrassing—for her, and judging by the red spreading up from his collar, him, too. "The robbers—"

"Are dead. You're safe."

"What day is it?"

"Friday. You've been out for forty-eight hours." He laid a damp hand over hers.

Hard to believe that only a few days ago, her boss had been transparently working up the nerve to ask her out. It now seemed harder to believe she'd considered accepting. Andrew (never Andy) was an efficient district manager, a good boss and a nice man. Middle-aged, middle management, middle—everything. They fit together like chalk dust and dust bunnies. Easily overlooked. Ordinary. Pedestrian.

She flexed her elbow, pulling her hand from under his. "Is the bank open for business?"

"Yes, of course. They haven't yet replaced the front window, but the cleaning crew was able to clean the—oh. Sorry."

She forced her face muscles to relax. "I appreciate your visiting, Andrew, but I'm really tired, and…"

"Of course." Worried eyes scanned her face. "I'll come back tomorrow."

"Could you bring my laptop from the office? I have the monthly reports almost done."

"I submitted the reports yesterday. You're not to even think about anything work related until you get home." He patted her hand. "You're a hero you know. It's all over the news."

Some hero.

When he'd gone, she listened to the hospital

whispers, trying to get her head straight. Things felt different; as though the bullet that ripped through her guts had kept going, tearing a hole through her entire life.

She lay, testing the edges of the hole. How big was it?

Everything felt foreign. Off-kilter. While she'd slept, Andrew had changed from a possible beau to a well-dressed Rodney Dangerfield, but without the sense of humor. The bank manager role she'd been so proud of had morphed to a well-titled paper-pusher. Her apartment…

The shudder ripped down her spine so hard it woke the banked fire in her gut.

I can't go back to that apartment.

Everything was gone. All the satisfaction, peace and sedate joy she felt about her life just three days ago were gone. With a flip, it had become someone else's life. A boring person's life. This was too big to contemplate right now. There were no edges to the black hole. Pressing the morphine button, she tumbled in.

BEAR MERGED CERULEAN blue with a touch of mixing white until he had just the right shade, then, with one long brushstroke, created a shadow on the robe to give it movement. Three more swipes and he stepped back, set down the brush and put his fists to the small of his back. The uncovered bulbs of several desk lamps threw light against the bright white wall and the start of his mural.

It had come to him in a dream, so stark and clear that it haunted him for weeks, until he began sketching the scene. He did it more to get it out of his head than anything; after all, no one would ever see it. A warped floorboard creaked when he backed up to double-check the perspective.

His angel floated above the harsh desert landscape on his dining room wall, cool, detached, serene. He still saw her when he closed his eyes. The face he'd painted fast and easily from his vivid dream-memory. White-blond hair you only see on small children, wide-spaced winter-blue eyes that spread a balm of peace over the burns on his soul.

He'd left his parent's religion behind with his childhood toys. But you didn't need to be a shrink to see where the dream came from. He grabbed a turpentine-soaked rag from the pocket of his jeans and wiped his hands. This mural was penance. Exhausted, he shook his aching head. A ten-hour workday, then three hours spent repairing the house and a few more stolen ones, here.

He walked through the doorless kitchen to check the time. Cabinets squatted at the base of every free inch of wall space, and plywood sheets that impersonated a counter surrounded the chipped and stained porcelain sink.

Two in the morning. And another full day tomorrow. He walked to the sanded door stretched across two sawhorses that served as his dining table. He should eat something.

Screw it. He needed sleep more. Not that his nightmares would grant him much of that, but he had to try. But as he walked the hall to his cot, he felt better. Lighter. Maybe, given enough pigment, even mortal sins could be painted over.

HOPE OPENED HER eyes to yet another nightmare. Her older cousin, Jesse Jurgen, stood alongside the hospital bed, hand on hip, from the look, royally pissed from her towering blond hair to the shell pink toenails Hope knew were peeking out from strappy sandals.

"So I tell Carl, 'It must be a coincidence. There's no way that woman in the paper is my cousin, because she'd have called me, right off.'"

You didn't face a force of nature lying down. Hope wriggled as upright as she could get. Only a small whimper got past her clenched teeth.

"Oh, don't you try to make me all sorry for you, missy. You should have called." Jesse's words were tough, but she eased pillows behind her cousin, then straightened the sheets, threw away used tissues, and dropped her nosegay of daisies and delphiniums in the water pitcher on the lap tray.

"Jess, they only took out the morphine drip this

morning. I couldn't remember my own name before that, much less your number."

"I'm on speed dial, and you know it." She humphed, but the corners of her lips relaxed a bit. "Thank God our mothers have passed on, because they'd be having fits to see you now."

Hope winced, imagining those doll-like twin dynamos descending on her. "Thanks for reminding me that things could be worse."

Hope had always wondered if her father died young to escape his wife's small, but mighty grip on his life. Hope had wanted to escape, too, after she'd completed commuter college in her Portland suburb. She'd never have made it, if not for Jesse's help. Hope had loved her mother, but she was…exacting. Anything within Vivian Sanderson's sphere had to be rearranged to her satisfaction. Lives included.

But growing up with rigorous direction wasn't the hardest part. Her mother didn't let go until you not only did things her way, but felt less intelligent if you didn't believe it was for the best. Her mother whispered in her mind. *How can you face company without lipstick on, at least?*

For the first time in a long time, Hope ignored her.

Jesse pulled up a plastic guest chair, sat, crossed her legs and leaned in. "Enough small talk. Tell me."

Hope had been lying listening to hospital sounds for hours, thinking. But she could make no more sense of things now, than she had on morphine. It was as if, in surgery, they'd taken her old life along with her spleen. The more minutes ticked by, the more anxious she'd become. Her life may not have been titillating, but it was *hers*. She felt torn from her sheltered harbor, adrift in a huge, heaving sea of choices.

And Hope Sanderson wasn't used to choices.

She reached for the water glass, and knocked it over.

Jesse mopped it up, her eyes reflecting Hope's own worry. "You're upset. Talk to me."

She not only owed Jesse, she trusted her. But how could Hope explain something she couldn't wrap her own head around? "I think I'm possessed."

Jesse patted her hand. "No, we exorcised your mother when you moved here, remember?"

Hope snorted a laugh, then grabbed her stomach when it felt as if her guts were going to fall out. "Thanks, I needed that, Jess."

Jesse took her hand. "Just talk. Don't worry how it comes out."

Hope scoured her mind, searching for words to explain her feelings. "It's like my life has become a dress in the back of my closet from high school.

It's not only out of fashion, I've outgrown it. It's too tight, and too short and—" she shrugged "—not *me* anymore."

"How so?"

"Andrew, you know, my boss—"

"The one who clearly has a crush on you?"

"Yes. In the couple of days I was out of it, he changed from a hot dish to a cold fish."

"Hon, don't know how to break it to you, but he was always a cold fish." Jess gave her a canny smile. "You could do so much better than sushi. It sounds to me like you woke up in more ways than one."

"But I didn't ask to!" It came out louder and way more desperate than she'd meant. "It's more than Andrew. I can't go back to the bank. I can't go back to my apartment. When I think about it, I break into a cold sweat."

"Sweetie, you've been through a horrible experience. The memories of that night are going to take time to get over."

"The memories may fade, sure, but when I picture myself going back to life as usual, I get depressed, then panicky." She squeezed her cousin's hand. "Am I going crazy?"

"Oh, hon, you know what I think?" Jesse's eyes went soft. "I think the Hope your mother created died in that shoot-out." She reached up and petted her cousin's hair. "You get to decide who this new person is. How many people get that chance?"

CHAPTER THREE

BEAR TOOK THE sweepers into Santa Maria slow. His classic Harley-Davidson Fat Boy rode great on the straights, but the raked front end got squirrely through the turns, especially at high speeds. The sun's heat tattooed his arms, but the salt breeze off the ocean buffeted his beard. The road whispered a siren's song of freedom. There was a great cliff-hanging burger shack outside Big Sur. Maybe…he shoved the daydream aside.

You have to go through this to be free.

His leather gloves tightened over his knuckles. He forced the bike to lean in the turn to the crowded parking lot of Marian Regional Medical. No motorcycle parking here. He finally found an open space, pulled in, shut down the engine and lowered the side stand. He threw his leg over and studied the white Spanish-style facade as he unbuckled his skullcap helmet. He'd rather be rolling asphalt in a Vegas summer than walk into that group. But since that wasn't an option the parole board would accept, he dropped his helmet into the leather side bag and headed for the door.

The old man at the information desk directed him down a series of rat-maze hallways that echoed his boot-falls. Outside the door, he took a deep breath and forced himself to turn the knob.

The room was small and windowless. The yellow paint was probably chosen to be cheery, but in the fluorescent lights, looked nauseous. Five of the six plastic chairs pulled into a cozy circle were occupied. Four of the attendees looked up at him with various shades of alarm.

He forced his face muscles to relax. He didn't mean to scare people, but between his size, the ponytail, wild beard and heavy brows hooding his eyes, his natural look came off as crazed. And that was okay; it kept people out of his face. And his life.

Only one didn't flinch. A small soft coffee-skinned woman with long black hair checked her watch. "You are late." She had a light, floating, East Indian accent.

"Yeah." He wasn't saying he was sorry, when he wasn't. It wasn't as if he had to get a passing grade for this thing. He just had to attend. He slouched to the only open chair beside her, slid it a foot back from the circle and sat.

"Well." She uncrossed her legs. "We were getting started. My name is Bina Rani, and I'm a family psychologist with the hospital. This is a new group, and an unconventional one at that, so let me detail how all this works, so you're not apprehensive."

He let the blah-blah flow around him as he checked out his classmates. He glanced to his left. At least he wouldn't be the only guy in the group... The twentysomething kid was lean to the point of stringy. Legs crossed like a girl, he twirled a lock of limp strawberry blond hair on one finger. When he saw Bear watching, he dropped him a wink.

Lovely.

Bear didn't have anything against being gay. Live and let live. But he didn't like having it shoved in his face either.

He moved on to a large mousy woman, squirming in her chair as if trying to make herself smaller. Lifeless hair and baggy clothes, she had the flat, not-too-bright stare of a soap opera addict.

Directly across the circle sat a guy with his nose smashed flat, and a worm of red scar tissue bordering a trench-like depression running from his forehead, across his pancake nose, through his upper lip. The scar distorted one eyelid, making him look constantly surprised. Noticing Bear's stare, the guy looked away.

Bear looked to the last chair beside the Rani woman. His breath reversed, sucking in so fast he choked. He coughed into his fist, but couldn't look away. Shoulder length white-blond hair framed ice-blue eyes. His angel's eyes. He felt his blood throbbing at his throat. He heard it in his ears. The resemblance sucker punched him, then rolled him along in a shock wave.

Watching him, her eyebrows disappeared into her bangs.

No, not your angel.

His artist's eye compared the differences: her jaw was broader, her face not as heart-shaped. Though small, she was built more sturdy than willowy, and there was no balm of peace in this woman's eyes. Quite the opposite.

"Douglas… Hello, Douglas."

Bina Rani's stare didn't penetrate his agitation any more than her calling his name.

What does it mean, meeting a woman who resembles— "What?"

"Would you like to begin?"

"Begin what?"

She huffed a breath, not quite a sigh. "Introduce yourself, and tell us what brings you to trauma group."

Even before his prison stint, the thought of "sharing" made him want to puke. He swallowed acid at the back of his throat and shifted in his chair. Shit. He had to say something. "I'm Bear." He put his elbows on his knees, laced his fingers and looked to the dude to his left to pass the introduction baton.

Bina jumped in. "So it's Bear, not Douglas. Bear Steele."

The boy beside him laughed, but when Bear glared, he stopped, midtitter.

"I think it fits you." Bina gave the kid a stern look. "Now, Bear, what brings you here?"

"The state correctional system," he growled.

With a look of horror, the kid scooted his chair away.

Bina did sigh this time. "I mean, what trauma brought you to us?"

He sat back and raised his face to the ceiling, hoping for a way out. "Well, prison is pretty traumatic. But you probably mean my Afghanistan tours."

"Yes, that's what I was referring to. You were a soldier. What did you do over there?"

He challenged her with his glare. "Not going there, Oprah." They could force his attendance, but no one could make him talk.

She sat relaxed, unintimidated by his death ray. That was odd. "I understand. Hopefully once we all get to know each other, you'll feel more comfortable opening up. Next?"

The kid beside Bear perked right up. "I'm Bryan. I'm gay," he chirped in a crisply enunciated voice.

Now there's a news flash.

"I was the victim of a hate crime. My boyfriend and I went to dinner. A gang of mouthbreathers jumped us in the restroom." His voice got wobblier as he went. "Curtis tried to fight them off, but…" He sniffed. "It was horrible. I just don't understand how people can…" He put his fingers to his mouth and shook his head, eyes liquid.

Great. A drama queen.

"Bryan, thank you. Hopefully this group will help you come to terms with your experience." Bina looked to the soap opera woman. "Next?"

The woman stared at the carpet, her oily hair curtaining her face. She mumbled something unintelligible.

"Sorry, I didn't catch that."

"I'm Brenda. I don't need to be here."

"And what brought you to us?"

"The court made me come, too." She slanted a skittish glance in Bear's direction, then focused again at the floor. "They gave me a choice—this or a battered women's program. But that's not me, so I came here."

Bina allowed the silence to spin out until Brenda looked up. "Thank you, Brenda. I look forward to hearing more about that." She looked to the scarred dude. "Next?"

"I'm Mark. And no, I'm not wearing a mask."

He looked around, his weak chuckle dangling in the air.

No one laughed.

"I was in a car wreck. Went through the windshield." He raised his hands. "There goes the shaving cream commercial."

Silence.

His shoulders slumped. "I can't sleep. Going out in public is excruciating." He tucked his hands in his armpits and shrugged. "I'm to have a series of surgeries, but in the meantime, I have to…deal."

"Good, Mark. Congratulations on getting here today. That in itself is a big step."

When Bina looked to his angel, Bear leaned in.

"I'm Hope. I'm a…*was* a bank manager." She sat straight, hands working in her lap. "I was kidnapped and—"

"I heard about that!" Bryan chirped. "Oh, honey, what you went through!"

Bina's eyebrow lifted. "Let's let her tell it, shall we?"

"Sorry."

"Go ahead, Hope."

"Three men broke into my apartment and after a long, awful wait until morning, they made me drive to the bank and open the safe. There was a standoff with the police and I was shot. I was released from the hospital ten days ago." She spoke as if discussing the weather.

Bina said, "That's a very traumatic thing to go through. Hopefully we can help you put it behind you."

"I don't want to put it behind me. That's not why I'm here."

Bina lowered the pen she'd been taking notes with. "So why are you here?"

"Because I think I'm going crazy."

Bear knew a bit about PTSD. He studied the woman for signs. Her hands shook a bit, but he didn't note a startle reflex or jerky movements. But then, he'd known this woman all of ten minutes, all of them silent.

"What makes you think that?" Bina's soft voice was calming, but it wasn't working on this girl.

She threw up her hands. "I can't go back to my apartment. I can't go back to my job. I can't go back to my *life*. Not after everything that's happened." She rolled her lips in and down, thinking a moment. "I feel like I've got amnesia. Except I remember everything." She glanced around the circle. "My old life isn't mine anymore. The future is a blank wall."

Bina picked up her pen. "Since the past can't be changed, all anyone can do is move forward. We'll try to help you explore what you want your new life to be, Hope." She clipped the pen to the small notebook and uncrossed her legs. "This group brings together people that normally wouldn't be in the same group. As I said before, this is an experiment. I believe however, your diverse experiences can lend you all insight to help each other, as you seek solutions yourselves."

Bina gave them her bio, and how she came to the idea of the group. More blah-blah, as far as Bear was concerned. Finally, she smiled at each of them. "I hope you prove me right. I'll see you on Wednesday."

All but the therapist stood and headed for the door. Bear waited until he could bring up the rear. They shot glances and smiles at each other as they walked down the hall in that awkward, what's-appropriate-in-this-situation, getting-to-know-you, dance.

He watched his angel—Hope—walk away. She dressed a step above the rest—neat and tidy in slacks, a blouse and loafers. Clearly a "good girl." What did it mean, meeting someone who so closely resembled a symbol that sustained him? He didn't believe in fate any more than he believed in the saints, sacraments or shrines of his Catholic upbringing.

But he hadn't believed in prophetic dreams before, either.

As if feeling his regard, she shot a nervous glance over her shoulder. He fell back a step or two, for once sorry for his size and appearance which kept people at bay. If he followed and tried to talk to her, at best, she'd think him a stalker.

Better he just watch and wait. It wasn't as if she'd know the answer to any of his questions anyway.

TWO MINUTES AFTER Hope stepped into the sunny summer day, Jesse's pretty black truck pulled up at the curb. Hope opened the door, tripped and stumbled into the blinding-bright poodle skirt–pink seat covers. "I appreciate this Jess, but I could have driven myself."

Jesse, eyes hidden behind movie star shades, waved her red manicure. "Are you kidding? I have the afternoon off. Who better to spend it with? Besides, we're on a mission."

Hope buckled her seat belt, then stroked the pink fuzzy dice that hung from the mirror. "I've searched through the paper, Jess. The only places for rent are the same generic apartments I was in before." Shivering, she aimed the A/C duct at the ceiling, though she wasn't cold. "I can't move into one of those."

Jesse checked her mirror, then pulled away

from the curb and headed for the exit. "Well, then it's a good thing your cousin owns The Farmhouse Café, Widow's Grove equivalent of the office watercooler." She pulled onto King's Highway and headed out of Santa Maria.

"You know of someplace else that's for rent?" Hope squinted through the glare at the green hills she'd loved since the first time she'd seen them, six years ago.

"Not just someplace." Jesse winked. "I know *the* place."

"But how could you, when I don't even know what I'm looking for?" All Hope knew was that everything she'd seen so far reminded her way too much of her old place.

"Trust me, sweetie. I know this place. It's perfect. You'll see."

"I hope so. I feel bad, putting you and Carl out, taking up your guest room."

Eyes on the road, Jesse felt for Hope's hand. Finding it, she squeezed. "You're my cousin, and I love you. Frankly, I wish you'd stay with us permanently."

"Oh, heck, no. I overstayed my welcome last time." When Jesse and Hope had ganged up on Hope's mother, she'd finally agreed to Hope's move to Widow's Grove, providing Jesse keep an eye on her younger cousin. Apparently Jesse thought the vow extended posthumously, since Vivian Sanderson had given up her iron-fist grip on life two years ago.

"Shut up, we love having you. Besides, you dust."

"Hello." Hope rolled her eyes. "You met my mother, right?"

"Yes, hon, and you met mine. Did any of that domestic goddess crap rub off on me?"

"You have a point." Jess may be a whiz mathematician who gave up Massachusetts Institute of Technology for her childhood sweetheart and his family's business, but she wasn't a housekeeper.

Hope looked past the beach houses to the light fracturing off the ocean's chop. In the ten days since she'd been released from the hospital she'd slowly put her cousin's house in order, down to organizing Jesse's two walk-in closets and alphabetizing Carl's considerable CD collection. Organizing her surroundings usually helped organize her thoughts. But not this time.

So far she'd resigned from her job, said goodbye to her baffled boss and looked for somewhere to live. Jesse had retrieved her clothes and personal items, since Hope still couldn't face her apartment. She had no idea what career she wanted, moving forward. Like her apartment, going to work for another bank was out. Her palms sweated just thinking about it. What was she going to do for a living for the rest of her life?

The edge of town was easy to discern. It was where the line of Victorian houses began, standing like colorful titled ladies in a receiving line. Jesse pulled over, consulting a scrap of paper before peering out the window.

"Oh, Jess, this can't be right. You know I can't afford to rent a house." Hope traced a scrolled fretwork with her finger on the window. "But what a dream. Look at the paint on that one. Who would have thought to use light gray, French blue and rose together?"

Jesse turned off the engine, snatched her purse from the floor and cracked her door. "Honey, if the local jungle drums are in tune, your dream is about to come true."

They stepped into the hammered Central California sunshine. Jesse waited until Hope came around the car, then grabbed her hand, checked both ways, and crossed the street, low-heeled sandals clacking.

"I think I'm capable of walking across—oh." Hope breathed.

The home they approached was in the ornately spindled Eastlake-style Victorian in lavender and white. The frothy gingerbread on the porch also adorned the tiny balcony on one second-story corner.

Jesse adjusted her huge sunglasses. "A little foo-foo for me, but whatever makes your hips wiggle."

"This from the woman with Pepto-Bismol–inspired seat covers."

Jesse just tsked and led the way up the steps to the covered porch. When she pressed the doorbell "God Save the Queen" chimed through the interior.

"That is too adorable for words," Hope whispered.

The door opened. A tiny old lady in a flowered dress and orthopedic shoes stood on the other side of the screen, a messy bun of white hair on top of her head. "Yes?"

"I'm Jesse Jurgen. I called about your guest cottage?"

Guest cottage. Hope even loved the sound of the words.

"Oh, yes. Please, come in." She unlatched the screen door and ushered them in. "I'm Opaline Settle." She led them into a formal sitting room scented with old furniture–mustiness and old lady dusting powder. "Would you like some tea?"

"I'm fine, thank you." Hope settled on the ornate but faded wingback sofa and looked around. "What a delightful home you have." Threadbare antique rugs covered wooden floors. Dusty floor-to-ceiling damask drapes were drawn back.

Opaline perched on the edge of a wingback chair. "Why thank you. Mr. Settle bought it for me as a wedding gift over sixty years ago. He's gone, but the old lady abides," she said in a soft, wobbly soprano. "Both of us."

"I'm Hope Sanderson. Jesse's cousin. I'm the one looking for a place to rent." She shot an optimistic smile across the ornate wooden tea table. "You have marvelous antiques, as well. I have a few Tiffany pieces myself." She nodded at the stained glass lamp on the gateleg table in front of the window.

Opaline's faded blue eyes sparked. "You have antiques?"

"Yes, quite a few that I inherited from my mother. She—eeep!" Hope jumped up when something bounced out from behind the sofa.

The old lady tittered. "Oh, that's just Euphengenia. She's named after Mrs. Doubtfire." She bent and lifted a large buff-colored rabbit into her lap.

A flop-eared black-and-white rabbit hopped in from the hall, followed by a black one. Soon there were ten.

"They're curious. We don't get company often. I won't bore you with introductions."

Hope scooted back into the couch, wishing she could lift her feet onto the cushion. She wasn't afraid of animals, exactly. She'd just never been around them much. Her mother wouldn't even allow Hope a goldfish, declaring that animals in the house were filthy, disgusting and unmannered.

"They're just bunnies, for cripes sakes. Deal," Jesse whispered out of the corner of her mouth. "Is the cottage still for rent?"

Don't they carry fleas? Hope watched the rabbits to be sure none ventured close. *The plague?*

"Oh, yes." She watched Hope like a bird eyes a scarecrow. "I have to be careful to choose the correct tenant. I don't want any wildness back there. You know—" she lowered her voice to a wavery whisper "—that sex, drugs, and rock and roll stuff."

Jesse coughed into her hand to cover a laugh.

Hope smiled. "I don't do any of those things, I assure you, Mrs. Settle. I live a very quiet life." But the words pinched, coming out. That was her old life. Her new one would be different. Different how, she didn't know, but different.

Opaline looked her over from her headband to her hands, clasped in her lap. "You appear to be a well-brought-up young lady." She gathered the rabbit, bent and returned it to the floor, then stood. "Would you like to see the cottage?"

"Oh, yes, please." Hope and Jesse stood.

They followed the little woman through the front hall, to the kitchen, then through the door that led to the back porch. Hope counted eight more rabbits on the way; she'd had to hug the wall to avoid two that chased each other toward her in the hall.

I've heard of crazy cat ladies before, but never a crazy bunny lady.

But when they stepped through the back door, all her concerns blew away. In the corner of the huge yard sat a cottage—a perfect, tiny gingerbread Victorian cottage. It looked like one of the painted ladies, only one-fifth the size, dressed in the same lavender and white trim as the main house.

"Ohhhh…" Something in Hope's chest moved. It was her heart, cracking open. "Oh, my gosh, it's precious!"

The tiny covered porch wrapped around a bay window, with room only for two painted white rocking chairs. Fretwork graced the roof's peak, and window boxes spilled bright pansies and geraniums.

As they walked the flagstone path to the cottage. Jesse asked, "How many square feet is it?"

"Five hundred and fifty, I believe." Opaline took the one step, crossed the porch, and unlocked the door. "It's small, but I think you'll find it has everything you need."

Hope followed her inside. Light from the bay windows shone on the polished wood floor of what she'd call a "sitting area," since it was too small to be a living room. To the right, a diminutive fireplace with a stone hearth sat, wood laid, awaiting only a match. She walked toward the kitchen at the back of the room.

My little dining table would be cute as a divider between the two areas.

Behind a door on her left, a cubby guest bath had a round window which saved the tiny space from feeling like a closet.

She stepped to the kitchen area. Matching yellow tieback café curtains hung in the windows over the kitchen sink in the corner, and over the Dutch door that led to the backyard.

Sighing, she took in the ambience. Snug and sweet. It was a happy place; she felt it in the empty spaces within her.

Opaline pointed to a tight spiral wrought-iron staircase that disappeared into the ceiling. "You'll need to climb up to see the loft. The stairs are beyond me, I'm afraid."

Hope led the way, Jesse on her heels. The stairs rang with their steps. At the top, Hope looked around. "Oh, wow."

Jesse's fingernail poked her butt. "If you'd move, I could see, too."

Hope took the last stair and moved aside. This floor had the same footprint as the house below, so it was a large room, with small windows at either end. But it was the skylights on either side of the sloping ceiling straddling the painted brick chimney that caught her eye. "Jess, if I put the head of my bed against the chimney, I could see the stars through those skylights at night!"

"It's like a little Hobbit house!" Jesse walked to the door at the far end of the room. "Come see this."

Hope walked over and stuck her head into an old-fashioned bath, complete with a deep claw-foot tub and faux Tiffany lights over the wash-basin sink.

She and Jesse looked at each other and squealed. Hope grabbed her cousin's arms and waltzed her carefully across the bathroom floor, singing, "I feel lucky. I feel lucky. I feel—"

"It's perfect, sweetie. But if you keep cater-wauling, Mrs. Settle is going to think you're into that rock and roll stuff."

Hope giggled for the first time in… *I've never giggled.* "Jess, that song is country, not rock and roll."

Jess grinned. "Let's hope Opaline knows the difference. Now, get down there and offer a de-posit before she rents this baby out from under you!"

This place would be way more than an out-of-work bank manager could afford, if not for her mother's estate. Hope hadn't touched the money,

but not needing it was only part of the reason.
Every time she'd thought about spending it, her
mother's voice haunted from the grave: *you're
spending my hard-earned money on that? Surely
I didn't scrimp and do without so you could
squander...*

This time, Hope wasn't listening. The money
would give her time to get her feet back under
her, and find a new career. A new life.

Thank you, Mother.

She took one last look at her new bedroom before she walked down the spiral stairs. Her old
life may be gone, but her new life yawned like
a black hole, but she now knew where it would
take place.

In a world where nothing was familiar, inex-
plicably, *this* cottage somehow fit.

"Home," she whispered to the room. The word
felt right on her lips.

CHAPTER FOUR

BEAR UNLOCKED THE padlock on his rickety barn, still chewing his energy bar breakfast. He'd rather have had eggs, but money came from work, not from cooking. He left the door open to get a cross breeze, flipped on the big overhead lights and walked the narrow corridor formed by crates and various flotsam he'd moved aside to create a work area in the center. He bent over and gave in to an explosive sneeze.

Maybe someday there'd be time to clean the place, too. But he wasn't being paid to do that, either, so it was going to have to wait.

Bear had saved his soldier pay, invested it and let it to grow while he was in prison. He liked the golden rolling hills he'd seen from behind the razor wire–crowned fence at the California Men's Colony in San Luis Obispo. So when he got out, he scouted around until he'd found this place; a remote tumbledown cabin and barn, outside Widow's Grove. It didn't look like anything. Hell, it wasn't anything. Yet.

He flipped on his pole lights, strode into the

open area in the center of the spotless concrete floor and sank to his knees beside his latest job, a 1989 Harley-Davidson Electra Glide Classic. On the tank, orange-tipped gold flames rose through the black paint—some of the best ghost flames he'd ever done. He'd laid the last clear coat two days ago, and returned the tank to the bike last night. Two coats of wax this morning, and it'd be ready for pickup this afternoon, right on schedule.

This was what brought in money. He'd opened The Gaudy Widow Custom Paint Shop six months ago. Turned out, Widow's Grove sat in the heart of some of California's best motorcycle roads, as well as being a stop on the custom car circuit. He had all the business he could handle.

He smoothed a finger over the edge of the tank. "Pretty damned sweet, if I do say so myself." Pushing himself to his feet, he walked to the back of the barn to open the big door there, then put on a pot of coffee.

A half hour later, he was in the loft, trying to locate a custom-welded metal easel to hold his next job, when he heard a scuffle and a kid's awestruck voice.

"Oh, wow."

He strode to the ladder, and had to grab it to steady himself. A brown-skinned kid was on his knees in front of the Harley. He didn't look much like the kid from Bear's waking nightmare, but that didn't stop his mind from running through the stop-action film anyway: a boy around the same age, in a traditional long shirt and long linen pants, a round kapol on his black hair. But it was the eyes, huge and black with panic that chased Bear through his dreams.

Bear used to like kids. Before.

The one downstairs reached his fingers to the tank.

"*Don't* you touch that!" Bear's voice was too loud and splintered with pain.

The kid jerked his hand back as if the ghost flames had burned him.

A young woman with black spiky hair stepped from the box corridor and looked up at Bear, mouth open.

He glared down at them. "Do. Not. Move."

The warning wasn't needed. The two stood, shocked to stillness.

He turned and started down the ladder, anger building with every step. Last week some kids had broken in and stolen a case of spray paint. Where were these kids coming from? Why couldn't they just leave him be?

At the bottom of the ladder, he turned, and hands fisted, stalked to them. "Goddamn kids. You come to rip me off, too?"

Eyes huge, the kid just stared.

"Hey!" The woman, too young to be the kid's

mother, stepped between them. "Back off, dude. He's not hurting anything."

He had to give it to her, she had balls. She turned her back and took the kid's hands. He shook her off, raised his chin and hung his thumbs in the belt loops of his baggy jeans, a kid's version of chilly.

"I had a break-in last week. I thought—"

She spun. "Bet you get a lot of repeat customers by scaring the crap out of people."

Damn lights make it cook in here. He reached into his pocket and pulled out his purple bandanna, folded it lengthwise and tied it around his forehead. "What do you want?"

The woman stepped from between him and the kid, but not far. "My brother needs to talk to you."

A NANOSECOND OF pure terror crossed the kid's face. "Um. I didn't steal your paint." His eyes darted. Probably scouting the nearest escape route. "But I used it." The rest of his breath huffed out. "For tagging."

Bear frowned down at the kid, knowing it made him look even scarier. "Where?"

"The Bekins warehouse." His voice shook, but he stood his ground.

He'd seen that. On the long wall of the building that faced the road, black letters, leaning back, as if they were zipping by. Yellow and orange flames trailing every letter. He bit back a smile. Kid was young, but had a set on him.

The spiky-haired spitfire watched close, ready to step between them again.

"Oh, yeah, I saw that." He squinted down at the kid. "What's your name?"

"N-Nacho."

"Well, N-Nacho, not bad work. For a beginner."

The kid looked like a prisoner whose firing squad had just taken a smoke break.

"But." He pointed, and put every bit of badass into his voice. "Defacing private property is a crime, and accepting stolen property can land you in jail." He leaned into the kid's personal space. "Did you learn anything?" He raised an eyebrow. He was having a tough time holding his face hard. He hadn't had this much fun in a long time.

"Y-yessir."

"What?"

"Crime costs more than it's worth."

He couldn't help it. His lips quirked, but they probably wouldn't see it through the beard. "Good answer."

The woman let out a breath and put a hand on the boy's shoulder. "Okay, we can go now."

The boy shrugged from under her hand. "Um, sir?"

"Name's Bear."

"Mister Bear—could you tell me how you did this?" He pointed to the flames on the bike's gas tank. "They're epic."

Bear chuckled. The kid was cute. For a delinquent. "It takes years of practice kid, and the right tools."

Nacho looked up at Bear, hero worship plain on his face. "Would you show me?"

The woman put her hand on the back of the kid's neck. "Getting late. We gotta go. Sorry to bother you." Steering him ahead of her, they motored for the exit, then disappeared among the boxes.

The prison priest had told him he could atone, by helping children. That was bullshit.

Most likely bullshit.

But there was something about this one. The odd combination of innocence and hardcase made Bear wonder what the kid's story was.

None of your business.

Another, not so different pair of eyes shivered through his mind.

He raised his voice, and it boomed through the barn. "If you come back sometime, we'll talk."

He could always tell the kid to get lost if he got irritating. Besides, from that woman's body language, that was probably the last Bear would see of…what'd he say his name was? Nacho? "THANK YOU BOTH. I don't know how this would have happened without you." Hope stood in her new doorway, rubbing moving day bruises, trying to choke out a goodbye to her work crew. They'd refused to leave until every picture was hung, every drawer was full.

"Our pleasure, sweetie."

Maybe, but her cousin looked very un-Jesse-like. In faded shorts, a stained T-shirt and holey Keds, she was downright disheveled.

Hope reached out to tuck a hank of Jesse's blond hair behind her ear. "I feel bad, making you two do all the work." She'd had every intention of packing up the apartment herself, earlier in the week. But she'd only gotten the door open—her feet refused to cross the threshold. Even after fifteen minutes of trying.

Today, with Jesse and Carl there, she'd managed to step inside. She'd even managed to pack the kitchen, probably because the men hadn't gone in that room that awful night. But she still hadn't been able to force herself down the hall to her bedroom. Even picturing Carl packing her underwear drawer couldn't get her to budge.

She was bone tired and emotionally spent, but if she felt past those, there was a tiny warm spot of pride. She hadn't done it all, but by God, she'd done *something*.

"Are you sure you're okay here alone?" Carl studied her from under creased Nordic brows.

She considered her injuries—emotional, as well as physical. "You know, I think I am."

"This place is the start of your new life." Jesse reached up and cupped Hope's face in her hands. "Go find out what it holds for you."

"I will, Jess." Hope closed the door of her cottage, then waved to Jesse and Carl through the bay window as they walked the flagstone path to the driveway. She sank onto her mother's antique settee and hugged herself, only partially to quiet the bullet track burning in her gut.

The antiques fit the cottage's Victorian style so perfectly, she felt she'd fallen through time. In the quiet, a delicate peace came and settled like a cat in her lap.

Mine.

It was as if, with the closing of the door, the cottage wrapped itself around her, new, yet familiar. Comforting. It already felt more like home than anywhere she'd ever lived, including the house she'd grown up in. Maybe this was an omen. A bridge, between her past to the life she felt coming, emerging from the darkness, touching the edges of her present.

She'd always been good at waiting. She'd

waited to grow up. She'd waited for the chance to live her own life. But looking back, she could see that when the cage door had opened, she'd just built another.

Maybe because a cage was all she knew.

She'd moved to Widow's Grove and still, she waited. Waited in her adequate career, her adequate life, for something to happen. Something wonderful, that would transport her from a little church mouse to…she didn't even know what.

It had taken her almost dying to realize that with all the waiting, she hadn't yet lived.

Well, that ended today. Jesse was right. No more waiting. If she wanted a different life, it was up to *her* to find it.

Now she just had to decide what that was. She stood and walked to the kitchen, pulled a steno pad and pen from the drawer, then sat at the tiny round table she used as a dining table. At the top of a blank page, she wrote "New Life" in tidy cursive. Then she sat, staring at the wall for five minutes.

How can you not know?

Well, maybe a place to start would be to consider what she admired in other people. Who would she be if she didn't have to consider anyone, or anything else?

"Who would you be, if you weren't afraid?"

Something about the question broke the logjam

in her head and she wrote fast, trying to catch the thoughts before they floated downstream.

Adventurous Independent
Pioneering Brave

A fizz of thrill, like bubbles of champagne, coursed into her blood. Oh, yes, she'd admire someone like that. She wanted to be someone like that. But how?

What would a person like that do in their leisure time? She jotted:

Surf Skydive
Outdoorsman Jog, ride a bike, sports

Who knew you could plot out your life? So, what career would a person like that have? She wrote what came to her, without filters.

StewardessWilderness guide
Park rangerPilot
ParamedicBusiness owner
Tennis proTruck driver
HitchhikerMountaineer

Okay, so the last two weren't careers, and some may not be practical, but dang it, the cage door had been blown off its hinges, and she was going to open herself to all possibilities.

So there, Mom.

Smiling, she added to her list.

THE NEXT DAY, Hope walked into the empty basement classroom of the hospital, nervous, but determined. So far, her new life was just pages of lists. Today it would exist, because she'd say it out loud. Once it was out, and people heard it, she couldn't back out. After that, she'd get started living it. She tugged to straighten the collar of her best business blouse, walked to the circle of orange plastic chairs and sat in the same one as last time.

Then she got up, and sat in one across the circle. She was going to have to watch herself. Habits, held long enough, became cages. And she was done with those. She unbuttoned her blazer and retrieved the newsprint from the pocket:

WANTED: Full-time Retail Specialist. Room for advancement. Apply to: The Adventure Outfitter in Widow's Grove—Your gateway to adventure!

"WELL, GOOD MORNING, early bird."

Bina sat across the circle. Hope hadn't even heard her come in, but there she sat, two chairs to Hope's left. "Hello, Ms. Rani."

"Please, I'm Bina."

"Okay. Bina." Hope smiled.

The rest of the group must have shared an elevator, because they all filed into the room and sat. Hope tried to recall their names. A minute later, Bear walked in and took the last open chair, beside her.

She had no problem remembering his name, because it fit him so well. He was well over six feet tall, and built like a bear—thick, and muscular, with hair the red-brown color of a grizzly, pulled back into a ponytail, a bushy beard. His plain white T-shirt pulled tight across his upper arms and chest, displaying the fact that though he may be big, he was lean.

It wasn't just his body that took up room, either. She could feel attitude rolling off him. With a furtive twitch of her hips, she scooted her chair an inch farther away.

The chair tips made a loud screech across the tile.

His big head swiveled her way. Under heavy brows, his eyes were a dusky shade of chocolate brown. And not angry at all. In fact, she saw more curiosity than animosity. And pain. Those eyes had seen more than they wanted to. She didn't know how she knew, but she knew it sure as her mother's rules of deportment.

She continued her study. His big forearms

rested on his thighs. On the back of one was a tattoo. She recognized the eagle and anchor, but in the center, where the globe should be, were the crosshairs of a rifle scope. A shiver shimmered through her.

"Well, let's get started, shall we?" Bina's voice broke into her thoughts.

Realizing she was staring, Hope looked away fast, her face hot enough to be glowing. She scrubbed her palms over her dress slacks, crossed her feet and tucked them under her chair.

"The last time we talked a bit about why each of you is here," Bina began. "Today, I'd like some of you to share your stories in more detail. I know it will be hard, speaking about such emotional events with strangers, but this is a safe place, and talking about it will help your mind process the traumas you've suffered. It will help ease the horror and begin the healing." She glanced around the circle of faces. "Who would like to start?"

The left side of Hope's face tingled as Bear's regard slid across her skin.

The redheaded boy raised his hand. "How do you heal from something that could happen again at any time?"

Bina nodded. "Traumatic incidents tend to make us aware of how dangerous the world is, and how fragile we are, Bryan. Will you tell us what happened that night?"

He looked down at his hands, twisting together in his lap. "Curtis is an IT guy. He works crazy-long hours. Weekends, too. So we don't get to go out much." His face relaxed into a small, intimate smile as he stared, unfocused at the empty center of the circle. "That night we went to Aurelio's, our favorite trattoria. I chose it the first time we went out, because it was like Curtis—Aurelio means golden in Italian, you know."

Beside her, Bear made a strangled sound.

Bryan's face flushed blotchy pink, the way only a redhead's can. "Are you some kind of ho-mophobe?" He put a fist on his hip. "Because I really don't need that kind of judgment right now."

Bear held up a hand. "Peace out, dude. I just swallowed wrong."

"Go ahead, Bryan," Bina urged.

"We sat in our usual secluded corner. The candlelight loves Curtis. His eyes, that blond scruff…" Bryan sighed. "He looks like a god." His body seemed to shrink into itself. "Curtis paid, and we were leaving. It was late, and the room was almost empty. We stopped at the bath-room on the way out. It's down a brick corridor, next to the back door." He dropped his head, and watched his hands gripping each other, knuck-les white. "Three men came in and blocked the way out. Thugs. Said they watched us through dinner, and since Curtis was obviously infatuated with me, they wanted to know the reason." His breath came faster. "Ugly, filthy men. They leered at me. Curtis put me behind him and told them to go away. That we didn't want any trouble." His mouth twisted. "They laughed. One grabbed Curtis. I started forward, but he put a knife to Curtis's throat." His shoulders rose to earlobe level. "I had no choice. They were going to hurt Curtis if I didn't!"

"Take a breath, Bryan." Bina's calm voice was in stark contrast to the tension-filled air. "It's in the past. You're safe now."

His shoulders lowered maybe a quarter of an inch.

"If you didn't what, Bryan?"

"The last guy, the leader, he made me…you know. Go down on him." He threw his head back and said to the ceiling, "I had to! He said he'd kill Curtis!"

Lowering his head, he pulled a halting breath through his nose. "They made Curtis watch, the whole time." He put a hand across his mouth. "I can't tell you—" He choked a sob.

Someone hissed in a breath. Beside her, Bear whispered, "Jesus."

Hope sat stunned, suddenly and thoroughly grateful to have only taken a bullet.

"Afterward, they beat us. We tried to fight, but

there were three of them." He looked up, his horrified eyes liquid. "Do you know what steel-toed boots sound like, hitting bone?" He shuddered and tried to gather himself. "I was in the hospital for a week. Curtis…" He pulled in another shuddering breath and his shoulders collapsed. His elbows hit his knees. He buried his face in his hands. "Curtis is upstairs, still in a coma."

The room's air felt heavy, saturated with shock, shame and silence.

Bina's soft voice cut through it. "I'm so sorry, Bryan."

"That's horrible. Did they catch those bastards?" Anger tinged Mark's face red, leaving his horrific scar a bloodless white.

"Not yet." Bryan sniffed. "It's been a nightmare. I think I see them everywhere. At the hospital, at work, in the grocery store."

"Do you think they're still following you?" Hope asked.

"I think I'm just paranoid. From worry and not sleeping." He looked at Bina. "But they're still out there, so…how do you ever get over something like this?"

"You know this isn't in any way your fault, don't you, Bryan?"

He nodded.

"Good." Bina's shoulder-length helmet of black glossy hair swung when she tipped her head to the side. "How do you feel now, after having talked about it?"

He thought a moment.

Hope knew from experience that he was feeling around the edges of the hole in himself.

"A little calmer, I think."

Bina's smile was soft as suede. "Then I think you may have the beginning of your answer."

She stood. "Why don't we stand and shake off the tension? This work can be intense, and it helps to loosen our muscles." She demonstrated, shaking out her hands and rolling her shoulders.

Hope stood and took a deep breath and did neck extensions to break the grip of muscle tension.

Popping came from her left, where Bear cracked his knuckles, then, with a hand under his chin, twisted his neck until several vertebrae popped. She winced.

Bina lowered herself into her chair. "We have more time. Does anyone else have anything they'd like to share?"

The rest of the group settled.

Hope threw back her shoulders, excitement and worry sparring in her stomach. *Write it, talk about it, do it.* She took a breath and pushed the words out. "I have some good news to report."

"I think we all could use some of that," Bina

said. "Will you begin by telling us about your trauma?"

Hope walked them through the events of that day, feeling an odd detachment, as if she stood outside herself and watched. She couldn't help the comparison to Bryan's story. Not the story itself, but the emotion. She felt his experience in her gut—as if it had happened to her. Her own story felt as though it had happened to someone else.

She trailed off at the end, leaving the last words dangling in the air.

Bina's brows pulled together. "You sound very detached from the trauma, Hope."

Feeling the regard of the others, especially the solid presence on her left, she shifted in her seat. "I am. That's because it happened to the old me."

"The old you?"

"I can't go back to that life. I have no interest in it any longer. So I'm starting a new one. I've rented a wonderful little Victorian cottage. I moved in just yesterday." She tightened her muscles, her resolve and her courage. Once said out loud, this would be real. "And, after this meeting, I'm hoping to begin my new career."

"Congratulations," Mark said.

Hope didn't know Bina well, but her face seemed to be held carefully neutral. "What is your new career?"

"I'm applying for a job as an adventure specialist." She loved the way it rolled off her tongue, the words round and fat with promise.

"Oh, that sounds fascinating. What exactly does that entail?"

"I'm not really sure." She smiled, projecting a confidence that would be real soon. Hopefully. "But I'm excited to find out."

CHAPTER FIVE

"YOUR PRIOR EMPLOYMENT is a bit…light in adventure. Retail experience is completely missing." The man across the counter looked up from her application, one brow raised. Travis Kurt, the manager of The Adventure Outfitter certainly looked the part. He had brush-cut brown hair and bronzed skin with starburst laugh lines at the corners, and he had the long muscles of a gymnast. His big hands resting on the glass looked capable and trustworthy. Hope could easily picture him putting up a tent with one hand, while squeezing the life out of a venomous snake with the other.

She checked to be sure her shoulders were directly over her hips, then tilted her chin up, just a fraction. "I learn fast. You won't find a more committed and dedicated employee." She brought his attention to her résumé with a tapping fingernail. "My references will tell you—"

"That you were a good bank manager, I'm sure." He nodded. "But the skills required of an adventure specialist are very different."

"I'm sure they are. That's why I'm applying for

a retail position." She clasped her hands in front of her, in an attempt to hide their fine tremor. Widow's Grove was a small town. Santa Maria, its closest neighbor, wasn't a big city, either. The employment pool was kiddie-sized. Which probably wasn't a bad thing, since she wasn't a strong swimmer. Okay, dog-paddler. "I plan to begin as a clerk, then work my way up."

She hadn't known laugh lines could look skeptical.

"Ookay." He breathed the word out like a sigh, and pushed the papers aside with the edge of his hand. "Can you tell me what the tools in this display are used for?"

She glanced into the lighted case. The top shelf held compasses of many types, the bottom held clear plastic arm boards with Velcro straps. In the middle, plastic maps and small white marker boards. Thank God she'd reconnoitered yesterday, and done her research. "Orienteering. It's a family of sports that require good navigational skills to go from point to point in a diverse and unfamiliar terrain, at speed. Participants are given a topographical map, and—"

"You know the definition. But have you ever done it?"

"Well, no. But—"

"How about skiing?" He pointed to ski tips, just visible over the tent display to his right.

She knew about skiing. "Alpine, cross-country or snowboarding?"

One side of his mouth lifted a fraction. "Any of them."

"Actually done them? No. But—"

He pointed to the long delicate rods on a rack to his left. "How about fishing?"

Her brain skipped pages. "Spin cast, fly rod, Spey rod or—"

"Let's say any of the above." His eyes reminded her of the close-up photo of a hawk she'd happened upon while researching camping. Watchful. And a bit predatory.

"No, not actually, but—"

"Miss—" he glanced down at her résumé. "Sanderson. You've done your homework. That much is apparent. But our clientele actually participate in these sports. Our retail specialists require more than a Wikipedia education." He looked her over, from her dress flats to her carefully arranged hair. "And be honest, given your background and education, why you would you want this job?"

Her courage melted like candle wax under his hot focus. When her sweaty hands threatened to slip apart, she laced her fingers and hung on. Her career ambitions were shrinking like the rear end of a galloping horse, leaving her in the dust.

Her mother's rosary bead litany started up. *You*

*give up a perfectly respectable career, what do
you expect? I scrimped and did without to see
that you had an education, and you throw it away
for what? To become a store clerk? You don't
have the sense God gave a paving stone. I am a
total failure as a mother if this is what—*

Hope cut off the tape, midscreech. She'd lived
with it while her mother was alive, plus two
years. She had no intention of living with it any
longer. Or the life her mother had so carefully
steered her to. She forced her hands to relax, letting blood return to her fingertips.

*Come on, Hope. How do you expect to live a
life of adventure, if you give up this easily?*

She lengthened her spine and opened her
mouth to say something. Something brilliant, to
convince this man that she was the one for this
job.

Nothing came out.

Her only fallback strategy was to pour out her
sob story and hope for the best.

But she couldn't.

Hope snapped her mouth closed so fast, her
teeth clicked. She'd be darned—no, she'd be
damned (take that, Mom)—if she'd gain passage
to her new life through pity for her past one. Courageous people didn't behave that way.

She took a breath, a step forward and a chance.
"Have you ever in your life wanted a do-over?"

He tipped his head to the side, which she took as encouragement.

She forced her shoulders square. "You know, you go day to day through your life, not really thinking. But one day, something happens to make you stop and realize the path you're on isn't leading where you want to go. So you look back, and see all the steps you took to get you to where you stand now…see all the missteps that took you off the path to where you want to be." She released her hands, spreading them in a shrug. "This job is my step back onto that path." She glanced around the store, then back to the gatekeeper of her future. "Mr. Kurt, you may be able to find an applicant who has more experience. But I guarantee you won't find one who learns faster, or will work harder than I will." She curled her fingers into a fist and dropped it, soft but solid, on the glass case before her. "I have more at stake, and I refuse to lose."

"I believe you." The white lines at the corners of his eyes disappeared with his squint. "Okay, I'll take a chance."

Hope's muscles relaxed just enough to get a full breath.

"But—"

Her muscles snapped back to attention.

He leaned on his hands, bringing his face closer. "Training is expensive, so you'd better be sure you want to do this. You'll be required to take lessons from our experts in three sports that we sell equipment for. Your choice which."

Not trusting her voice, she nodded.

"You won't need to be an expert. You just need firsthand knowledge and familiarity with the equipment and how to use it."

This man was taking a chance on her. What if she wasn't up to the task? Was her mother right, keeping Hope sheltered all those years? Did she know something her daughter didn't? A wisp of panic must have escaped on to her face, because he asked, "But if you're not sure about this…"

Gravity weighed heavier than it had a moment ago, pulling the blood to her feet. She swallowed. Audibly. "Nope. I'm sure."

He gathered the employment papers. "In the meantime, you can start as a cashier. I assume you won't need much training there, given your background. When can you start?"

"Tomorrow." The word, pushed from her diaphragm, came out too loud.

He smiled. "We're closed on Sundays. Let's make it the day after that."

THE RUMBLE OF his truck's glass pack mufflers vibrated through the seat, settling into Bear's chest like a cat's purr. A crazy extravagance, but the mufflers were a promise he'd made to the '64

Chevy beater. He knew it looked like shit, with rust and primer spots, but he was saving the paint job for last. He wasn't sure what he wanted yet, but it was going to be epic. He patted the plastic steering wheel. "Hang with me, honey. We'll get you a makeover as soon as the bank balance comes up."

Checking both ways at the stop sign, he turned onto Monterrey. The spring air blowing in the window cooled his sweaty face. Maybe a new A/C compressor before the paint job. A long low brick building on his left caught his attention. No, actually it was the sign out front—The Bar None. A neon Schlitz sign flickered in the small window, and the door stood open. He slowed, trying to peer through the typical bar murk to see if it was crowded.

Damn, I'd love a beer.

He could almost feel the vinyl bar seat under his ass.

But after his last visit to a bar, he had no interest in a repeat performance. Prison claustrophobia squeezed, making him feel trapped in his own clammy skin. He hit the accelerator.

I'll get a six-pack at the store.

At the Piggly-Wiggly, he scanned the breakfast aisle, hunting for Pop Tarts. Spying them on the bottom shelf, he bent and took two boxes of strawberry. The Walmart in Santa Maria was cheaper, but the place was so crowded and noisy that he couldn't relax there.

Not that he could here, either, today. He tossed the boxes in the little plastic basket he held in his other hand, and sidestepped a harried woman trying to lift a toddler headed for a full-on meltdown. He walked away, fast.

Turning into the bread aisle, an old lady in a print housedress stood on tippy-toe, trying to reach a loaf of organic whole grain. He reached and handed it to her.

"Oh, thank y—" Looking up to see him towering over her, a look flashed in her eyes. The look of a rabbit, in the shadow of a hawk.

"You're welcome, ma'am." Feeling the sting of being innocently intimidating, he turned away and pulled a loaf of the whitest, fluffiest, empty-calorie bread he could find. After the bland slop in prison, he now ate whatever he damned well pleased, and white bread reminded him of lunches when he was a kid.

At the checkout stand, he snagged a box of Cracker Jacks. Ducking the cashier's stare, he paid cash and beat feet for the truck.

His jaw loosened when he turned off King's Highway onto the road that wound through the hills that would lead him home. The hills were still green, but soon they'd shift to the brushed gold tint he loved so much. When he turned in at the ruts that constituted his driveway, grass shushed along the underside of the floorboards. Bordered by barbed-wire fences, the trail wound a quarter mile to the copse of trees that hid his cabin and barn from prying eyes. The privacy was one of the reasons he'd loved this place on first sight. He rolled into his tree-shadowed cave.

A dusty sedan stood in the packed dirt yard.

Warning sirens wailed in his head.

A skinny man in a white shirt stood on the porch, hand cupped, peering in the front window. Bear's guard-dog temper woke, and snapping and growling, lunged to the end of its chain.

The mufflers burped as he hit the gas and roared into the dooryard. "What the fuck do you think you're doing?" he yelled out the passenger window, threw the truck in Park and shut down the engine. Then he was out the door and stalking for the cabin, fists clenched.

First its kids stealing paint, now it's some nosy salesman asshole. Why the hell can't people just leave me be?

The guy turned. His eyes got bigger the closer Bear got. "I was just checking to see if anyone was home. I didn't mean anything by it."

Skipping the concrete block step, Bear launched himself onto the porch. "This is private property, and you're trespassing."

The guy backed up a step and put up his hands.

"I—I've got a car. A '72 Camaro. I heard you do custom paint."

Oh, shit. His temper whimpered, and tail between its legs, slunk back from where it came, leaving Bear alone with his mess. "Oh. I do business out of the barn. I don't like people in my personal stuff." When he held out a hand to shake, the guy flinched back. "I'm Bear Steele. Tell me about your car."

"Um. I just remembered. I've got an appointment in town." The guy sidled to the broken slats of the railing at the edge of the porch and past Bear, without turning his back. "I'll need to stop by…some other time." He scurried down the cinderblock step.

"Wait." Bear reached in his back pocket for his wallet.

The guy froze, his eyes huge.

What, does he think, I'm going to shoot him? Bear pulled out a business card and handed it down, not wanting to spook the guy by getting closer. "I'm sorry to scare you. Give me a call sometime. I'd love to see that Camaro."

"Um. Yeah. Sure. Sometime." He scuttled to the sedan, slammed the door, fired the engine and hit the gas.

Dirt sprayed from the tires, and Bear watched the car disappear in the trees. He hiked to the truck to retrieve his groceries, swearing the whole way.

When the hell was he going to learn to control his temper? Hadn't it made him lose enough?

BEAR STOOD WAITING in the hall outside what he'd started thinking of as The Interrogation Room of the hospital. He'd gotten here first on purpose. He leaned, one motorcycle boot propped against the wall, hands in his front pockets. Waiting.

The dream came to him every night, and now his angel appeared twice a week in his waking time, too. He had to talk to her. Had to find out if this meant something, or if it was just one more of fate's cruel jokes.

But he knew he intimidated her, and after what she'd been through, she was skittish to begin with. He practiced a smile and tried to relax. A bit rusty maybe, but he knew from practicing in the mirror this morning that it made him look less…brooding.

He heard the elevator door ding, followed by Bryan's high-pitched voice. He and Mark, the scarred guy, came around the corner.

Mark kept walking, but Bryan stopped in front of Bear. "You know, I get hater vibes from you. Do you and I have issues?"

The elevator dinged again.

Crap. That's all he needed—to be in a touchy-feely discussion when Hope showed up. "Hard to believe, dude, but you star in your own life. Not mine." Bear glanced from Bryan's pursed lips, then back down the hall. "I told you. I've got nothing against gay. You don't believe me? Not my problem."

Bryan let out an exasperated sigh and rushed into the room.

Her white-blond hair caught his eye first. Even when he was ready, her face still held him for the space of several heartbeats. She was beautiful. And not because of his dream, either. Her ice-blue eyes held secrets that her open face belied. She was all business, even in khakis and a denim short-sleeved shirt. But her lips…her lips were pure sex. They made him want to bow his head and worship them.

Noticing him notice, she looked down and kept walking.

Before she could brush by him, he reached out, and touched her arm. She shied back, the lines of her body full of alarm.

"Wait. Please. I just wanted to talk to you for a second. I'm Bear—"

"I know your name."

"I just wanted to tell you…you don't have to be afraid. I can't help how I look, but that's not who I am."

She looked up at him, head cocked. But her eyes softened. "Okay."

How do people do this chitchat thing? He put his foot back on the floor, and his hands back in his pockets. "Um. How's that adventure thing working out for you?"

A tiny self-satisfied smile softened her mouth. "Nailed the interview. I start today."

"Nice. Congratulations."

"Thanks." She took a step toward the door.

"Wait." He took a hand from his pocket, reached out, but didn't touch her. "Were you serious about wanting to be more adventurous?"

She looked at him as if he was a vacuum cleaner salesman on her front porch. "S-sure."

"Then how'd you like to go for a motorcycle ride?" He pulled his mouth up into what he hoped was a benign smile. "I've ridden a hundred thousand miles without an accident. I promise I'm safe."

"I don't even know you." She slapped a hand over her mouth, as if shocked at her own abruptness.

"I get that, but—"

"I mean, you don't ever talk, in group." Those ice-blue eyes probed his face, looking for a crack to get into. "How can you expect people to feel comfortable around you, if you just sit and glare at us?"

He could give a crap if anyone was comfortable around him. Except her. "Oh."

"Excuse me." She brushed by him.

The Rani woman came around the corner, talking to the big woman in the shapeless dress, who walked head down, hair hiding her face.

He ducked into the room. *What now, Slick?*

It was pretty clear that he wouldn't get closer to Hope without giving something up. But talking about himself in a group like this? He'd feel as though he was on a Dr. Phil show. *No way. Not happening.* He grabbed an empty chair and scooted it back from the circle.

Then slid it back in.

He sat, crickets playing "Dueling Banjos" in his stomach as the last two settled into the remaining chairs.

"Happy Monday, everyone," Bina said. "Who would like to share first this morning?" She patted the soap opera lady's hand. "Brenda? How about you?"

She just shook her head.

"Brenda, this is a safe space. Feel free to keep it to whatever you're comfortable sharing."

The woman pulled at her dress, trying to make it even looser. "I'm not from around here. My husband, Phil, got transferred to Vandenberg six months ago."

"He's in the air force?" Mark asked.

"No, he's a civilian inventory management specialist."

"Do you like it here, so far?" Bryan asked.

Hands in her lap, she picked at a cuticle. "It's okay."

"Why did the court mandate that you be here, Brenda?" Bina leaned forward, trying to get the woman to look at her. It didn't work.

"I don't know."

Bear heard it only because she sat beside him.

"You'll have to speak up, dear," Bryan said.

"We've got bossy, nosy neighbors." Her voice hovered, just above a whisper. "Phil, he gets mad sometimes." She tucked a hank of hair behind her ear, eyes still on her lap. "For good reason. I… I'm kind of a mess."

The group waited. Bear swore he could hear dust falling.

"What makes you say that, Brenda?" Bina asked.

She heaved a sigh, and rolled her eyes until they landed on Bina. "Oh, please. Just look at me. I'm fat, I'm ugly. I'm pretty useless."

Bina frowned. "I don't think that's true. Tell me one good thing about yourself. Something you're proud of."

Brenda sat like a female Buddha, contemplating the meaning of the universe. Finally, she said, "I married well."

"Really?" Mark said. "Pardon me for saying so, but your husband sounds like a major jerk."

"You don't even know him." She glared across the circle. "See? This is what I knew would happen."

"Why don't you tell us about you, instead?" Bina jotted a note on the small notebook in her lap.

"Like what?"

"Oh, I don't know. Why don't you tell us your happiest memory?"

When Brenda's head lifted, the crease between her brows was gone, and she looked different.

He realized that it was her eyes. Well, not her eyes exactly, but it was as if she was looking out them instead of looking inward, for the first time since he'd seen her.

"I had a puppy once. He was sweet, and all mine."

"What kind of dog was it?"

"Oh, I don't know, just a mutt, mostly. I found him in a parking lot of a grocery store, digging in the trash for something to eat."

"What did you name him?" Hope asked.

"Bucky."

When Brenda smiled, Bear could see the woman behind all that fat and sadness. She was pretty.

"Bucky and me, we went everywhere together. He loved me."

"Where is he now?"

The pretty woman dissolved into the washed-out housewife. "Oh, he died. It was a long time ago."

Hope asked, "Why don't you get another puppy?"

"Phil doesn't like animals." Brenda's head dropped, and she started worrying her cuticle again. "Besides, he's allergic."

She should develop an allergy to Phil. Not that it's any of my business.

"Thanks for sharing that, Brenda. It's nice getting to know you a bit better." Bina crossed her legs. "Who else would like to share?"

Bear almost squirmed in his chair, but caught himself in time. *Say something.* But what? Hope made it clear he was going to have to give to get. But what would constitute sharing, without revealing anything? Any thread he picked at could unravel his carefully woven blanket of solitude. And he couldn't allow that to happen. He chewed his lip. What then?

"You are now looking at a retail adventure specialist," Hope said.

"Hey, congrats," Mark said.

"That's the job you wanted, right?" Bina watched Hope from under one raised eyebrow.

"Yes. I start later today. I'm manning the register to start, but I'm going to take lessons in three adventure sports, to better be able to sell the equipment."

"You're not going to skydive, are you?" Bryan's long-fingered hand splayed on his chest. "I'm terrified of heights."

The kid looked so aghast, Bear couldn't help it—he chuckled.

Bryan shot him a glare.

"No way. I'm looking for adventure, not terror." Her fond smile, aimed Bryan's way, pinched Bear. "No, I think I'm going to start with surfing. It looks so… I don't know, freeing. You're riding a force of nature, harnessing the power for your own happiness. You've got to feel free then, wouldn't you think?"

The longing made her face glow. It pulled words out of him. "That's what it feels like, when I'm on my bike."

Bina jumped in, fast. "How so?"

"Well, you're not harnessing nature, but you're out in it—almost a part of it. You smell what's in the wind, feel the flow of the land underneath you. The changes in temperature, the weather. It affects you in ways there aren't words for. You can only feel it."

"It sounds amazing." When Hope turned that fond smile on him, it warmed him. Or maybe it was embarrassment. Or both. He ducked his head. "It is."

"Tell us something else about you, Bear." Bina's voice was soft, but it poked him.

"I have a business, doing custom paint jobs, out of my barn."

"Cool," Mark said. "Where'd you learn to do that?"

"My dad had a repair shop when I was growing up. He hated painting. Turned out, I liked it. So I took over that part." He checked the clock on the wall over the door. Five more minutes. Surely he could keep this up that long. Surely Hope would consider this "sharing."

"Why did you join the army, Bear?" Bina only sounded innocent.

He shrugged. "Those people brought their shit to my country. Thought I'd give a little of it back."

"Wooah," Mark said.

"Amen, brother."

Bryan rolled his eyes.

"I understand you were a ranger." Bina consulted her little notebook. "A sniper, is that right?"

He ground his teeth. She couldn't lead him anywhere he didn't want to go. He glanced at

Hope. She nodded, encouraging him. How had he walked into this ambush?

Bryan's strident voice broke the silence. "What I'd like to know is why he was in prison."

CHAPTER SIX

THE LIGHT LEFT Hope's face. Along with most of the color. "Prison?"

Brenda, the soap opera queen flinched.

Mark leaned back in his chair. "Dude."

So much for not sharing. Outed by a gay guy—the ultimate irony. *Son of a bitch.* Noticing his clenched fists, Bear forced his hands to relax. His temper would do more than cost him a customer, here.

"You don't have to talk about that if you don't want to, Bear," Bina said.

"Oh, yeah. It's kinda the pit bull in the room now. Thanks a lot, asshole."

The little pissant sat arms crossed, as if owed an explanation.

Bear chewed his lip, trying to figure how to make a steaming turd smell like room freshener. He glanced again at the clock. In four minutes. It was impossible. He almost heard his chances ticking away. "A guy gave me crap about being a soldier. I punched him. He hit his head on the way down. It was an accident, okay? A freaking, stupid, accident."

"What were you charged with? How much time did you do?" Mark asked.

He looked to Bina, but she just nodded encouragement.

Fuck. This is never going to end. He'd have blown them off, if not for the fact that Hope was hanging on every word, looking as though she wanted to believe the best. "Involuntary manslaughter. Ten months." He ground the words between his jaws and spit them out.

"The guy *died*?" Bryan's mouth was an O of horror.

Let that be a lesson unto you, asshole. He forced his fists to relax. Again. "Hence the prison term." If sarcasm could slice, this guy would look like a teen in *The Texas Chain Saw Massacre*.

Bina must have sensed his potential for eruption. "I think we'll leave it there for today." She stood. "Good session. I'll see you all back here on Wednesday."

Bear would have caught Bryan outside for a meeting of minds, but it turned out weasels could move—he scuttled away, fast. That was probably for the best. The kid was just a distraction anyway. What Bear really wanted was to talk to his angel. He waited outside the classroom, while Hope lingered inside, talking to Bina.

They walked out together. Two pairs of eyebrows went up when they saw him.

"Hope, can I talk to you for a second?" He waited, dangling at the end of his last chance.

She shot a look at Bina, then back at him.

He held out his hands, palms up, trying to look unimposing. "I just have a question to ask. I promise I won't keep you long."

Hope glanced around. The classroom was in the basement of the hospital. The halls were deserted.

Bina locked the door. "The cafeteria is on the ground floor to the right of the elevators, if you two would like to get a cup of coffee."

Bina's comment seemed to shatter Hope's indecision. She checked her phone for the time. "I have a half hour before I need to get to work."

He let out the breath he'd been holding. "That's great."

As Bina brushed by him, he could swear she winked, but since he only saw her profile, it was impossible to tell for sure.

The cafeteria was prelunch busy. He bought them coffee, and they sat at a small round table near floor-to-ceiling windows that looked out on a sloping landscaped courtyard. Hope stirred her coffee, waiting for him to say whatever he had to say.

If only he knew what that was. He wasn't even

sure why he needed to talk to her so desperately. Maybe in talking, he'd hear the answer. He took a sip of coffee he didn't want, then set the cup down. "This is going to sound crazy, and given what you just learned about me. See, the thing is…" He focused on her eyes. They reminded him of the lapping waters of the Caribbean: soothing, yet incessantly restless at the same time. And like those waters, they calmed him. "Have you ever felt that a stranger held the answers to all of your questions?"

Her head tilt held curiosity and concern at the same time.

"I know that sounds bizarre. I swear to you, I'm not a stalker. I don't want anything from you. I just had the oddest feeling when I met you." The past hour's tightrope walk had worn on his nerves. Now, when he needed words more than ever, he was spewing nonsense. He looked down at his coffee cup. He lifted and set it down in precise one-quarter turns. "Oh, never mind. I'm sorry to have—"

"I believe you."

He looked up at her soft words.

"I don't really understand what you're trying to say, but I can tell you're sincere."

He blew out a breath. "Well, that's something anyway."

Her laugh tinkled over him. "You should

see your face. You look like you just got a stay of execution."

He kind of had.

She checked her phone. "I'd like to know more about this. But right now, I've really got to go."

"Then we're going to have to do this again. Maybe by then, I'll be able to explain better." He wanted to ask her out. But the straight line of her back and the tight line of her lips told him if he pushed right now, she'd be in the wind. So instead, he stood and held her chair as she gathered her things and rose. "Come on, I'll walk you out."

They chatted all the way to the parking lot, where he'd scored a slot in the first row.

"Is that your bike?"

"Yep."

"Wow. Did you do the paint job?" Her hand hovered, a hairbreadth above the tank, tracing the ghost flames.

He shivered as if she'd almost touched his skin. "Yeah. You like it?"

"It's beautiful. So real you expect to feel the heat."

He sure felt it.

He took his helmet from the fringed leather side bag. "Maybe you'll take me up on that ride sometime. When you know me better."

Her mouth said "Maybe." Her eyes said *No friggin' way.*

"Hey, you wanted adventure, right?" He smiled and threw his leg over.

"Yes, but one adventure at a time. Right now, I've got a first day at my new job adventure to live through." Her smile was a parting gift. "I'll see you Wednesday. Thanks for the coffee."

"Thanks for listening to my incoherent babble." He strapped on his helmet, watching her walk away.

At least she hadn't run screaming, or called the cops. He was going to call that a success.

He turned the key and cranked the throttle. The bike fired up with a roar. Wednesday suddenly seemed a long time away.

"OKAY EVERYONE, QUIET DOWN. The store opens in a few minutes, and we have things to discuss."

Travis Kurt leaned against the counter in the break room of The Adventure Outfitter, addressing his Monday opening crew.

Hope scanned the athletic bodies draped over chairs and perched on counters, feeling like a measly mortal in the Hall of the Mountain Kings. They wore the company uniform of ivory button-down shirts with the sleeves rolled, khaki cargo shorts and lightweight hiking boots as if they'd been born in them. Healthy, tanned and self-assured—any one of them could have starred in a granola commercial. She crossed her legs in a futile attempt to hide their ghostly pallor.

Of course you feel ridiculous. You don't belong here. You were a gently raised young woman, not a person who does their business in the woods. A cashier. I suffered, to send you to college, and you end up a—

She squelched her mother's voice, midscreech.

"First, I want to introduce our newest team member, Hope Sanderson." He held out a hand, palm up, in her direction.

She just offered a timid wave to the curious look-overs.

"She's new to adventure sports, so she'll be a champion of the checkout line while she's in training. Have you decided which three departments you want to specialize in, Hope?"

No need to worry about her pallid skin, because she was now pink all over. "I'm not sure about the other two, but I'd like to try surfing, first."

"Ah, good choice. Hope, meet Arthur Bogart Chase, our surfing expert." He pointed to a young man leaning on the wall beside the minifridge, built taller and bigger than she'd imagined any surfer would be.

But what did she know?

He nodded at her. "Let's talk later, and we'll coordinate your first lesson."

Coordination. Another skill that she didn't possess. Yet.

Travis handed out a list of outdoor events within a two-hundred-mile radius of the store, so they could keep their customers informed. He highlighted storewide markdowns and upcoming sales, then had each department head explain one of their lesser known items and its selling points.

Hope took notes.

He released them with a booming "Let's go get people fired up about the outdoors!"

He paired Hope with another cashier, Grace, and in no time, Hope was ringing up sales. Maybe it wasn't the most mentally stimulating job she'd ever held, but she enjoyed chatting with customers and trying to guess what some of their purchases were used for.

A few hours later, she checked out the last person in her line and then a leggy blonde employee stepped up to her counter.

"I'm Lori Olsen. Goddess of all that is camping. Can you do lunch?"

Hope glanced around. "Um. I'm not sure. Can I?"

Grace made shooing motions. "You go ahead. I'll hold the fort and go when you get back."

"Okay. I'll be back in…" She reached under

the counter and retrieved her purse. "How long do we have for lunch?"

"Forty-five minutes," Grace and Lori said together.

"Okay. Lead on, Goddess."

"No need for formalities. You can call me Lori." She flipped a lock of waist-long golden hair over her shoulder and took long strides to the door.

Hurrying to follow, Hope couldn't help but notice her lunchmate's muscular thighs and heart-shaped butt.

Common. Her mother chimed into Hope's thought. *A lady never wears clothing that tight. Or revealing.*

Maybe my butt will look that good in the uniform, after I try all these sports. That shocked her mother to silence.

Lori held the door. "You okay with eating at the drugstore? There's a great café there."

If Hope ate lunch out, it was always at The Farmhouse Café, with Jesse. But Hollister Drugs was just down the street. "I've never eaten there. Sounds good."

"Oh, you've got to order a milk shake. Sin makes the best in town."

Hope checked out Lori's fat-free frame. "Where do you put them? If I drank a milk shake, it'd be on my hips in thirty seconds."

"I'm a runner. Three miles every morning means I earn a treat for lunch."

"Run? Morning? I'd rather just have a salad for lunch, thanks."

They strolled down Hollister, Hope walking on the outside, ducking from under the canvas awnings of the stores they passed. The sun felt good, warming her naked thighs. She'd never owned a pair of shorts higher than the top of her knee before. They made her feel daring and exposed, all at the same time.

Kind of like my new life. Her mouth spread in what had to be a goofy grin. "Thanks for being the welcome wagon for a newbie."

Lori walked to the glass doors of Hollister Drugs, and pulled one open. "I have an ulterior motive."

"Now I'm worried." Hope stepped in, but caught her toe on the doorsill, and stumbled into Lori. "Sorry."

Lori caught Hope's arm to steady her. "Hope was a much better name for you than Grace."

"Very funny." Heavenly scents distracted her. French fries, bacon and...was that hot fudge?

Beyond the cashiers, the aisles of products led through the store to the pharmacy against the back wall. But Hope's nose directed her left, where an old-fashioned soda fountain perched in a sea of black-and-white checkerboard tile. The huge mirror behind it reflected the stacks of sundae boats and parfait glasses. All of the white wrought-iron tables were occupied.

Lori led the way through the babble of the lunch crowd to the bar where they snagged the last two seats. "Hey, Sin."

The young woman behind the bar didn't even look up. She dispensed a soda from the old-fashioned draft handle and flipped a burger on the grill at the same time. She wore a pink throwback A-line dress with a white frilly apron and pink pillbox cap perched on her turquoise shoulder-length hair. The rims of both ears were encrusted with studs and her lipstick and nail polish were lime green. "Do I look like I got time to chat?" She snapped gum like machine-gun fire. "The McDonald's is closed for redecorating, and everybody got ravenous at the same time. Holy shit." She planted a hand on her bony hip and pointed a spatula at Hope. *Snap snap.* "What's her problem?"

Hope closed her mouth and focused on arranging paper napkins in her lap.

"Ah, she's new, don't mind her," Lori said.

Sin slapped the burger on a bun, tossed on a tomato, lettuce and pickles. She spun, pulled a fryer out of the oil, shook on salt and dumped some fries on the plate. She put the plate and the soda on the counter. "Hey, Bert, come get it!"

She wiped her hands on her apron. "What do you two want? Reubens are off the menu today. No time."

"Strawberry milk shake." Lori didn't even hesitate.

A moment on the lips, a lifetime on the hips. "I'll have the same."

"Ah, easy. I can do easy." She whirled, and took a milk carton from the minifridge and closed it with her foot. "Simon, you want a coffee refill, you'll have to come back here and get it yourself."

Hope watched the girl, amazed at her skill, concentration and *interesting* uniform/personal-style pairing.

"So, Hope, you went from bank manager to retail cashier. How come?"

Hope turned to Lori's frank perusal. "You know."

"Everyone does. In that place, gossip travels faster than a hang glider in an updraft. So, spill. Why the drastic career change?"

Sin set two sweating fountain glasses in front of them. The straw stood up on its own and chunks of strawberry hung suspended in the glass.

Hope ran a finger down a drip on the side and tasted. "Hmm. You were right, she's a whiz."

Ladies don't pry into private affairs. This one is pushy, brash and—

Maybe so. But Lori had extended a hand of welcome to a stranger. Hope could use some friends, especially as she navigated the unknown waters of her new job. Besides, she obviously already knew the facts of the robbery, and the standoff. "When I woke up in the hospital, I realized that I had been living the life my mother chose for me." She bounced the straw in her glass. "I hadn't even realized it. But sadder yet, when I thought about what career I'd rather have, I had no clue." She glanced at Lori. "Pathetic, I know." She took a sip. It was thick, cold, rich— and damned fine. Worth every stinking calorie that she felt sliding down her throat to settle in her butt.

"The only thing I'm sure of is that I don't want to die without having lived. I know that sounds dramatic, but I feel like if I don't do it now, I never will."

"I totally get that." Lori used a long spoon to scoop up a chunk of strawberry. "Which brings me back to my ulterior motive—why don't you choose camping as one of your departments to learn? You and I would have a blast. I can teach you everything you need to know."

"Snakes and spiders and peeing outside?"

Hope wrinkled her nose. "I appreciate the offer, but no, thanks. Besides, I want adventure!"

"Yeah, but—"

"Once I learn to surf, next I think, is sailing. Then, maybe rock climbing. Or skydiving." She pictured herself, tanned and athletic, hanging off a sailboat on one of those rope sling thingies, with the sun setting behind her.

"Really?" Lori's eyebrow disappeared into her bangs. "Are you sure? Because you don't seem to be the most…um…coordinated…"

"Oh, thanks for the vote of confidence."

"Hey, don't discount camping. Hiking is a great workout. Besides, you're out in nature. It's not only good for you physically; it's good for your *soul*."

"Want some granola in that milk shake?"

Lori chuckled. "Oh, shut the hell up."

THAT AFTERNOON, BEAR knelt in the barn beside his current job, a royal blue 1971 Camaro. He airbrushed a curling baby blue pinstripe onto the rear quarter panel, then pressed his wrist to the bandanna on his forehead to blot sweat. It was cooking under the spot lamps, but he needed the light. He bent again, tracing the motion of the stripe without spraying, to get the feel; like a golfer taking a practice swing.

"Hey, Bear, incoming!"

Shit. This place was getting to be like a government building, with all the people coming and going.

Priss, the spikey-haired girl who'd been with the kid the other day, stepped out from the box wall. Following her close was a clean-cut guy with short brown hair.

He set the sprayer down on a towel and shoved his safety glasses back on his head. "What the hell do you want now?"

"I wanted to talk to you."

He stood. "So, talk."

The guy's eyes got big, and his throat clicked when he swallowed.

"Nacho has his heart set on learning to paint cars." She reached a hand out, to lean on the car. "With you."

"Don't touch that!" He took a step forward. She jumped.

"Hey," the guy said from behind her. "No need to yell."

Bear eyed him. Maybe six feet, but still a good six inches shorter than he. And a lot less muscular. "Who're you?"

"That's Adam." She crossed her arms over her chest. "Look, I don't want to offend you, but I hear you've been in prison."

He pulled a rag from his back pocket to wipe

his hands. "Well, you got balls, lady. I'll give you that."

The little thing held his stare. "I'm responsible for Nacho—I'm his sister and his guardian. It's my job to ask all the questions."

"You're assuming I want a kid around the place."

"You told Nacho to come around and you'd show him some stuff. It's all he's talked about since." She stuck out her chin, probably trying to look badass. She almost pulled it off. "Are you the kind of guy who would lie to a kid?"

Your own fault. Why the hell did you tell the kid that? Because something about that kid's dark eyes and black hair reminded him of another kid, a world away. He stuffed the rag back in his pocket. "Follow me."

He walked to the back of the barn, where he'd set up a card table and chairs next to the huge back door. He liked to take breaks here, where he could watch the looming trees stir in the breeze. He waved at the old coffeemaker and mugs on the table. "Take coffee if you want it." He poured a cup and doctored it with enough sugar to put a diabetic into a coma.

Priss poured herself a cup, and perched on one of the chairs. Adam took a chair and straddled it, though he didn't look relaxed in the least.

This went against Bear's nature. He didn't owe anyone an explanation.

Penance, remember?

Maybe, but he could volunteer, teaching kids to box, or by being a baseball coach. No one had to know why. That felt right. That felt doable.

But he'd been a Catholic his whole life. He knew that easy didn't count as penance. He picked up his coffee, donned his hair shirt and sat. "Since you had the guts to show up, I'll tell you the deal." He watched the trees sway, dredging for the words. "I was pretty wild when I got back from Afghanistan."

"Army?" Adam asked.

"Sniper." He nodded. "Anyway, back stateside, I was playing pool one night, minding my own business. A guy heard I'd been over there, and started yapping off. You know, all about how our 'Imperial Army' was just there for an oil grab, yada, yada. Normally I ignore it, but I'd had a few that night, and he was more obnoxious than most. Anyway, I punched him. He hit his head against a table on the way down. Broke his neck. The doctors called it a freak accident. If I hadn't been a champion boxer in high school, they wouldn't have prosecuted." He really should stop here. "I swore I'd never lose my temper again. And I haven't. I don't."

He looked over at her. "I keep to myself. Don't

want trouble with nobody." He drained his cup. "But I like kids. Always have. They're honest. If you want to let the boy come out here, I'll give it a shot, working with him."

He knew what it looked like when someone sized you up on a tough judgment call. He'd done it himself, every day, in Afghanistan. He just looked back. *Easier for me if she says no anyway.*

"I'll pay you."

Adam stood. "Priss, I don't think—"

She ignored him. It was clear Momma was in charge here. "The only thing is, I don't have much money."

"Let's see if he's really interested, first." Bear put the coffee cup on the table and stood. "If he screws around, or is a hassle, he's out. I'm not a babysitter, and I can't afford to redo work."

Priss stood, and put her untouched coffee on the table. "I'll make sure he understands. Nacho needs something of his own to hang on to. Something he's good at. He really respects your talent." She stuck out a hand.

It disappeared into his. The class at the hospital was the state's last condition of probation. It was probably time he started on his own condition: atonement.

CHAPTER SEVEN

BEAR WAS WAITING at the door of the hospital on Wednesday. Hope looked him over as she approached, pinballs of conflicting impressions whizzing through her brain. He was *so* big. The top of her head hit him around biceps-level. But now that she was getting used to his looks, she realized that his face wasn't made up of angry lines; what made him look frightening was his intense focus. No one looked at other people that way—as if he saw past the mask people wore to what they really were. *That* was scary. Not that she had anything to hide, but it was unnerving to be stripped bare like that. Like he was looking at her now.

But his eyes—he must have seen so much death and pain—heavy shadows of it remained in their chocolate depths. She recalled his story from the last group. *Not all of that pain belongs to others.*

What does he want from me? His stumbling admission over coffee two days ago told her only that he didn't know, either. But she didn't get spooky stalker vibes from him, which was odd, because her mother had trained her to be afraid of pretty much everything.

She took the stairs to his tentative smile, and the questions in his eyes. "Hello, Bear."

"Hope." He held the door open for her. "How's the new job?"

Her shoulder bumped the door frame on the way by. "The cashiering part is easy. I don't know about the 'adventure' part yet. My first surfing lesson is Saturday."

"Surfing?" He watched her rubbing her stinging shoulder. "For some reason I can't picture you as a surfer girl."

"Well, it's going to happen." She stabbed the elevator button as if it had offended her.

"Oh, I believe that."

She glanced over as the doors whooshed open, to see if he was laughing at her.

"I think you could do anything you put your mind to." There was a touch of awe in his voice, and a touch of pink in his cheeks.

"Thanks for the vote of confidence. I can use it."

"Why?"

Maybe he couldn't see through her mask, after all. "I'm a bit of a klutz. And I don't really swim all that well." The bell dinged for the basement, the door opened and she stepped out, shoulders square, chin out. "But I'll be better at it, after Saturday."

Bryan stood outside the classroom door, sniffing and looking at the ceiling. As Bear walked past, a tear rolled down the kid's pronounced cheekbone.

Not your problem. But Bear stopped, just the same.

"What is it, Bryan?" Hope put a hand on his forearm.

He sniffled again, and swiped a sleeve across his eyes. "I just came from Curtis's room."

"He's no better?"

Bryan just shook his head and took a deep breath, trying to pull himself together.

A dart of sympathy hit Bear in the chest. The guy had an attitude problem, and he'd been an ass, but... "Ah, that sucks, dude. Really."

Bryan squinted at Bear, as if searching for sarcasm. "Thanks." He nodded. "Sorry for blindsiding you last time. But getting it out and talking about it really helps."

Right. You were trying to do me a favor. He walked away before the sarcasm could slip out.

Once they were all seated, Bina asked, "Who would like to start today?"

She waited a full fifteen seconds. "Mark, we haven't heard much from you. Why don't you start?"

His face reddened. The scar blanched white, making him even harder to look at. "I don't know what you want me to say."

"Can you tell us about the accident?"

He huffed out a breath. "I don't remember much." His eyes darted, avoiding the circle's occupants. His gaze finally settled on the wall, somewhere over Bina's head. "The doctors say that's not uncommon."

They waited.

"It was late at night. I was driving through Santa Barbara. I don't even remember why I was out that late. But I either fell asleep, or maybe I passed out. I woke up in the hospital, a day later, after Doctor Frankenstein put me back together." He looked down at his hands clasped to white in his lap. "As much as he could anyway. They told me I ran headfirst into an overpass abutment. And that I was lucky to be alive." He snorted. "Oh, yeah, I feel lucky."

"Alive is always better," Bryan said.

"Really?" Mark sneered. At least the unscarred side of his mouth did. "You live like this for a few days, and I'll ask you for your opinion then." Anger spilled into his voice, making it come out ugly. "Children run screaming from me. Literally, screaming. But at least they're honest. Adults, they go through stages that flash across their faces: fear, curiosity, then embarrassment—

for me or for themselves—I'm never sure. Then, the *pity*." He spit the last word as if it tasted foul. "Then they get away, as soon as politely possible. Because, God knows, they have to be polite."

The room was full of Mark's anger and the silent imaginings of everyone else.

"Oh, I don't know," Bryan whispered. "I think Curtis would trade places with you. I know I'd be happy to have him back—no matter how he looked."

Mark, in the grip of his own pain, wasn't ready for anyone else's. "Happy to oblige. More than happy." He looked up at Bryan. "Now, can someone tell me how we do that?

"See, I've got nobody. My parents are long gone, buried in Missouri. I came out here to work as a 'blue screen' tech for Hollywood. I hadn't planned on starring in a horror flick."

Hope shifted in her chair, as if the tension in the room made her restless. "Surely there's someone—"

"I used to have a girlfriend. I was going to marry her."

Hope winced. "Don't tell me she left you when this happened."

His mouth twisted. "Oh, no. She turned me down before the accident." He sighed. "Good thing, too. At least I know it wasn't about my looks. It was only about my personality."

What the hell can you say to make that better? Not that Bear would try. But you couldn't help but feel for the poor guy.

"I understand you have another surgery coming up?" Bina asked.

"Yeah. They're going to try to reconstruct my nose. Kinda like slapping a coat of paint on a haunted house." He shrugged. "The scar is the biggest problem. But they say if they try to fix that first, when they reconstruct the nose, it'll pull it all out of shape."

"Have you made any progress on getting out more?" Bina asked.

Mark's turn to shift in his chair. "I make it here. That's enough. I mean, why tear myself up, seeing people's reactions? What the hell good does that do?"

"You may find that it makes you stronger. That you feel better."

"If it doesn't kill me first, you mean." He scrubbed his hands over his ruined face. "Besides, I don't need to go out. I do that every night in my dreams."

"You dream about going out in public? Tell us about that," Bina said.

"I have horrible dreams. Like I'm the walking dead, and everyone is running from me. Even people I know from work. My parents, my old girlfriend..." His voice cracked.

When he didn't continue, Bina asked, "You may find you're not alone in this. Who else has nightmares?"

Bryan's hand shot up first. Then Hope's. Brenda's went up, tentative and half-mast.

All eyes turned to Bear. They made his skin heat. A platoon of army ants double-timed down his spine. He'd stand up and walk out if it hadn't been a bigger admission than simply raising his hand.

Oh, fuck it. They couldn't make him talk about it. His lifted his hand.

"See, Mark? Nightmares are very normal for those who have suffered trauma."

"Knowing that doesn't help when I'm in the middle of one."

"Yes, I can see that. They do fade with time, though."

"Yeah, but then I wake to this." His hands bracketed his face. "And this is not going to fade."

"I have homework. For you, Mark, as well as everyone else." Bina uncrossed her legs and closed her notebook. "I want you all to do something in the coming week that pushes you. Something that's hard for you to do. When it gets hard, and it will, you'll have the comfort of knowing that you're not alone. Okay?"

When the meeting broke up, Bear turned to Hope. "Do you have time for coffee?"

Her brows in profile furrowed, and she shot him a wary look out of the corner of her eye.

She still doesn't trust you.

"Hey, guys," she called to the rest, who had begun to stand and gather their things. "The hospital cafeteria is just on the way out. Want to go for coffee?"

Oh, Christ. Two hours a week wasn't enough time with these people?

"I'd love to," Bryan said.

"As long as you're ready for the looks you'll get with me there." Mark slung a carrier's bag over his shoulder.

"Don't be silly, of course we want you to come." She stood, and bent her head to try to see past Brenda's hair. "Brenda? What about you?"

The woman shuffled her feet and picked up her purse, which looked as if it belonged to a bag lady. "Oh, I couldn't. Phil will be calling. I need to get home."

"Come on. Twenty minutes couldn't matter."

Hope touched Brenda's arm and she jerked as if she'd been burned. Her eyes were wild. "I can't." She hustled for the door, leaving Hope staring after her.

Bryan chirped. "Bina? Would you like to join us?"

"I have another appointment." She stood. "Besides, I think it'd be great if you got to know each other better—without teacher around."

That had been the plan. Bear sighed, and trudged after the others.

Once they were seated with their coffee, Hope played hostess. "So, you know what I do for a living, and Mark told us he's an IT whiz with Hollywood. Bryan, what do you do?"

"I'm a jewelry designer. It's my passion."

"Wow. How wonderful it must be to make a living doing what you're passionate about."

"Oh, it is. I design commissioned jewelry for stores, but I'm also doing my own designs on the side, and selling them online." He pulled out a small stack of business cards, and passed them out. "You can check them out on my website."

Hope scanned the card. "You have more in common with Bear than you may guess. He's an artist, also."

Bryan's sour expression probably matched Bear's. "What do you do? Chain saw carving?"

A dry chuckle bubbled from his chest. "Funny how you thought *I* was the one who stereotyped people."

Guilt flashed as that volley hit home. "You're right. That was not only not nice, it was hypocritical." He extended a pale long-fingered hand. "I'm willing to start over if you are."

Bear shook the guy's hand, lightening up when he winced.

Bryan retrieved his hand. "Okay, so what *do* you do for a living?"

"You know those wooden bears that they sell at the swap meets?"

Red spread up Bryan's neck and his Adam's apple worked, as if trying to swallow words he'd already said.

Bear chuckled. "I'm just messing with you, man. I do custom paint jobs. Cars and motor-cycles."

"Oh, cool," Mark said. "I'd love to see how that's done. Maybe someday I could come out there and watch you work."

Bear took a gulp of his coffee to give him time to think of an excuse. He felt sorry for the guy, but invite him? Coffee seared through the soft membranes on the roof of his mouth. *Shit, goddamn, hellfire, stupid...* He couldn't spit it out in front of Hope. Finally, the lava cooled enough to swallow, though it still burned all the way down.

Hope rescued him. "Bryan, my cousin Jes-se's birthday is coming up. I don't have a ton of money, but I'd love to get her something special. Do you have any ideas?"

That began an animated discussion of unique costume jewelry that even Mark jumped into.

Bear sat like a...bear in a costume jewelry discussion. He was happy to sit back and become invisible.

It was impossible to untangle how much of what he felt was due to his dream, but one thing was fact: Hope was beautiful. He didn't think he'd ever tire of the innocent softness overlaying the hard bones of her face. It reminded him of the tawny coat over the rocky hills of Widow's Grove; just as pretty, just as enduring. Her eyes were the elusive blue at the heart of icebergs. True windows, they sparkled with delight, and sparked in anger. He hoped she didn't play poker. From what he'd seen, those eyes were incapable of deceit.

God that sounded stupid. Especially since he hardly knew her. But the odd...connection he felt was undeniable. As if he really did know her. But how could that be?

"Earth to Bear." Hope waved a hand in front of his face. "You know you're doing that scary-face thing again, right?"

"That's me, thinking." He shook his head to clear his thoughts, and his expression.

"What are you thinking?" She drained the last of her coffee.

Here is your shot. Maybe it would even help to have the other guys here. More nonchalant. Less intimidating.

Hopefully.

"I was wondering if you were ready for that motorcycle ride." He held up a hand when she would have spoken. "I know you have to go to work now. And I know you're surfing Saturday. How about Sunday?"

She chewed her lip. "I don't know. Surfing is about as much adventure as I can—"

"You should go. Remember, we have homework to do," Bryan said.

"It'll be good for you," Mark said.

She frowned, considering. Hard.

"I'll go out, if you do." Mark crushed his empty paper cup in his fist.

"And I'll go to dinner alone, if you go," Bryan said.

She looked at Bear.

"Hey, I'm the loner who doesn't like people. I'm pushing the envelope by offering, right?" She didn't need to know he was at least partly lying.

He watched her throat work as she swallowed. Then she blew out a breath. "Okay, but only if you all pinkie-swear." She held out a crooked baby finger, and one by one, they clasped it.

Her tiny finger almost disappeared in Bear's. She didn't let go. "You don't know how big a deal this is for me. I never even learned how to ride a bicycle, much less a motorcycle."

He held her gaze, his heart hammering. "I'll

never let anything happen to you, Hope. I swear it." He tightened his finger, locking hers in his. This was a lot more than a pinkie-swear to him. It was a vow. He released her finger, glad his voice didn't give him away.

"You never learned to ride a bike? Where are you from? Mars?" Bryan asked.

"Nope. I'm from the planet Vivian."

"Huh?"

"Never mind." She stood. "I've got to get to work, but this was fun." She looked down, into his eyes. "Let's do it again."

Bear stood, feeling his heart pumping and the rush of blood through his veins. His chest filled with something lighter than air. It took him a minute to recognize the feeling.

It was joy.

"PREP WORK IS seventy percent of painting. And it's the most important part." Bear rolled the Harley Fat Boy into the center of the barn work space. The spot lamps warmed the area, though the rainy day had never warmed up.

Nacho followed him, taking in every detail. Priss, his sister, had dropped him off after school, then hung around to be sure Bear wasn't going to eat him before she finally left, promising to pick the kid up before dinner.

"So, what do you do, wash it?"

The kid's age, brown skin and black hair and eyes still resembled the shadows in Bear's dreams. But maybe getting used to seeing them in the flesh would rob the nightmares of their power. Like exposure treatment for a phobia.

"First, you have to take it apart. Every single nut, grommet and washer needs to be removed. Luckily, this one doesn't have any stickers or vinyl on it. That can be a bitch—um—a real pain."

The kid rolled his eyes. "I'm not a little kid."

How was he going to handle this? Be the good-guy, mentor type? The tough cop? The badass motorcycle dude? He lowered the bike on the side stand, then tightened the bandanna around his forehead to give him time to think. And study the kid.

Bear had noticed the hand-lettered tats on the back of the kid's fingers. He had caught the hard look in his eye, as well as the vulnerability it was meant to cover. His sister was his guardian, so the parents were out of the picture—either dead or dangerous. From his attitude, the kid had seen bad stuff in his nine years, Bear had no doubt.

It wasn't his job to be a surrogate dad, or a cop. Best to just be himself, and they'd work out the rest as they went along.

He gave the kid a glare of his own. "I guess you're old enough to hear adult words. But if that scrappy sister of yours chews my ass because you're spouting them at home, we're done. Hear me?"

The kid stood a little straighter and hiked his jeans to keep them from falling down. "I'm hearing you."

"Okay. You ever been around tools? Do you know a box end from an open end?" He squatted by the engine of the bike.

"Course. My dad showed me before…well, before."

He peered under the engine. "Okay, go to that toolbox, second drawer down, and get me a three-eighths-inch hex."

Nacho hustled to comply, and returned with the right one, first time.

"Good. Now, squat down here and watch me." He slipped the wrench on and broke the first bolt loose. "You have to drain the tank first—don't forget that. Fuel is heavy, and you can bust a nut trying to carry the tank once you've got it off."

"Got it." Nacho watched close.

"You also don't want to let the wrench slip off and scratch the paint." He worked the wrench until he could finger-loosen the bolt.

"Why not? You're gonna paint it anyway, right?"

"Yeah, but it's more sanding if you have a gouge in the existing paint." Bear pulled out the bolt, and the nut from the back fell into his waiting hand.

"Oh, that makes sense." Nacho watched close.

"Hand me that metal dish over there." He pointed to the shelf on the toolbox. "You always want to keep the pieces together. Lose them, and you're gonna be screwed when you go to reassemble. Waste of time. And since I charge by the job, not by the hour, it's a waste of money. See?"

"Got it." Nacho retrieved the pan, and Bear dropped the parts in.

Then he handed the wrench to the kid. "Go ahead, you try."

With utmost concentration, Nacho knelt, slipped the wrench on the bolt, and pulled.

Nothing happened.

He put some weight on it.

Nothing.

Red-faced from holding his breath, he pulled until his knees came off the floor. He hung for a second, until the bolt broke loose.

"Maybe you are big enough for this, after all."

A huge grin broke over the kid's face, before he remembered he was tough, and the scowl took over once more.

Bear was careful to keep his own smile hidden. The kid reminded him a bit of himself, at that age—eager to be tough, and to please, all at the same time, with a little pissed-at-the-world thrown in, besides.

Maybe this would be okay, after all.

CHAPTER EIGHT

THE NEXT MORNING, Hope stood shivering in the sunrise on Pismo Beach. If she'd realized that the good swells happened at five thirty, or "dawn patrol" as Art called it, she may have chosen differently.

Art looked as at home in a wet suit as a seal in his skin. "Your lesson will be different than most, because besides learning to surf, you need to understand the equipment and the terminology in order to sell it. So listen up." He launched into an explanation of long board versus short board, Styrofoam versus fiberglass, rails and rockers.

She filed the information while she shivered. The onshore breeze was slight, chilling her sweaty face. Getting into a full wet suit was like donning a body girdle—embarrassing in private, but mortifying with an audience.

Sure, she wore a bathing suit underneath, but it was a tank-style racing suit, with a high French cut and plunging back that barely covered her butt. Lori insisted it was standard, and Hope had a lot of them come through her checkout line, but she'd never worn anything so revealing.

When she'd gotten her leg stuck in the wet suit and had fallen in the sand, Art had taken pity and helped her. Which was even more embarrassing. And now, with every movement, the sand trapped between her and the tight wet suit chafed. She felt like the Michelin Man. With sand fleas.

"That's the basics. Now, let's get out there." He handed her a Styrofoam long board. The wind caught it, pushing it across her body, and she almost fell again.

He looked her over. "You don't look very strong. It's a good thing we've got a glassy morning. I should probably have brought you a set of webs. They're gloves with webs between the fingers, to help you paddle."

Her stomach roiled as she watched the surfers out beyond the breaking surf near the pier, bobbing like sea lions on their boards. "I can paddle," she said through her clenched jaw. She'd checked with her doctor, and he'd cleared her for any sport she wanted to attempt, so there was no physical reason she couldn't do this. She swallowed, tamping down her worries and her shakes. Maybe watching Gidget movies on the internet wasn't the best way to prepare for actual surfing.

But her hair and her spirit both lifted when she turned into the wind and took a bracing lungful of salt tang, seaweed and cold. Here she was, living her own life, not her mother's ill-fitting, out-of-date, hand-me-down one. A thrill spiraled up through her, exploding in her head like confetti. "Bring it on." She smiled up at Art.

He smiled back. "Okay. Now, watch the waves. See how there are a few larger ones, then small ones in between? Those are set waves, and those are the ones you're going to ride. But first, you have to get out past them." He pointed to a cresting wave. "It's not that easy to do, if you don't know how. My short board will duck-dive under them, but yours won't. Remember why?"

"The rocker on mine is different."

"Right. So, when you come up to the wave, you hold on to the board and flip over. It'll take you right through." He knelt in the sand, and attached a Velcro band around her ankle that was attached by a cord to the board. "This is your leash. It keeps you from losing your board." He attached his own to his ankle and stood. "Watch me, and follow, okay?"

Not trusting her voice any longer, she just nodded.

He took a few running steps, holding his board out in front of him. When his feet hit the water, he launched, landing on his stomach on the board. He paddled a few strokes, then sat up and waved to her.

Here goes nothing. Hoping that saying wasn't literal, she managed not to trip as she took the running steps and flung herself down. Ice water covered her hands. In shock, she let go. And slid right off the nose of the board into a small breaking wave. It rolled over her, and down the back of her wet suit. She struggled against the shifting sand and the suit's restriction, and came up yelling. "Holy mother of God!" She pulled in air—having lost all of hers when the frigid water hit.

Something tugged. Her foot was ripped out from under her, and she fell again. She fought the surf and panic, though she knew she was only knee-deep in water. She came up spitting salt water and sand.

"It's your leash. Grab your board!" Art called from his comfy spot. He didn't act at all concerned that she was drowning.

Breathing like a buffalo, she caught her board and pulled it under her. The wind running over her goose bumps seemed warm in comparison to the surf. "That water is arctic!"

He chuckled. "Now when someone tells you they've been flushed, you'll know just what they're talking about. It's that delightful rush as the water goes down your back."

"I'd have been good with just the definition, thanks." She paddled over to him.

"Nah, you're gonna love this." He lay back

down on his board. "Now, remember, paddle into it, and roll upside down as the wave face breaks over you, okay?"

She lay down and watched the waves come at her, trying to decide on one like she had when she jumped into a skipping rope as a kid. She ignored the big ones. *No...no...that one!*

She paddled like a madwoman toward the one-footer that looked more like seven at water level.

When the end of her board touched the wave face, she rolled, gripping the board for dear life.

Bubbles, bubbles and darkness, the surge pulling at her. She let go with one hand and pushed to the surface.

Art lay on his board beside her, grinning like the Cheshire cat. "Excellent."

She craned her neck. The waves broke behind her. "I did it!"

"Course you did. Now, let's go." He started paddling out to sea.

Looking out at the open ocean, alarm shot through her core, heating it. It didn't extend to her hands and feet, though. Those were still ice-bound "Why? The waves are behind us."

"You have to paddle into a wave, so you have to get a ways behind it."

"A ways" turned out to be far enough out that her arms were rubber from paddling. She turned her board so it faced the beach and sat up, straddling it, trying not to imagine her legs from below, looking like chicken fingers to a shark.

What had she been thinking, choosing surfing? The sum total of her swimming experience had been in a pool, except one time she'd played in the shallows in the gulf. That ocean was way calmer than this coast. And way warmer.

"Why aren't we over with those guys?" She pointed to the surfers near the pier. The more chicken fingers, the better her odds the sharks wouldn't choose hers.

"They're regulars. They wouldn't welcome a kook—um, a beginner."

She was starting to think anyone in this frigid water at dawn was a kook, but didn't say so.

"Besides, they ride different waves than you. You're going to be looking for small ones; one to two feet max. Oh, look at that!" He pointed out toward the open ocean.

"What? Where?" Her feet were up on her board before her brain processed the information.

A dorsal fin broke the surface, twenty feet away.

"Was that a shark?" She squealed like a bopper in full crisis.

"No, dolphins! God, look at them."

A whole pod passed within feet of them, close enough for her to glimpse shiny laughing eyes, smiling mouths and flipper tails. They moved as if one, rising and falling in silvery sinuous waves, almost close enough to touch. Heart banging in her throat, she sucked in a breath and held it, wanting to burn the picture into her memory. But even more, wanting to capture the feeling—as if she could almost touch the exhilarating and terrifying wildness. It struck an instinctive thrum in her chest, making her recall a forgotten time when her species, too, was wild. When they were just imagined dots in the distance, she breathed, "Oh."

"See? There are advantages to getting up early." Art pointed to the shore. "Let's get to why you're out here to begin with."

He spent a few minutes explaining wave structure, the board's "sweet spot" and regular versus "goofy foot."

"Waves move faster than you think. You've got to dig in and paddle your ass off to catch one. There'll be a small window, where you'll feel the wave take your board and lift you. That's when you push up with your arms, and in one smooth movement, stand. Catching your balance may take a few tries, but when you hit it right, and you're on the face..." His expression went slack in bliss. "It's heaven."

She knew that look. It was the look of a man during sex. The blood pounding in her cheeks warmed them.

"You'll feel a small drop, then you just ride to the whitewash and kick out. Or, more probably, just step off."

The steps, cautions and details wheeled through her mind like the gulls over her head, screeching and calling.

"I'll be right behind you, and I'll push you into the wave. Just feel for that lift." He nodded. "You *can* do this."

Equal parts of "what have I done?" and "I'm so doing this" cycled through her mind. She nodded back, watching for a wave. "I'm *so* doing this."

She chose one, and before she could change her mind, flopped on the board and paddled, digging in and pulling with everything she had. Even so, she'd have missed it when she felt a push from behind that propelled her. From beneath, a swelling lifted the board slightly.

Now!

Everything happened fast, and in slow motion at the same time. She pushed with shaking arms, got her feet under her, but as she rose, the world tilted and fell from beneath her. Water shot up her nose and closed over her head. She came up sputtering and thrashing in a foot of water.

"Good first try!" Art shouted from beyond the swells. "Come on back and try it again!"

Well, at least I'm warm now. She pulled her

board back under her, and headed for the incoming waves.

Four tries later, when the surf rolled her battered body onto the beach, she leaned back on her elbows, staring up at the cloudless sky, trying to breathe. Her arms were useless rubber bands, her sinuses were swamped with seawater and the sand inside her wet suit was making inroads, eroding her skin.

Art looked like a board-short god, perfectly balanced, carving a wave. He rode it in to the whitewash, then stepped off into ankle deep water. "We're done."

She wouldn't have argued, even if she'd had the breath for it.

He untethered his leash and hiked his board under his arm. "You didn't do too badly for your first day."

"How can you say that?" She rolled over, groaning when she had to use her arms to push to her feet. "I never even came close to riding."

He knelt and unzipped the Velcro around her ankle. "No, but you will. Give it time."

"Art, come on. There's no way I'm ever going to get this. I don't have good balance walking, much less on something that's moving under me in every direction." On wobbly knees, she began the trek across acres of loose sand to the road where Art's van was parked.

"Just because you're a bit coordination-challenged, it doesn't mean—"

"It's more than that. This just isn't *it* for me. Don't get me wrong. The ocean's gorgeous in the early morning, and those dolphins were incredible." She jerked down the zipper of her wet suit. Now that she was out of the icy water, the sun heated the black neoprene, boiling her in her own sweat. "But I hate being cold, feeling like shark chum, getting up early—" She tripped in her neoprene bootee and would have gone down if Art hadn't caught her elbow. "And this *stinking* wet suit!"

AT TEN O'CLOCK on Sunday morning, Bear turned into the gravel parking lot of The Farmhouse Café, slow and easy. Even so, the back tire tried to slide out from under him. He turned around with the tail facing the door, so he could pull out straight. He didn't want to freak Hope out on her first ride. Apparently she trusted him enough to ride, but not to see where she lived, because when he called, this was where she told him to pick her up.

He shut down the engine, dropped the side stand and unbuckled the deep purple full-faced helmet behind his left thigh. It should fit her; it was a youth size that a customer had offered up since his son had grown out of it. Bear smiled, running his hand over the skull and crossbones on the back. Not Hope's style maybe, but he bet she'd look great in it.

The door opened and Hope limped out, a blonde in a skintight jumpsuit teetering in her wake, checking him out and watching her heels in the gravel at the same time.

He was happy to see that Hope had taken his suggestions about appropriate attire to heart. She wore hiking boots, jeans and a T-shirt under a suede jacket.

He stepped off the bike. "Why are you limping?"

"Surfing is harder than it looks, trust me. Bear, this is—"

"I want you to know you've got some precious cargo right here." The blonde steamrollered in. "You'd better not be riding crazy, or going to meet some biker gang for wild drinking, or some drug-crazed sex orgy."

She pulled a pen from behind her ear, and a slip of paper from *somewhere* in her clothing, though he didn't see where a slip of paper would have fit.

Stepping to the back of the bike, she wrote down his license plate.

Hope toed the gravel, clearly mortified. Pink cheeks behind her white-blond hair answered a question he'd asked himself riding over. The attraction he felt may have started with the dream, but had grown to something else now. When she glanced up, her odd, ice-blue eyes caught and held him. Something wild broke loose in his chest to race through him. An odd mix of lust and...tenderness? The surge was so strong that he looked away first, afraid she'd see, and be afraid.

"Bear, this mother hen is my cousin, Jesse Jurgen. Jesse, this is Bear. Don't you dare scare him off after I've mustered the courage to ride."

Bear chuckled. As if this buxom blonde had a chance of scaring him off.

Jesse looked him over from boots to his helmet. "You are a big fuzzy one, aren't you?"

"Jesse, jeez." Hope's cheeks escalated to scarlet. "I'm sorry. She's not usually rude. She's just channeling my mother at the moment."

The blonde frowned. "I am, aren't I? I apologize. It's just that..." She turned to Hope, fingered the lapels of her jacket, smoothing them. "This is my favorite jacket." Her words got crumbly and her voice higher as she went along. "Don't you get it...scuffed or anything."

"Jesse, will you stop worrying? You're making me more nervous." Hope enveloped her cousin in a hug, then released her. "You go back inside. You know they've got to be yelling for more coffee by now."

Jesse sniffed once, shot Bear one more momma-tiger look, then turned and tottered back the way she came.

"Don't worry, ma'am. I'll take good care of her," Bear said to her back.

Jesse turned at the door. "Don't you ma'am me. And you come in for coffee when you bring her back. I want to know more about you—Bear-person."

When Hope made shooing motions, Jesse turned and flounced inside.

"I'm so sorry." Hope took the helmet he handed her.

"I'm glad you have someone looking out for you." She was so small beside him that he felt like a clod and a superhero, all at the same time.

"One mother was more than enough for me. I'm looking out for myself now." She turned the helmet this way and that, studying it.

"Here." He took it and settled it on her head, moving it around to test the fit. "That's just right. Watch me, I'll show you how to buckle it." He demonstrated with his own, and when she was done, checked to be sure hers was tight enough. "Now, to be a good passenger, you only need to know three things."

She frowned in concentration.

"One, stay behind me. If I lean, you lean. But

only as much as I do. If you stay upright, it throws off the balance and makes it harder for me."

She nodded. He saw her throat work as she swallowed.

"Two. Don't put your feet down at the stops. I'll handle that part."

"Got it."

"Three. Lighten up."

She cocked her head, as if trying to discern if that was a biker term.

"Have fun. Relax. Shut off your mind and open your senses. Riding isn't something you have to work at. It's something to experience."

She took a deep breath. "I'm ready."

"No, you're not." He put a hand on the grip. "Not until you smile."

Her tension broke in her smile. So did his. The day ahead shifted, from fear to promise. The road whispered of adventure and the breeze blew across his face in a scattering of wishes.

He hadn't known a smile could do all that.

"Then let's roll." He threw his leg over and settled onto the sun-warmed seat.

She glanced from the seat to him to the seat. "Um. How?"

He set his feet and hauled the bike upright. "Put your hand on my shoulder and throw your leg over, like you would a horse."

The suspension hardly moved with her weight.

"Okay. Now put your feet on the pegs. They should be just behind your calves."

"I'm there." Her voice came out shivery.

"You're not smiling."

"How do you know?" She half laughed. "You can't see me."

"Haven't you heard? Motorcyclists have eyes in the back of their heads. Now, put your arms around my waist."

Her palms settled light on the top of his hip bones.

He fired the engine, and her hands clamped down.

When he eased the clutch and the bike inched forward, her arms came around locked in a death grip, her body plastered to his back. Smiling, he pulled to the entrance, then turned left onto King's Highway, heading downtown.

It was going to be a good day.

AT LEAST YOU have clean underwear on, when they scrape your body from the pavement. This is what happens when you...

The banging of her heart and the sound of the wind overrode her mother's voice. It was a nice break, except that it meant they'd sped up. Eyes slammed shut, Hope perched on the tiny leather pad like a jockey on a runaway horse, trying to become one with Bear's leather-clad back.

She'd thought she understood when he told her she had to trust him. But this took a lot more trust than could have germinated in their brief acquaintance. Bear's solid body was all that separated her from roadkill.

She'd also underestimated how intimate riding double was. Feeling the rise and fall of his chest through her own. Feeling the muscles in his waist tense when he leaned into a turn. Inhaling his scent—leather and something darker. Something that made her aware of the parts of her plastered against the vibrating seat.

The flush she felt had nothing to do with the sun.

The engine growl changed pitch as the bike slowed. Bear put his feet down and stopped. Her foot was off the peg and reaching for the ground before she realized what she was doing. It was instinct—to help balance, and connect with the sweet, sustaining earth.

"Feet up."

His deep voice rolled like thunder through his back, and kept going, reverberating through hers.

"Sorry." She squeaked. They were at the stop sign corner of King's Highway and Foxen Canyon Road.

"You're not smiling."

Her lips were pulled back from her teeth, but it probably wasn't a smile. "I'll try."

"Look at it this way. You wanted to push the envelope, right?"

"Yeah, but I didn't want to fall off it."

"I won't let you fall." He took a hand from the grip and patted her arm, locked around his waist. "Nothing bad will happen to you when you're with me, Hope. I'll see to it."

In spite of the fact that it was an impossible promise, the bedrock belief in his voice rumbled through her, loosening her from the inside. Where do you get that much confidence in yourself and your ability?

He'd been a sniper. He'd faced death—probably many times. Could confidence only be earned by facing your fear?

If so, she was making serious inroads today.

"Try to relax. Trust me." He squeezed her forearm, then returned his hand to the handgrip.

"I do trust you." She realized when the words were out, that they were true. If it were within his power to keep her safe, he'd die doing it. His broad back was like an impenetrable wall in front of her, and she turned her head and leaned against it. "I'm ready."

"There's a girl." He twisted the throttle and the bike vibrated between her legs. She felt the throb, deep inside. She now understood at a visceral level why bikes were always linked to sex.

Bear eased across the road, and onto Foxen

Canyon. "This is one of the best motorcycle roads on the planet." The wind brought his words to her, clearer than she'd thought possible. "Close your eyes and *feel* it."

The closed eyes she had no problem with. After a few minutes, with the ebbing of panic, her senses came to life. She felt the difference in temperature from full sun to shade. The smells surged, until she could almost taste the smell of cut grass and cool, damp, boggy places. Even the occasional eau de cow drifting by her nose wasn't unpleasant.

If he'd have bobbled in the curves, or been the least bit tentative, her muscles would've remained locked. But when he didn't, her fear lay down before his skill—Bear rode the bike as if it was a part of him—a modern day mechanical centaur. Her arms loosened and when cooler air brushed her eyelids, she opened them to find herself in a tree-lined tunnel of dappled shadows.

She stole a peek around his shoulder as they broke into the splashed sunshine. The black road curved gentle between the hills, like the yellow brick road; except here, the road was gray, and the hills were gold. "Ohhh."

"Told you." His smile traveled through her body as easily as his throaty rumble.

Joy swelled in her chest, as thick as warm condensed milk and just as sweet. She hugged him in a paroxysm of happiness.

The road twisted and she watched over his shoulder as they took a curve, one way, and then the other. They were flying! The wings fluttering inside her spread, and delight burst from her in a laugh. *So this is what the edge of the envelope looks like.*

"That's my place, there."

They flashed by a sign that read "The Gaudy Widow."

"Wait, I want to see it!"

"Some other time. It's past lunch, and I'm hungry."

She glanced at the sun's position, shocked to see he was right.

"Which would you rather, fancy or casual?"

You are not going into a nice place, dressed like that! Mother was right, this time. "Casual."

"You got it." They pulled up to an intersection that could only be Pacific Coast Highway—across the road, across the sand, the sun turned the ocean chop into a blinding disco ball. He waited for traffic to clear, then turned right.

The traffic made her nervous—cars whipped by, the bike's rear end perspective making them look bigger. Menacing. She focused instead on the ocean. From this angle, it looked tame, a kid's pail-and-shovel beach rather than the wild, raw force that she'd experienced surfing.

She liked this ocean better.

Bear slowed, and turned in at a weathered clapboard burger shack, perched on the edge of a cliff overlooking the ocean.

When he pulled up and stopped, she managed not to put her feet down until he shut down the bike and told her it was okay. She put her left foot down and slid off, but her boot caught on the seat. Panicked, she hopped on one foot until she could extricate herself.

He laid the bike on the side stand, swung his leg over, and unbuckled his helmet. "Well? What do you think?"

She undid her chin strap. "I think the Russian judge is going to ding me for the dismount."

"Ah, you did fine. You're a good passenger." He took the helmet from her, and set it under the bike next to his.

Her chest expanded. She *had* managed to relax, for a minute or three.

He bought them burgers and sodas, and they split an order of fries. He carried it to where the land ended and the ocean began—after a hundred-foot drop-off. He sat, legs dangling over the edge.

She crept as close as she dared, then got on her hands and knees and crawled the rest of the way, butterflies in her stomach fluttering hard enough to support her if she fell.

"We can sit at a picnic table." He started to get up.

She stopped him with a hand on his arm. "It's okay." She hung on until her legs dangled next to his. "This is so beautiful."

Below, the surf broke over rocks on either side of a secluded cove and a tiny half-moon strip of beach that could only have been accessible by boat.

"Whoa."

His head came up. "If you're dizzy, we can move."

"It's not that. There's a naked guy down there." She pointed.

"Well, damned if there isn't."

Thirty feet down the almost vertical cliff face, a naked man was sunbathing on a ledge not much bigger than he was. She couldn't see any path. "How the heck did he get down there?"

"He must have climbed down, somehow. I just hope he had clothes on when he did it. That could be painful."

To distract herself and cool her blush, she reached for her soft drink. They ate in silence for a few minutes, enjoying the view and the breeze off the ocean.

She was too aware of his huge thigh a foot

away, and his shoulder, even closer. "What was your childhood like?" It was hard to imagine him any smaller.

He rolled his eyes to her. "Group isn't until tomorrow."

"I just want to get to know you better."

He took a bite and chewed on her words as he looked to the horizon. "An All-American blue-collar mountain boy. That about sums it up. My mom and dad raised my brother and me in a tiny 1950s house outside of Boulder. I hunted, fished and basically ran wild."

"So being a sniper was kind of a natural for you?" She knew just when he shut down—his squint and his mouth both hardened. His beard twitched with the tick of a muscle near his ear.

"You don't like your mother much, do you?" His lips barely moved.

The lightning subject shift jolted her. "Why do you say that?"

He turned to her and reached for a fry. "You never have a smile in your voice when you mention her."

Hope pushed in the dimples on her soda lid. "Oh, she did the best she knew how, I guess. It was just that she was afraid of everything. I imagine she thought she was protecting me when she tried to make me afraid, too."

"But you don't agree."

A casual answer was faster. And easier. "All day I've ridden on a motorcycle, holding on to a guy I hardly know. What do you think?"

"I think your mother would be horrified. What was your childhood like?"

"The complete opposite of yours." She picked up her soda and took a sip. "Have you ever sat in a room so quiet that you became aware of the clock ticking, the house settling?"

"I think. Once."

"That room was my childhood. Polite, ladylike and asphyxiating."

"It sounds awful."

"Actually, if a bird is born in a cage, does it know to want the out-of-doors? It's all I knew." She put her soda down and pressed the dimples again. "So when the door opened, I didn't leave." She took a breath and pushed the last of the shameful truth into the light. "It took a bank robbery and me almost dying to realize that the cage was *my* choice." She kept her head down. "But you know what I think?"

He sat, waiting for her.

"How do you know where your limits are, if you don't go to the edge to see?"

"You know what I think?" His soft chocolate eyes drew her in. They weren't a stranger's eyes. There were places she knew in there... warm, comfortable, peaceful places. He leaned and reached across the paper-wrapper picnic between them. His fingers hovered, not touching her skin, but so close that she felt them on the hairs of her cheek.

"I think you're far braver than I." Eyes open, he leaned in.

Surprise blossomed, shifting to a fluttering disquiet. But when his lips touched hers, a tidal surge of mixed emotions pulled her off balance, as the surf had yesterday. Before she could sort it out, he was gone—only cool air caressed her lips.

"I apologize. I had no right to do that." He crumpled the empty paper between them, wadding it in his fist.

She sat, dumbfounded, sorting emotions, fingers touching her lips.

"We'd better get you back, before that cousin of yours comes after me with a gun."

CHAPTER NINE

BEAR SAT IN the circle the next day, only half listening to Bryan prattle on, hyperaware that Hope's bare knee was inches from his denim-clad one. Those hiking shorts may be only a work uniform, but he applauded the owner's taste.

She hadn't acted any different when she came in today—she said hello with the exact same tone she greeted Bryan with. But she didn't fool him. The blush was for him alone.

He hadn't expected her to sit still for a kiss yesterday. But then, he hadn't expected to kiss her to begin with. But the way she looked when she told him of her fear, it drew him, and—

"Bear?"

He realized it was the second time Bina had called his name. His own cheeks heated. "Yeah?"

"Tell us what it was like for you in prison. Were you angry? Sad?"

He shot a glance around the circle. They watched him with the intent stare of vultures, spotting roadkill. He had to say something. If he shut this down, Hope would probably shut him down.

At least she didn't ask about Afghanistan.

He swallowed. "It was enlightening. You can never judge anyone by how they look. A tattooed gangbanger who was my size and looked rabid, was in for kiting bad checks. An old guy with a cane had killed six people, one of them in prison."

Bryan's inhale was loud in the quiet room.

"One time, when—"

"I'm sorry, Bear," Bina interrupted. "But we're not interested in prison stories. We want to know how prison affected *you*."

"I want to hear the stories," Mark mumbled.

Bina shot him a "come on" look.

"You're in a cell twenty-three hours a day, so you have a lot of time to think." He shrugged. "Of course I felt bad. I never meant to really hurt the guy." At least he didn't think he had. But some of that night was lost in a haze of beery fury. "I'll tell you one thing I learned." He looked to each person in the circle, in turn. *This* he could talk about. "I vowed to never lose my temper again."

"Have you had a problem with your temper before, Bear?"

He flinched. He should've known a shrink would dig. He glanced at Hope, who nodded in encouragement. It was his own fault. He was a bear caught in a trap of his own making. "Yeah."

"Tell us about that."

He sifted memories, searching for an innocuous one. "I was hunting with my brother. I was a senior in high school, he was a freshman." His brother's innocent freckles floated through Bear's mind. "He'd always had a happy trigger finger. I told him a couple dozen times to hold—to wait for a solid kill shot." He shook his head. "He'd listen, but then get excited and forget when he got a deer in his scope."

"Oh, this is not going to end well," Bryan said.

"He was about fifty yards to my right when I heard the shot. When I got there, my brother was gone. I tracked him a half mile. Found him in the dirt, over a doe who'd been dragging her intestines a good ways before dying."

Brenda made a coughing sob.

He didn't look up. He was watching the film of that day in his head. "I picked him up by the jacket. He'd been crying—his face was covered in snot." He gripped one fist in the other. "I punched him between the eyes. Broke his nose."

"How do you feel about that now?" There was a pardon in Bina's soft tone.

It was a pardon he couldn't accept. "How do you think I felt? He was sorry; I knew that before I hit him. I knew he'd never again sight down a gun without being sure of his shot. I hit him anyway." He scrubbed a hand through his hair. "He learned his lesson from that day, but I didn't learn mine." His voice got smaller as he went. "It took me killing a man for that."

"You didn't do it on purpose," Hope said.

"Yeah. Tell that to the guy's mother." He kept his eyes on the floor.

"Thank you for sharing, Bear. I know that wasn't easy for you."

Easier than the rest. The nightmares were bad already, the lack of sleep abrading his nerves, rubbing his patience raw. What would happen if he actually talked about Afghanistan? His sniper instincts were still solid—he sensed it would be a firestorm.

"Brenda? Would you like to share something with the group?"

The woman threw her head up like a spooked horse, the whites of her eyes showing. "What?"

Bina spoke slow and calm. "Oh, I don't know. Tell us about yourself. Do you work?"

"No. Phil prefers it that way. We wouldn't want anyone thinking he can't provide for his family."

The way she said it, Bear knew those weren't her words. Besides a paper-pusher, Phil was also a ventriloquist.

"What do you with your days?" Bina asked.

"It's my job to keep house, and have dinner on the table when Phil gets home," the puppet said.

"Do you have a big house? Does it take a lot of upkeep? A garden, maybe?" Bina asked.

"No. We're renting an apartment."

"Are you a gourmet cook?"

When she chuckled, Bear glimpsed even white teeth. It had to be the first time he'd seen them—because he was surprised that Brenda had a pretty smile.

"Hardly. I'm more tuna casserole than lobster bisque."

"So, that must leave you with a lot of time on your hands. Do you shop a lot?"

Not unless you count the thrift store.

"Oh, no. Phil does the shopping with me. We have only one car." She picked at a nail bed. "I read a lot."

"What do you like to read?" Bina prompted.

"Lots of things, but mostly romance. Phil takes me to the library once a week and I stock up, so I won't run out."

"That Phil. He's a gem," Mark said, deadpan.

Brenda frowned. "You don't know him. He is." She ducked her head, to pick at her skin. "Almost always."

Bina jumped in. "I like to read romance, too. Why do you like it, Brenda?"

She looked up, then away. "The happily-ever-after."

"Then why don't you dump that asshole, and find your own happy ending?" Mark asked.

Brenda glared fire at Mark. "You talk big for someone who won't go out by himself."

Good for her. Phil hasn't beat all the spirit out of her.

Mark's mouth opened and closed, but no sound came out.

Brenda nodded. "Not so easy when it's you, huh?"

"Remember those thoughts. We'll start there on Wednesday."

Bina checked her notebook. "Now, how did everyone do with the homework I assigned?"

Mark raised a finger. "I went to dinner. At a restaurant. By myself."

"That's wonderful, Mark. How was it?"

"I sat in a dark corner of a pub, so I don't deserve a star or anything. But I did it." He looked around the circle. "It helped to know that everyone was doing stuff they were afraid of. I didn't feel so alone."

"I'm proud of you. How about the rest of you?"

Bear started. "I invited—"

"I rode—" Hope began.

They smiled at the same time, too.

Bryan piped up. "Bear took Hope for a ride on his motorcycle. And he didn't kill her." He slapped a hand over his mouth. "Oh, I didn't mean that how it came out. Sorry." He spoke from between his fingers.

"How was that, Hope? Bear?"

"Great," they said together. Then blushed together. *This was getting ridiculous.*

Thankfully she moved on. "Bryan, what did you do?"

Bryan's face fell. He went from amused to dismal in an eye blink. "I talked to the doctors."

"About Curtis?"

He nodded, eyes closed. "I can't talk about it now. Okay?"

"We'll talk about it next time, all right?" Bina waited for another nod before moving on. "Brenda?"

"I thought," she said from behind the hair curtain.

"About what?" Bina asked.

"About how ya'll see Phil."

"And what did you decide?"

She sniffed. "I'm not ready to talk about it."

"We can save that for later, too. Good group, everyone. I'll see you Wednesday." Bina checked her watch, stood and bustled out of the room.

Bear turned to Hope, just as she said, "Coffee, everyone?"

They all nodded. Except Brenda.

"I have to get home. If I miss the bus, I'll be very late. And Phil…"

"Where do you live?" Hope asked.

"On the Vandenberg base." She stood and gathered her bag-lady purse.

"It has to take a long time to get there by bus. Why don't you come to coffee with us, and one of us will run you home."

Brenda squinted through dirty bangs. "Why would you do that?"

Bryan said, "Because you're one of us, silly."

"We'd be happy to," Mark said.

Brenda stood considering, like a mouse eyeing the cheese on a trap. "I'd better not. Phil wasn't feeling that well today and he may come home early."

"Okay, maybe next time, then?" Hope bent to see the face under the hair.

"Maybe." Brenda scuttled out of the room.

"That lady is wound way too tight," Mark said, looking after her.

"I wish I could help her." Hope sighed.

"Someone ought to take out that husband of hers," Bear said. All heads swiveled his direction. "Hey, I said *someone*, not me. It's none of my business."

"It's all our business. We have to help each other," Bryan said.

"You're right, Bryan." Hope glanced at Bear, then away. "Let's go get coffee. Then I have to get to work."

YOU NOT ONLY ride a two-wheeled death machine with a man you don't know, you allow him to take liberties, then agree to date him again? You are heading for a bad end, young lady.

Could her mother's ghost be right for once? Maybe. But when Bear had asked her out, she'd felt like when she'd seen those dolphins—exhilarated and terrified, all at the same time.

And she liked it.

I raised you gently, and I didn't do it so you could—

"Oh, piss off, Mom." Smiling at the shocked silence in her head, she shifted the borrowed gear to her other arm and pulled open the door of The Adventure Outfitter.

When she walked into the break room for the Monday meeting, everyone clapped.

"You made it!"

"Little surfer, little ooooone…" Art crooned.

"Yay, you survived!" Lori pumped a fist.

"Thanks, guys." Hope dumped the borrowed wet suit in the corner, next to Art. "But Gidget, I'm not."

"Well, even if surfing isn't for you, you can now work that department." Her boss, Travis, leaned against the wall, arms crossed. "What's next?"

"I think I want to try sailing. I love the raw nature of the ocean, but I think I'd appreciate it more if I wasn't part of the food chain, you know?"

Art chuckled. "I don't know about that. Ever seen *Jaws*?"

A guy at the table spoke up. "Hey, don't scare her before I've even gotten her on a Sunfish." He was older, and thin, with glasses and a beard. He had one of those rare faces—you could read the chapters of an interesting life in the cracks and crevasses. "Barry Nix, sailor and swashbuckler at your service." He stood and bowed low.

Hope smiled, willing to bet her next paycheck that this guy was a heck of a storyteller. "I'm Hope. When can we go sailing?"

"I'm working Saturday. How about Sunday, assuming the conditions are right?"

"Sounds great."

Travis briefed them, then released them to their stations. Lori caught up with Hope on her way to the register.

"So? How was the motorcycle ride?" she sing-songed like a third grader.

"Good."

"You have a hunky guy between your thighs for an afternoon, and that's all I get?" She aimed a finger in Hope's direction. "You and me. Lunch. And I'm warning you—you'd better spill the deets."

Hope waved her off. Being a cashier may not be the most exciting career on the planet, but at least she'd made a friend.

"STOP!" BEAR WOKE to his own shout, his body twisted in sweaty sheets. *Shit. Again.* One foot still in the dream, he sat up and put the other on the floor, to anchor himself in his bedroom reality. If he didn't, he might fall asleep, where the heat and blood of Afghanistan waited. It always did.

He glanced to the clock on the wire spool he used for a nightstand.

Four. He glanced to the window full of dark. A.m.

Elbows on knees, he scrubbed his hands over his face to wipe away the sticky cobwebbed nightmare. It didn't take a shrink to know what had conjured the dream this time—the kid. Nacho's features weren't the same; Mexican was a world away from Afghan. But they were about the same age and both had brown skin, black hair and huge dark eyes. That old saying was wrong. Eyes weren't mirrors—they were glass. Too easy to see what was beneath. Horror was the only word Bear had for what he'd seen.

Such an inadequate word, that.

He heaved himself out of bed and walked to the bathroom to wash off the stench of sweat and regret. His feet chilled on the new slate floor and the bare stud walls reminded him to order Sheet-rock as soon as he got the check for that Fat Boy he'd finished last week—well, that he and Nacho had finished. The kid waxed and buffed the bike after the paint was cured. Did a good job, too.

He stepped to the mirror suspended from a spiral shank nail. His hair was wild, his beard a fuzzy nest. He looked like a Charles Manson mug shot. Maybe it was time to shave. Summer was coming, and it'd get hot in the barn…

Oh, bullshit. He smoothed down the bush. Would Hope appreciate a clean-shaven man?

And when was the last time you worried about shit like that?

He was a loner. For good reason. He ran his fingers through his beard. Maybe he'd just trim the shrubbery a bit. Stepping to the corner, he dug through his cardboard box of toiletries for the electric trimmer.

A half hour later, clean, trimmed, showered and dressed, he walked past his makeshift dining table and through the kitchen, not pausing to admire his newly hung cabinets.

In the dining room, his angel's tranquil image welcomed him from the wall, calming the burning inside that sizzled his nerves and the lining of his stomach.

He was ahead of schedule. Maybe he'd just spend a few minutes roughing out the shadow of the mountains behind her. Eyes on the wall, he reached for a brush.

CHAPTER TEN

THE SETTING SUN'S rays splashed the cottage's porch with gold. Hope sat amid the riches, sipping iced tea and listening to bird gossip.

It'd been six weeks since the bank robbery and her new life had begun. The time before already felt like a different lifetime. How could she have guessed how wonderful a cageless world would be? If she'd had an inkling, she'd have run away from home much earlier. She closed her eyes, pulling in the braided scents of Opaline's blossoming lemon trees, and the jasmine in the bed below the porch.

The sound of a screen door slapping stirred her. Opaline, in an aproned housedress and orthopedic shoes, herded a batch of bunnies into the yard. Hope couldn't hear the words, only the rise and fall of her baby talk. Shading her eyes, the old lady spied Hope and waved, then toddled down the path to Hope's porch.

"Hello. You've been coming and going so much, I haven't been able to catch you for a chat."

"Hello, Ms. Settle. Come sit and talk to me."

Hope leaned over to pat the rocker on the other side of the tiny round wicker table. "Would you like some tea?"

"No, thank you. And it's Opaline, dear." As she squeezed by Hope, she reached into the pocket of her apron and pulled out a tiny caramel-colored bunny, and put it in Hope's lap. "You pet Buckwheat while we talk."

Hope started, then grabbed the thing before it fell off her lap. It appeared fragile, and— "Ooh. It's so soft."

"Of course it is. Are you going to tell me you've never held a baby bunny before?" Opaline settled into the rocker with a small, ladylike sigh.

Its little whiskers twitched when Hope ran a finger down its back. "I've never held any bunny." It didn't look as if it had fleas. But how would she know?

"Well then, it's high time you did. Baby bunnies are good for the soul." She sniffed. "How do you like your new home so far?"

"I feel like when Dorothy found Oz, and everything went from black-and-white to color."

"I know just what you mean." Chuckling, Opaline pulled a paper from another pocket on the apron to fan her face. "It was like that for me after I married my Virgil and we came to this house—like I'd finally found the place I fit in the world." She sighed. "Have you ever been in love, Hope?"

Hope rubbed the velvety bunny's ears. It seemed content. She just hoped it wouldn't poop in her lap. "I've had boyfriends. But love? I don't think so."

"Well, my dear, you have a wonderful world in front of you, if you're lucky enough to find it."

The creases in Opaline's face smoothed, Hope could almost see how she'd looked as a younger woman. She must have been very pretty. "How did you meet Mr. Settle?"

"Ah, we met at a church social. He was so handsome in his bow tie and Brylcreemed hair. To this day, when I smell Old Spice, it takes me back…" She fanned harder. "He was—how do you young people say it? A hunkster."

Hope bit her lip.

"He carried me over the threshold of that house, and my life changed forever." She sighed. "I wish every woman could experience that… space. It's like your world expands to fit just the two of you, and you can't believe you ever thought your life before was enough." She turned to Hope. "Are you dating anyone now?"

Hope looked down to dodge the question. All animal babies were cute. But this one would win a prize. She cupped her hand under the bunny and gently raised it so they could see eye to eye.

It sniffed her nose. "No. Well, maybe. No. I'm not sure."

"Well. You'll certainly never get anywhere with a wishy-washy attitude like that."

Hope laid the bunny on her chest and stroked it. "We've been on one date. He's asked me out on Saturday night, to the concert in the park, in Solvang."

"Oh, that should be fun."

"Would you like to come with us? I'm sure Bear wouldn't mind—"

"An old lady on your date? That would *not* do. How do you expect to get to know this boy, with someone else along? What did you say his name was?"

"Bear. Well, his real name is Doug. Doug Steele."

Opaline's brow furrow deepened, and her lips pursed. "His family must not be from here. I don't recognize the name, and I've lived here all my life."

Hope's guard snapped to attention. Opaline would certainly not find a felon a suitable suitor.

That's because he's not. You hang out with people like that, you're going to wake up one fine day, murdered in your sleep.

She spoke to override her mother's voice, and to turn Opaline's line of questioning. "No, he's

not from around here. And I don't know him well
enough to know what I think of him. Yet."

"There's the spirit." There was a gleam in the
old lady's eye. "If he isn't the one, you keep looking." She pushed herself out of the rocker. "And
if you decide you like him, after it gets dark, you
let him kiss you."

"Opaline!" Hope's face heated. She may have
had sex only a few times, but she wasn't pathetic
enough to get into a birds 'n' bees conversation
with an octogenarian. Besides, she'd already let
him kiss her. And she'd enjoyed it. So much so,
that she wished he'd do it again. But he'd backed
up, just as things were getting good.

Her landlady took Buckwheat from Hope's
hand and dropped her a wink. "How do you
think I snared my Virgil? You're a well-brought-
up young lady, but modesty and good manners
will only get you so far. You have to give a man
a sample of nectar to keep them coming back
to the flower." She nodded, and shuffled away.
"As well I should know." Her titter drifted over
the quiet yard.

Hope smiled into the dark, listening to Opaline's singsong voice as she gathered her herd of
bunnies. Hope sat rocking for a long time, thinking about where she was headed, and remembering the softness of Bear's lips on hers.

LATE THAT AFTERNOON, Bear was heading for the barn when Nacho skidded into the yard on an old-fashioned bike and jumped off before the wheels stopped turning. "Hi, Bear."

"Hey, kid, nice wheels. Did you ride all the way out here?"

Nacho wheeled the too-tall-for-him bike alongside Bear. "Course. It's only four miles. You think I'm some kinda baby?"

Yes. "No. But did your sister okay that?" At Nacho's glare he put his hands up. "Hey, I'm not checking on you. I'm just trying to keep her outta my face."

"Yeah, she knows." His nose wrinkled. "Her boyfriend let me use this." He patted the seat.

Bear led the way around to the back doors. "You don't like him?"

Nacho did a one-shoulder shrug. "He let me use the bike, so… I just hope he's not sucking up to me to get into Priss's pants."

"Hey, don't talk like that. Only punks disrespect women."

Nacho squinted up at him. "I thought you were tough."

"I am. Putting down people isn't being tough. That's being small, and trying to pull everyone else down to your height."

"I never thought of it that way before." He

leaned the bike against the door and followed Bear inside.

"What's the deal with your sister having custody of you?"

Nacho stopped.

"You don't want to talk about it, that's okay, too." Bear walked to the motorcycle tank bolted to a stand in the center of the concrete floor.

The kid followed, quiet so long that Bear moved on, running through his next steps for prepping the tank.

"My mom died a month ago. Priss showed up the day they buried her. That was the first time I ever saw her."

"I'm sorry about your mom, kid. So Priss came to take care of you?" Bear pointed to his toolbox. "Bring me some sandpaper, will you?"

Nacho stepped to the big cabinet and pulled out a drawer. "Four or five grain?"

"Five. Grab yourself one, too."

Nacho brought him the paper. "She didn't want anything to do with me. They put me in the kid warehouse—you know where they put kids when they got nowhere to go."

Bear didn't look up, afraid the kid would clam up if he looked too interested. "County?"

"Yeah. After a couple of days, I guess she felt guilty, cuz she came to get me."

Now he understood her mama bear attitude.

Score one for the spunky girl. "Bring me that fender. I'll show you how to do this." When Nacho brought it, he showed him how to feel for, and sand down, rough spots.

"So what about your dad—is he dead, too?" He felt along the bottom of the tank, sanding rough spots as he found them.

"Yeah. Even though he's still breathing. Meth head. He's doing a dime for armed robbery."

"Oh, man, that's hard."

"For him, maybe. It's nothing to me." Nacho turned the fender and started on the other end.

The kid acted like a hard case. But the case was about a millimeter thick. "How are you and your sister getting on?"

Nacho ran his fingers over the metal, eyes closed. "She doesn't know how to make beans, or sopaipillas, but I guess she's okay. She got Harry Potter at the library, and we're reading it together. It's pretty cool."

"Sounds like you've landed on your feet, then."

They sanded in silence for a few minutes.

"Hey, Bear?"

"Yeah, kid."

"You ever been afraid?" Nacho studied the fender, turning it this way and that.

"I've spent a bunch of my life scared." He blew sandings off the tank, making sure not to look up. "Why?"

"Oh, nothing. Just wondering."

Penance dictated that he do more for this kid than just teach him how to use an airbrush. He'd have to get involved—give something of himself.

Nacho bent over the fender, sanding as if it was an Olympic sport. He loosened a hard place in Bear. Would he have turned out different, if he'd let someone help him along the way?

Only one way to find out.

"Life is a scary thing, kid. Anyone who tells you they're not scared is either lying, or brain damaged. Even when you grow up, there's still a ton of crap you have no control over." He felt Nacho's attention, but didn't look up. The kid wasn't the only one who could play chilly. "People find different ways to deal with it. Some whine to anyone who'll listen. Some turn mean, like a beaten dog. Some retreat from the world, trying to limit the risk. But that doesn't work, either.

"There are a few that realize scary is just reality. They get on with their lives, trying new things, not letting fear stop them. Those are the bravest people." He turned the sandpaper and kept working. "I don't know your sister well, but she seems like one of those."

"And that's you, too, huh, Bear?"

Seeing the man he wished he was in Nacho's eyes, Bear looked down, focusing on the tank in his hands. "Nah, not me, kid. But I know some-one like that."

Someone with white-blond hair, and glacier-blue eyes.

HOPE STOOD AT the end of her landlady's drive, listening for the rumble of Bear's Harley. She wasn't taking any chances; Opaline would have a heart attack if he rolled up to the cottage on that.

Bear had told her to dress comfortably, and after some deep wardrobe mining, Hope had de-cided on the fitted leggings and scoop-necked T-shirt that Lori had talked her into buying. The T-shirt was long and covered her butt, but it was formfitting. She felt almost naked from the waist up, as if her boobs were falling out on top.

You have perfectly decent shorts, and a nice seersucker blouse that—

Hope slammed the door on the closet in her mind where she'd banished her mother to. She tossed Jesse's suede jacket over her shoulder and glanced up and down the street, butterflies bat-tering the walls of her stomach.

But her mother hadn't *always* been wrong. What was she doing? Was she going out with Bear because he was the opposite of someone her mother would have chosen? Rebellion wasn't independence, because it required someone to rebel against. Which made it just another cage, in a really good disguise. She'd learned that the hard way.

Maybe she should rethink this whole thing. Look around with her new eyes before choosing the first man who showed an interest...

An old-style truck with big round fenders, burnt-black paint and a deep purring rumble pulled up in front of her. Bear smiled through the open window. "You look as good as ice cream on a hot summer day." He threw the truck in Park, opened the door and stepped out.

The butterflies settled, and at the appreciative look in his eyes, the tension drained from her and she remembered. It was the odd dichotomy of vulnerability and sadness on the inside that drew her. Well, the outside wasn't shabby, either. "You shaved!"

He rubbed a palm over his razored beard. "Just trimmed back the brush a bit."

"Well, I think you look very dashing." She looped her arm through his, and he led her around to the passenger side, and handed her in. "I didn't know you had a vehicle other than your bike."

He patted the hood over her head. "She doesn't look like much, but there's lots of life in this old girl yet. I'll paint it when I get the interior finished."

He closed her door and jogged around the front of the truck. He'd been good-looking before, but with his hard jaw and soft lips exposed, he looked like a real-life action hero. Strong, handsome and man enough to make her woman parts perk up.

He opened the door and stepped in. "I brought us a picnic dinner, complete with blanket and wine. You ready?" He gave her a soft smile.

The butterflies inside took flight again, and her stomach plunged with the thrill of a roller coaster's first hill and as the ground dropped away, she found herself teetering on the edge of impetuous. The breeze blowing in the window whispered potential. She felt like a teenager with a crush. Thanks to her mother, she'd never had an unchaperoned date in high school. Maybe it wasn't too late for a do-over?

"Not quite yet." She slid across the bench seat, put her hands to either side of his face, pulled his head down and kissed him. God, how could he smell like leather and fresh air, when he wasn't on the bike? A pull of yearning fired in her chest, and what was meant as a flirty hello, shifted fast. Abandoning all reason, she tilted her head and opened her lips.

He made a rumbly sound deep in his chest, and his hands came up under her hair as his tongue touched hers. He explored, gently, reverently, slowing her headlong rush.

Her heart banged against its cage. The contrast of a huge man being gentle made her want to crawl in his lap and eat him alive.

He lightened the kiss, and with one last taste, backed up to gaze into her eyes as if she held the answers to the universe. "Wow. I don't know what I did to cause that, but if you'll tell me, I promise to do more of it in the future."

"To tell you the truth, I'm a bit shocked myself."

When his gaze wouldn't release her, she'd have ducked her head, but his fingers were there, stopping her. "Thank you, Hope, for coming out with me."

Suddenly, it was all right again. "My pleasure." She slid back to her side of the truck and dug for the old-fashioned seat belt. "Now, get a move on, big guy. I'm hungry."

He pulled the stick on the column, put it in gear, and said with a smile, "I noticed."

Solvang was a Danish town that used its history to its advantage. The downtown streets were crowded with shops, bakeries and strolling tourists. Bear found a parking spot in the municipal lot in the center of town. He let her carry the blanket—he took hold of the picnic basket and her hand, and led the way to the park, a block away.

In a bandstand with a gazebo, the band tuned up. The green expanse of lawn before it was a colorful quilt, where families staked their territory in blankct-sized bites. Vendors had set up tents in the back. The smell of cooking sausage and popcorn wafted over the crowd.

"Let's find a place over there." Bear pointed to an area on the right near the back, under the trees. "The music won't be so loud."

They wended their way through the shifting crowd, dodging running children and beach balls. It was comparatively unpopulated under the trees, and Bear unfurled the blanket with a snap of his wrist, then bowed over it. "Milady."

She sat. He knelt and pulled a bottle of red wine from the picnic basket, along with two wine glasses.

"Wow. Real glasses, too."

He twisted the corkscrew in and pulled it out with a pop. "Plautus said, 'Let us celebrate the occasion with wine and sweet words.'" Easily holding both stems in one hand, he poured, nestled the wine back in the basket, and handed her one.

She clinked her glass to his. "Now there's a quote I can get behind."

He sat beside her, and, shoulders touching, they sipped wine and watched the crowd. The babble of voices blended in a rise-and-fall cadence punctuated by laughter and the screams of delighted children.

"Look at that sweet little boy with the chubby legs and ice cream all over his face." Hope pointed. "Isn't he adorable?"

The boy toddled to his mother, smacking his chocolate-covered hands together. She laughed, and reached for a wipe.

"Do you want kids someday, Bear?" She turned to see his thin lips and flared nostrils. "What is it?"

"Nothing." He took a deep swallow from his glass.

What hurt this big man so badly it could paint pain across his face? "I'm a good listener. I don't judge."

"Some things are better kept in." The words came out short, as if bitten off.

"I don't think that's true. Look at the group. Talking has helped all of us. Didn't you feel better after you talked about hitting your brother?"

"Nope."

Well, there's a slammed door.

The band crashed into their first song. It sounded like "Amarillo by Morning." Kind of. Bear knelt and lifted white carryout boxes from the picnic basket, along with paper plates and plastic utensils. "I took a chance on Thai food. It was either that, or chicken in a bucket."

"I love Thai. But I'm surprised. You seem like more a meat-and-potatoes kinda guy."

"Ah, but I'm full of mystery." He smiled and waggled his heavy eyebrows.

"You sure are." She spooned out chicken red curry, then beef broccoli onto the plates while he refilled their glasses.

The band was loud enough to preclude conversation, so when the sun went down, they sat companionably, watching kids dance in front of the stage.

And Hope considered the problems with big men, relationships and mystery. She liked him. Obviously they had chemistry. But a relationship needed to be so much more than that.

And it was the old Hope Sanderson who'd settled for less—the new Hope was aiming for more. A lot more.

An hour later, arms loaded, Bear led her through the crowd to the street. "Sorry about the band. They were pretty bad."

"Yeah, they were. But the band wasn't really why we came, was it?"

He glanced over, one lifted eyebrow asking a question.

She'd tested out the words in her mind, sitting next to him in the dark. It was time to say them. "I had a good time tonight, Bear. But I don't know about all this." She waved a hand.

"About all what?" He put an arm up to stop

her from stepping into the street until the traffic cleared.

"I mean, I get that you're a private person, and a bit of a loner. But how can I get to know you better if you're not willing to talk about yourself? And how do I trust you if I don't know you better?"

He took her hand, and led her across the street. The sidewalk was less crowded on this side. They walked through the shadowed parking lot, lit by only one sodium lamp. His head swung left and right, as if watching for threats and his fingers tightened on hers.

"What happened to you over there, Bear?"

He dropped her hand at the door of the truck to reach for his keys, his head still swiveled, probing the dark. "Shit happened. I'm not special. Shit happened to most guys over there." He helped her in, then jogged to the driver's side. Once he was in, he snapped the locks down, and turned to her. "I hear what you're saying. I really do. You're a single woman, living alone, and I—I'm not exactly every mother's dream." In the faint light, his eyes found hers. "I'm trying my guts out, even though it may not seem like it. Do you think you could hang in there with me for a little while longer?"

There it was again, that tug to her heart at seeing the soft side in this big man. She may not know everything about Doug Steele, but whatever it was that had damaged him, she sensed he was more afraid than she. Reaching over, she touched his cheek. "I'd be proud to."

CHAPTER ELEVEN

LATE SUNDAY MORNING, Hope took the scenic route to Morro Bay State Park. Her Mini purred along the deserted road, allowing her time to process last night's events. Bear had been the consummate gentleman, parking in the street and escorting her to her door.

She'd wondered if Opaline had watched through the curtains as they kissed good-night on the porch. Or maybe Hope was just projecting her mother.

The old-fashioned setting and his old-fashioned manners made her feel treasured. But that kiss…it made her want to rip her manners away, right along with his clothes. She put a hand to her hot face. How he could stir feelings in her that no other man had, she didn't understand. But for once in her life, understanding, common sense, lists and logic didn't matter. When Bear kissed her, she just wanted more. She wanted to follow the trail of sweetness to see where it led. Hopefully to a bed somewhere.

Her thoughts were blowing like trash in a

whirlwind by the time she'd closed the door behind her last night. To collect them, she sat at her table with a pen and pad and started making a list—a list of what she was looking for in a man. And after ten minutes with nothing written, she had to admit, yet again, she had no idea.

In the past, if a man who was acceptable to her mother's standards asked her out, she went. Even after her mother died, Hope used the same worn, outdated yardstick.

She had no intention of doing that again. She threw the yardstick in the closet she'd locked her mother in, and focused once more on her list. Which looked more like a blank slate.

Okay, if she didn't know what she wanted, at least she had a clue what she didn't want. She wrote that, instead.

Dictatorial—All about HIM
Boring—Elitist
No like interests yardstick worthy

She scratched out the last one, because, though it was tempting to discard a man just because her mother would like him, it smacked of rebellion. And down that road lay yet another cage.

That list led her to the one she was really interested in.

Attributes of a Boyfriend According to
Hope Sanderson:

Interesting
Courageous
Respects me and my opinion
Earns a living
Doesn't think he's all that
Makes me laugh
Is my friend, first
We can talk about anything

She'd sat staring at the list for a long time.
Funny, Bear had all those attributes, except the
last. And he promised he was working on that.

Could she have happened upon a guy who
could make her happy, before she even realized
what she needed to be happy?

That only happened in romance novels.

Didn't it?

She turned in at the parking lot of the state
park, and pulled to the edge of the sand dunes
leading to the bay. Her heart skipped to a jit-
terbug beat. Just to be sure it was okay to sail,
she'd called her doctor. He'd told her that she was
healed—she was cleared to parasail, feed lamas,
jump out airplanes (with a chute, of course), rock
climb and box with kangaroos if she liked.

If she wanted to visit the moon, however, it

would take special clearance, and to call back and make an appointment if that was the case.

She got the hint. She was being a baby.

Hope pulled up her big-girl panties, snatched her windbreaker from the seat and stepped into the brisk onshore breeze.

Barry, in board shorts and a windbreaker, waved to her from the water's edge, beside two boats not much larger than a surfboard sporting happy, multicolored sails.

She was huffing by the time she negotiated the strip of loose sand between them.

He gave her a one-eyed squint. "Avast, matey! Are ye ready to give up the life of a landlubber?"

She chuckled. "I hope your lesson is better than your pirate imitation, or I'm doomed."

"Critics, even on the high seas." He sighed. "Have a seat. Let's go over some basics, first."

They perched on the edge of the boat, and Barry pulled some index cards and a golf pencil from the pocket of his shorts. "A sail on a boat works like the wing of an airplane, only vertical rather than horizontal." He sketched a sail. "The air moves faster over the belly of the sail—the rounded part—the low and high pressure areas pull the boat forward."

"I always thought the wind pushed it."

"That depends where you're going, and which way the wind is blowing."

He explained terminology and parts of the boat. She was surprised to find out that a "sheet" wasn't a sail, but a rope. Who knew?

"Now, let's go over how to maneuver where you want to go." He stood and led her to the edge of the water. The sand dunes created a cove, where kayakers and wake boarders took full advantage of the smooth, sheltered water. "The whole purpose is to get your sail into a position that takes full advantage of the wind. That's really all there is to it."

"Um. Okay." She frowned, filing information as fast as she could.

"You can figure this out. Let's say you're running downwind. That means the breeze is behind you. Where does your sail need to be to get the most wind?"

She thought a second. "It'd have to be at a ninety-degree angle to the boat."

"Aye, matey. I knew you were smart. And if you want to sail upwind—into the wind, where would your sail need to be?"

Scenarios flashed through her brain like still action shots. "You can't."

"You can. But you're going to have to tack."

"The only tack I know is on horses and bulletin boards."

He shook his head. "You keep the sail parallel to the boat. Tacking is just turning the boat left

and right, to keep wind going across your sails."
He jotted a stair-step path. "See?"

"Oh, I get it. That makes sense."

"And if you want to turn and go right? How
would you position the sail?"

She'd always been good at spatial relationships.
It was personal relationships she had problems
with. "Somewhere in between parallel and ninety
degrees. Say forty-five?"

"Oh, you're going to do well." He high-fived
her. "Now. Rate of movement. If you want to
speed up or slow down, you change the angle of
the sail, or the amount of belly in the sail." He
demonstrated the pulley system, and how to take
in and let out rope. *No, sheets.*

She was actually getting this! Sailing appeared
to rely more on knowledge than coordination.
Opposed to say, surfing. She cupped a hand over
her eyes and looked beyond the cove, to the open
sea. "I'm going to love this. I just know it."

Barry smiled and straightened. "We'll get out
there in a minute. First, we need to go over safety.
You know how to swim?"

She started. "I'm not going to be in the water,
am I?"

"Not if all goes well." He bent and lifted an
orange life vest from the small well in the boat.
"But shit happens. And it can happen fast. Put
this on."

"I can swim."

"Not if you're unconscious, you can't."

Picturing herself as a shark canapé, her hand shook a bit as she took the vest. "You're scaring me."

"Then listen up. Even though this is a tiny sailboat, you need to be aware at all times of the wind, and its effect on the sail. If the wind shifts, or you lose focus, the boom can come across and hit you. If you're lucky, you'll just see stars. If you're unlucky, the cold water should wake you." He pointed a finger at her. "Never get on a sailboat without a life vest. You hear me?"

She shrugged into it and only nodded, not trusting her voice. Or her knees. She sank back onto the edge of the boat. Why hadn't she tried something safe—like rock climbing? She might fall, but at least she wouldn't drown. Or get eaten.

"You're going to do fine, don't worry." Barry extended a hand. "You may want to leave your watch and your phone here."

She handed them over.

If you insist on getting on the water, what's wrong with a motorboat? Or a cruise ship? This is foolhardy and—

Shut. Up. Mom.

Hope pushed the door shut in her mind that had come open while she was concentrating. Now was not the time for negativity. She conjured pictures of herself, tanned and smiling sitting on a wave-slicing sailboat, hand on the tiller, wind blowing her hair back. Like a commercial for suntan lotion, or beachwear, or—

Shark Week. Her mother mumbled from behind the door.

Hope tightened her stomach muscles, slapped her hands on her knees and pushed herself to her feet. "Argh. I'm ready, skipper."

"That's the spirit." He patted her on the back. "You get in, put your feet in the footwell and get ready to lower the centerboard."

She did as he said, and he pushed her off the sand. Soon she was floating free.

Barry shouted. "Trim your sails, then hold tight. I'll be right there."

She pulled in the "sheet" through the metal "cam cleat," dropping the extra into the footwell. The breeze blew her hair back. She smiled into the wind, feeling more and more like that commercial.

Barry drifted within a few yards of her. One hand on the sheet, one on the tiller, he looked a part of the boat. "Okay, what should you do now?"

"Tack!" She steered the boat to the right. *Star-*

board. The sail billowed and the boat tacked, slicing the small waves, picking up speed.

"Nice, now tack port," Barry said. "Mind the boom!"

She steered left, ducking when the boom came across. The boat turned. The water raced under her, the spray wetting her hands. "Wooooeeee, I'm flying!"

A gust of wind heeled the boat. It tipped away from her.

"Lean out! Counteract the wind with your weight!"

She leaned over the edge until the boat was balanced.

"Tack again!"

She scrambled back to the center, moved the tiller, ducked the boom and tacked. She giggled. "I'm doing it!"

"Yes you are. Watch the kayak!"

The kayaker's eyes were huge by the time she completed another tack to move away from him.

"You are doing really well. How does it feel?" Barry stayed with her easily.

"Fantastic! This isn't as hard as I thought it would be." Maybe she'd actually found something she was good at. The wind gusted and she leaned out over the water when the boat heeled. *I wonder how much one of these cost? Maybe Travis will give me a deal...*

"It's as crowded as an LA freeway in here. You ready for the ocean?" Barry lifted one eyebrow in challenge.

"Bring it on, skipper."

"Okay, head to starboard. We'll go out the mouth."

She let out the sail to a forty-five degree broad reach and adjusted the tiller. Her little boat took off, skimming to open water. Her heart rose with the bow, pride and happiness bursting onto her face in a huge smile.

The waves looked much bigger out there. And the closer they got, the bigger they looked. Surely that was an optical illusion due to her sitting so low in the water.

The first wave smacked the side of the hull and the boat rocked. She scrambled to pull in sheet. Soon she was scooting along again, but her Sunfish was so lightweight, instead of slicing the waves, she bounced wildly between them.

"Mind the wind!" Barry yelled from somewhere behind.

The boom came around and smacked her in the shoulder. She teetered for a few heart-stopping seconds, then remembering, ducked. But the wind kept gusting and the boat heeled over. She grabbed and leaned out, but it was too late. The boat tipped the last few inches…and the sail fell onto the water. And she fell off the other side.

The shock of cold water drove the air out of her lungs, and she came up sputtering.

"—on the centerboard and pull it upright!" Barry yelled.

Holy crap it's cold! Her clothes swirled around her. What was he saying? She had to get out of the water before she flash froze like fresh salmon for market. "Do what?"

"Climb on the centerboard, your weight'll pull the boat upright." Barry sailed past, looking not the least worried that she was going to die.

She reached up and forced her stiff fingers around the gunnel and pulled her legs, weighted by soaked cotton onto the centerboard. The Sunfish came upright with a plop, dunking her again.

Barry came about. "Get in before you get too cold to work your hands!"

"Too late," she grumbled, and with a pull and a mighty kick, heaved herself up onto the side of the boat. Kicking, scrambling and imagining what she looked like from the back, Hope finally fell into the wildly rocking boat.

The breeze hit and she shivered.

"That happens to everyone. Don't worry." Barry cruised by. "Let out your sheets."

She managed to close her frozen claw around the friggin' *rope*, and pulled. Nothing happened. Dammit, it was knotted at the cam cleat. She bent and focused, trying to untangle it.

Her stomach rolled in a greasy wave. The boat rocked and she frowned, trying to focus. Suddenly all she could think of was the cereal she'd had for breakfast, sloshing in a sea of curdled milk in her stomach.

God, I've got a headache. The more she fumbled the tighter the knot became. And her hands weren't working right. She shivered in frozen, nauseated misery.

If you'd only listen to me—

"Shut the fuck up, Mom!"

"What'd you say?" Barry sailed alongside and grabbed her gunnel. "Are you all right? You look a little green—"

"Hooaaaahhh!" She heaved her breakfast over the side of the boat. Her head spun and her boneless body slithered into three inches of cold sloshing water in the footwell.

Her stomach was a washer, stuck on the agitate cycle.

Oh, please. Just let me die now.

THE ENTIRE WORLD was trying to get him to spill his guts. This stinking group, Hope, hell, even Nacho wanted to know things. But Bear's guts weren't liquid; they were a solid block of granite. That stuff didn't spill. He hauled that brick with him every day, weighting his guts and sapping his energy, filling his nights with blood and the slime of guilt.

Even if he'd wanted to, he wouldn't have a clue how to haul all that out of himself and into the light. What would people think if they really knew who he was? If they knew that killing a man and serving time for it weren't his worst sins?

He knew what they'd think. They'd look at him with contemptuous eyes, as if he wasn't quite human—then turn away.

Much better to reject people than to have them reject you.

But. He'd promised Hope he'd try. That put him between the rock in his guts and a very hard place. The pull he'd felt when he and Hope met had increased with every new thing he learned: her courage, her unrelenting drive, her...*goodness*. He felt like a better person when he was around her. In her eyes he could see—she believed that man was real.

It made him yearn to *be* that man.

Yeah, as if that was possible.

Hope was the last one through the door of the meeting room. Her face lit when she saw him.

It just *had* to be possible.

When they were all settled, Bina said, "Hope? How is your new, more adventurous career coming?"

"It's great."

But her lips drew to a tight line when she said it.

"What is it?" Bina pulled out her notepad and a pen.

Hope shrugged. "Surfing was a disaster. I don't have the balance for it. I tried sailing yesterday."

"Did you like that more?"

"In the beginning. It was freeing. Kind of like riding the motorcycle."

She shot him a look that warmed his gut.

"Maybe, but there's a 'but' in there. I hear it," Bina said.

Hope looked at her lap, and a curtain of hair obscured her face. "I got seasick."

"That can happen to anyone," Mark offered.

Bina put up a hand to stop him from saying more. "Hope, look at me."

She looked up.

"How are you feeling about this new life that you've embarked upon? Does it seem to fit you? Are you comfortable in it?"

"Not really." She tucked her hands under her thighs. "But it's all new. That's bound to be the case."

Bina cocked her head. "There are a lot of things for you out there. Perhaps if you tried something—"

"No." Her shoulders hovered around her ears

as she pulled into herself. "I'm doing this. All I need is time." She glared at Bina. "I'm *not* going to fail at this."

"You told us at the beginning that this was an experiment. You can't fail at an experiment." Bina's voice was soft. "I just want you to consider, if this isn't working—"

"It is working." Hope stopped, as if realizing she'd just contradicted herself. "It *will* work." She glanced at her lap again. "I don't want to talk about this any more."

Bina hesitated, then moved on. "Bryan, you're obviously upset. Would you like to talk about it?"

Bear had been so focused on Hope, he hadn't noticed; the kid was a mess. Redheads didn't just cry—they looked on the outside what crying felt like on the inside. His pale white face was blotched with red and it had spread to rim his bloodshot eyes. Tears dripped off his chin. "Curtis..." He wrung a tissue in his hands, as if it could somehow hold him together.

"What is it, Bryan?" Bina asked. Pulling a backup box of tissues from under her chair, she passed it to Mark, who passed it over to the kid.

Hope was closest to Bryan. She reached over and took his hand.

"I just gave them permission to unplug his respirator." He covered his face and sobbed.

"I'm so sorry," Bina said.

Everyone mumbled their condolences.

Bear was last, and his, "Aw shit, man, that blows." Sounded loud in the sorrow-soaked room.

Bryan sat up and pulled tissues to mop himself. "I couldn't let it go on any longer. I know he'd hate just lying there..." He sniffed. "They've been pushing me to do it for a week, but I just couldn't stand to let him go..."

"That's a huge burden for you. Doesn't he have any family that could make that decision?" Bina asked.

Bryan's face went hard. "Curtis's mother died before I met him. He and his dad didn't have much of a relationship. When I called, the man told me 'I don't have a son.' And hung up." He sniffed. "Better someone who loves him..."

Shit, that's cold. As uncomfortable as Bear was with the emotion in the room, he couldn't help but feel sorry for the guy.

"When are they going to do it?" Hope asked, holding his hand, and rubbing his shoulder.

"When I get back up there."

"Then we'll be there with you." Hope looked around the circle. "Right, guys?"

"I think that's a wonderful idea. You all should," Bina said.

"I'm in," Mark said.

"I—can't," Brenda, the bag lady said. "I have to get home. Phil will be calling."

"Screw Phil. When are you going to quit being a doormat?" Mark said, distaste distorting his ravaged face. "Bryan shouldn't have to do this alone."

She sat up straight. "You don't understand. I have to—"

"You're right. I don't understand. Under all that hair and those frumpy clothes, I think there's a gentle, nice woman. I've been watching, and I've caught flashes of her." Mark hesitated, as if realizing he was exposing too much. "If you can't stand up for that woman, at least stand up for a friend, who needs our help. Have a little pride and grow a pair—"

Bina interrupted. "Okay, I think we need to take a breath and calm down."

Brenda's mouth opened and closed, looking pleased at the compliment and offended, all at the same time.

Everyone sat back and waited.

Her muddy-green eyes shifted to a sharper shade, and her head came up. "Fine. I'll stay, but I can't stay long."

"Good," Mark said.

Heads swiveled to Bear.

His face heated. Sitting with a dying man he didn't know with these people, and all that emotion, was right up there with picking up his gun at the bottom of his bucket list. But Hope was looking at him with beseeching eyes. And Bryan… he may be obnoxious, but his pain was palpable, pulsing in the room. How could a person not want to help? "What the hell, I've got time."

"Then I think we'll adjourn for the day." Bina stood. "Bryan, I'll check in with you later." She glanced at each person. "I'm proud of you all."

CHAPTER TWELVE

"POWER-HEAVING INTO the bay can be considered littering you know. Or polluting. You're lucky you didn't get a ticket." Lori took a huge bite of her bacon and avocado sandwich.

The lunch crush at Hollister Drugs was in full swing. Hope had a hard time hearing her friend across the table.

"So sailing's not your thing, either. You have one more activity to try, and it should be camping. At least you're not shark bait, and you can't get 'land sick.'"

Hope set her fork beside her half-eaten salad. Just remembering that day made her nauseated. "I'd still be a part of the food chain—there are bears out there."

"They're just small black bears." Lori took another bite.

"Holy jeez, are you saying you've *seen* bears?"

"Sure, but they won't bother you. It's the cougars you have to watch out for."

A shudder rattled down Hope's spine.

Lori laughed. "I'm kidding. I've never seen a cougar."

"In case you were wondering, you are not making a good case here."

A college kid who was helping Sin with the lunch rush stopped at the table. "You done with that?" He pointed to her salad, and when she nodded, he took it away.

"No, seriously, just listen for a minute." Lori moved her plate aside and leaned in. "The Pacific Crest Trail is within a hundred fifty miles of here. You get out on the trail, and the stress of the real world falls away. You can't even remember what home looks like without thinking hard about it." Her eyes went all soft and dreamy. "It's you and nature. That's it. The running conversation in your head stops, and you notice things: the wind in the trees, the smell of jack pine, a woodpecker hammering away."

"A rattlesnake, hissing at you." Hope grimaced.

"They don't hiss. They rattle. And not very often." She looked off, with a dreamy expression. "And the stars at night…you can see the whole Milky Way spread above you like diamond chips on black velvet. It's amazing."

"That part does sound awesome." Hope sighed.

"I know that trail like my own body. I've hiked there all my life. You'd have me to protect you."

She gazed at Hope with little-kid-digging-for-Disneyland eyes. "Won't you try it?"

Bugs. Peeing outside. Sleeping on the ground. Wild animals. Broken legs... Hope could come up with a dozen reasons not to, and doubtless her mother could fill in the gaps. But Lori had been a good friend.

And then there were those puppy dog eyes.

And the fact that Hope had been a dismal failure at her first two attempts. She threw her hands up. "Oh, buggers. I've gotta die sometime, right?"

"Whoop! That's the spirit!" Lori held her hand up for a high five.

Hope touched her fingers to Lori's palm, telegraphing tentativeness. "I can't believe you talked me into this."

"Well, you can't take it back now. We'll discuss the deets later." She propped her elbows on the table, and plopped her chin into her hands. "Now, tell me what's happening with Bear?"

Hope had needed someone to talk to about her budding relationship, but Jesse was on vacation, and the thought of talking to Opaline was...just wrong. Besides, Lori was a good listener.

She explained Bryan's horrific decision, and how all of them were there in the hospital room to support him. "Oh, you should have seen Bear. He was so uncomfortable with the emotion in that room he was about to bolt. But he didn't.

Granted, he didn't hold Bryan's hand, or cry when Curtis slipped away, but he did pat Bryan on the back and offered to take him for a beer."

"Wow, downright metrosexual, that one." Lori's smile took the sting out of her sarcasm.

"For Bear that was the equivalent, believe me."

Lori cocked her head. "You're getting hooked on this guy, aren't you?"

"Yeah, I think I kinda am." She shook her head. "I sat down and made a list of traits I wanted in a guy, and Bear has almost every one. But."

"But what? From what you've told me, he sounds like a great guy. Except for the prison stint, of course." Her shoulders lifted. "Nobody's perfect."

Suddenly, Hope viewed this from her mother's viewfinder. Hope, a gently raised dormouse, going out with a reclusive ex-con biker dude. How did she get from there to here? If not flat-out impossible, that should have been a very long road. But it hadn't been.

"Lori, please tell me what you really think. Adventure is one thing, but have I crossed over into completely reckless?"

Don't forget the death wish.

Back to the closet, Mom.

Lori's hand covered hers. "Hon, I don't know this guy. Only you can answer that." She squeezed Hope's fingers. "But remember, your eyes only see the top layer. Your gut sees deeper. Trust your gut."

She knew her gut's opinion. It trusted Bear.

"So? What's the next step? I'm between boyfriends, so you know I'm living vicariously through you, right?"

"Not sure that's a good idea." Hope opened her wallet and pulled out enough to cover her bill and tip, and tucked it under her plate. "You ready?"

"Yep." Lori pulled a ten and a five from her shorts and dropped it on the table. "So, has he asked you out again?"

"The bedside of a dying man wasn't exactly the best place—"

"Then you ask him." Lori stood and took off for the door.

Hope hurried to catch up. "I can't do that."

"Why not?" Lori held the door for a young woman with a baby stroller.

"I've never asked a man out in my life."

"Damn, woman, did you grow up in the '50s? Hello, it's a new century. Women ask for what they want today." When Hope cleared the door, she let it fall closed. "Right up to, and including sex."

"Could you keep your voice down?" Hope whipped her head around to be sure none of the tourists they passed were listening.

"You should ask him over for dinner."

"At my place?"

"No, your landlady's. That would be more romantic." She gave an exasperated sigh. "I see camping isn't the only thing I need to teach you."

Hope was so busy thinking, she tripped over a crack in the sidewalk.

"Add grace to the list." Lori dodged a kid with a drippy ice cream cone. "Seriously, Hope. Get him to your place. If things go well, and your gut tells you it's okay...hit the boneyard, babe."

"The boneya—oh." She put a hand to her face, which felt as if it was about to burst into flames. "Lori!"

"What?" She stopped in the middle of the sidewalk, creating a break in the flow of tourists. "It wouldn't be some one-night stand. You've been out with him a few times. You like him. What's the problem?"

Hope grabbed her friend's elbow and moved her along before she could say anything else embarrassing. "Come on. We're going to be late back to work."

I could make lasagna. No way I'd ever ask a man out.

Maybe steaks?

HOPE HAD WARNED him not to freak out her landlady, so Bear parked his bike two houses down and walked. He'd been surprised when Hope had called and asked him to her house for dinner.

He slid a thumb in the waistband of his jeans to be sure his dress shirt was tucked, then tightened his grip on the bottle of wine. Twice in a Blue Moon Merlot. The guy in the wine shop downtown said it had won all kinds of awards, and was the best the valley had to offer.

At least he could buy the best—maybe it'd help make up for his shabby ass. Hope could do a damned sight better than an ex-con with the social skills of the animal he was named after.

He turned at the driveway of the lavender Victorian. His stomach bucked, and not from hunger. When was the last time something in life excited him?

A long freaking time. Before Afghanistan, surely. After that, it seemed life had gone gray and dingy, like one of those gritty black-and-white urban photos.

Maybe meeting his angel was an omen—that his life was changing for the better.

If he didn't screw this up.

He passed the landlady's window, head down, hoping she wasn't looking out. His size and appearance tended to freak out old ladies and he didn't want her calling the cops. That would not be the romantic evening he'd hoped for.

He opened the knee-high gate, and walked the

paving stones to the Mini-Me cottage in the back. Cute and feminine, it suited Hope.

But God, it was tiny.

The door opened, and Hope's happy smile drew him. "About time you showed. I was about to feed the salad to Opaline's bunnies."

Shit. He'd left home early, so he'd ridden the neighborhood for ten minutes to burn off some time. "Sorry I'm late." He handed her the bottle of wine.

"I'm teasing you. You're right on time." She took his arm and led him through the door. "Come sit."

Spindly furniture filled the front part of the room. A stained-glass lamp sat on the fussy round table in front of the window. Everything looked fragile. He chose the couch. Since it was made for two, surely it'd hold his weight. Wouldn't it?

"This place suits you."

She beamed. "Thank you. I love it here."

"I barely fit."

Her tinkling laugh followed her to the kitchen area. "You look even more masculine by comparison."

The couch creaked when he sat. *Yeah, right up to the furniture failure.*

He noticed the photo on the mantel above the small fireplace. "Are those your parents? Your mother doesn't look like a dragon."

"Good makeup covers the scales."

"Your dad looks like a nice guy."

"He was."

She opened the oven, releasing the aroma of roasting meat.

"What smells so good?"

"Pot roast." Putting on oven mitts, she lifted out a covered pan.

"Oh, man, did you call my mother?"

She put the pan on the counter. "Nah. You just look like a meat-and-potato guy to me."

Mentioning his mother made him remember his manners. He stood and walked into the tiny kitchen. "Can I do anything?"

She turned, two salad plates in her hands. "If you'll open that gorgeous bottle of wine you brought, we're ready."

He poured the wine, held her chair for her, then sat. He lifted his glass. "'Thou hast no faults, or I no faults can spy; Thou art all beauty, or all blindness, I.'"

She flushed a pretty pink. "Wow, you're a poet, too?"

His turn to flush. "I looked it up before I came here, to impress you with my sophistication."

"Well, it worked." She clinked her glass with his. *"Salud."*

But neither of them drank. They were too busy drinking in each other. She wore a jewel-tone sweater that highlighted her incredible eyes. It was modest, but hugged her curves—her perfectly proportioned curves.

He would have been happy to sit looking at her until dark, but she blinked first.

He took a bite of roast and closed his eyes. "This is better than my mom's."

"Thank you." She smiled, then took a gulp of wine before picking up her fork. "How's your business doing?"

"It's good. In fact, I have a new assistant."

"You hired someone?"

"I think that'd be against child labor laws. He's nine."

"Really?" She took another sip of wine. "I somehow got the impression that you didn't like kids."

"I used to." He barreled on to discourage questions. "This kid is special, for some reason I can't understand. He's a delinquent waiting to happen, but he's also eager to please, and interested in painting things besides warehouse walls, which is what brought him to me."

"Do you think you'll want kids of your own, someday?"

"I don't know. If I could pick one out, like with a litter of puppies, maybe. How about you?"

"Oh, I wouldn't have any idea of how to be a good mother." She focused on her plate, arranging green beans with her fork. "Better to not take a chance on ruining some kid's life."

"Why would you assume you'd do that?"

She wiped her hands over the napkin in her lap. "Well, they say you become your mother as you get older. One of those was more than enough."

"Actually, I think people either end up like their parents, or the opposite. Role models can teach you what you want to become as well as what you don't want to be."

"I wouldn't want to pass my fears on to a child."

"What fears? You're the bravest person I know." He took a sip of wine.

"Are you kidding? I had to change my whole life, because I was afraid to go back to my old one."

"A life that, from what you've told me, didn't fit you. That's a move very few have the guts to do." He watched her over the rim of his glass. "And ever since, you've been challenging every fear you developed growing up, to see if it was your mother's, or yours. I'd say that's pretty courageous."

"Saving yourself is preservation. Courage is in saving others. I'm sure you did that all the time as a soldier."

"Women are much braver than men. Much stronger."

She snorted. "Why would you say that?"

"Are you kidding? Women bring life into the world. They create a family, make a home, then do their best to preserve it, despite tremendous odds."

"That sounds like personal experience talking."

He finished the last bit of roast, stalling. Maybe if he gave her the unobjectionable parts of his past, she wouldn't dig for the rest. He wiped his mouth on his napkin. "I was in high school during the last economic downturn. Business at Dad's shop fell off to the point that it couldn't support us. I offered to get a job, but Mom wouldn't hear of it—said my job was school, including the sports and clubs I belonged to.

"So she went out and got herself a thirty hour-a-week job at the local grocery store. Somehow she still managed the house, and had a hot meal on the table every night. We started calling her Supermom." He shook his head. "By the time Dad's business picked up, she'd been promoted to head of the produce department. She loves her job and refuses to quit. She's now the store manager, and making more money than Dad."

"Wow. Supermom is right. I think I'd like her."

"I think you and she are a lot alike."

She reached for her wine and knocked over her water glass.

He snatched it before it hit the table. It barely wet the tablecloth.

"Oh, buggers." She hopped up. "I'm sorry. I'm such a klutz."

He stood and caught her elbow. "I think you're adorable."

When she looked up, he wished he could burn the look of her face onto the wall of his memory. Open and vulnerable, and so...tender.

They stood, hesitating as the tension built in the room, a crackling in the air like just before a lightning strike.

"I think you're crazy. And chivalrous. And just about the most surprising man I've ever met." Her lips quirked.

He chuckled.

And just like that, they were laughing.

"Oh, God, if this was a movie, I'd walk out." She took a breath and wiped a tear. "Those were the cheesiest lines I've ever heard."

"We do stink at dialog." The skin of her arm felt like silk, as he ran his hand down it, to entwine her fingers in his. "What do you say we skip to the kissing scene and see if we're any better at that?"

WHEN HIS LIPS touched hers the tension in the air coalesced, jolting through her, raising her awareness and the hair on her arms. She twined her hands around his neck and pulled him closer, wanting—needing the current that sizzled, awakening the sensitive parts of her: her nipples, her sex and whatever parts of her skin that touched him.

His huge arms came around her, but he held her lightly, as if she was priceless china. A small sound escaped her. It might have been a whimper. She wanted him. In her, around her, any way she could get him.

They were both breathing heavy by the time she broke off the kiss. "I made brownies for dessert, but I've changed my mind. I'd rather have you."

His lips lifted in a slow, lazy smile. "I'm definitely fewer calories."

"Stop selling. I already bought." Tugging his hand, she led him to the tight spiral staircase to the loft.

"Just hope you won't have buyer's remorse," he said under his breath.

Smiling to herself, she led him upstairs. It helped to know she wasn't the only nervous one. "This is probably my favorite room in the house."

When he took the last step, he let out a breath.

"What?"

"I'm just glad your bed is more substantial than the couch. I was afraid I was going to break it."

He pulled her into his arms. "Now I just have to be afraid of breaking you."

Seeing his heavy brows gathered over worried eyes, second thoughts melted like snow before a Chinook wind. "Oh, Douglas, I really wish you would."

He moaned, deep in his throat, and lifted her in his arms as if she weighed nothing. "Since I met you, I've wanted this…dreamed of this. I hope you don't mind if I go slow. I want to savor every moment."

Since she didn't trust her voice not to give away her trembling inside, she let her kiss be her answer.

He lowered her onto the bed, then sat next to her. She braced herself for what came next. A quick fumbling of clothing followed by furtive coupling.

"I love your hair. Never seen that blond shade on an adult." He ran his fingers through it, fanning it on the pillow. "So soft. And your eyes." He ran a hand down her cheek. "They draw me in. It's like they're speaking to me, only it's a language I can't quite understand. Sometimes I have to look away, because I know I'm staring." He touched the exposed skin at her waist. "May I?"

She sat up, and stripped off her sweater in one smooth motion and kissed him for all she was worth.

He ended the kiss and laid her back once more. He smiled, lightly touching her bra. "Pink lace. That's so you." Trailing the backs of his fingers down her ribs, he looked his fill. "God, you're beautiful."

Between her awkward clumsiness and her mother's criticism, she'd never felt beautiful. But she did now, seeing the worship on his face, *Just for a little while*... Her expectations, inhibitions, her mother's rules hit the floor along with her sweater.

She reached for the buttons of his dress shirt, but he covered her hand. "You'll get your turn. I'm not done unwrapping the best present I've been given."

A flush shot straight to her crotch. Her rushing hands fumbled at the buttons of her jeans until he took over, loosening them with large, sure fingers. In a movie, clothes just seemed to melt away. In the real world, no way that squirming out of jeans could be anything but awkward, much less when she did it.

When her pants lay in a heap on the floor, he laid her back again, skimming his hands down her ribs, her thighs, the backs of her knees. He lifted her foot and kissed the arch. His loving attention to detail made her skittish at first, waiting for him to get to it. But when it became apparent he did indeed mean to take his time she decided to relax and enjoy it…at least as much as she could, given the sexual tension building in her like a summer storm.

"Close your eyes. Just relax. Trust me."

He undid her bra clasp with a practiced twist of his fingers. Before she could get nervous he kissed her again, long and deep. Thoughts swirled, none lighting long enough for consideration. Her body responded without her say-so as he trailed endearment-murmured kisses down her throat. In the lack of sight, her other senses took over. Her stuttered breathing—his, calm and deep. She smelled a hint of sex in the ozone. But mostly, she *felt*, as his hands made love to her skin.

Sweet. So…sweet.

His palm skimmed her mound and her hips bucked.

"That's what I'm talkin' about," he whispered, bent and blew a hot breath over her, through the silk of her panties.

"Bear…please." Frantic, she opened her eyes, and scrabbled at his shirt. "I have to touch you."

He sat still, and let her. When she finally negotiated all the damned buttons, she pulled out the tails and skimmed the shirt off. Dark hair covered his pecs, narrowed at the valley of his ribs, then became a line between his washboard abs, to disappear into the waistband of his jeans.

"Oh, nice." She bent and suckled his button-flat nipple. "I like my present, too."

He sucked in a breath, but his hands stayed at his sides.

She tasted her way down the trickle of hair, to nibble his ribs, and was rewarded with a moan. When she dipped her tongue into the edge of his jeans, he broke, grabbing her upper arms and lifting until he could capture her lips once more.

They were both caught by the storm, and things started moving fast.

He stood, unzipped his jeans and let them fall. His cock jutted and pulsed, bouncing off his lower abs. She sucked in a breath, and felt her heartbeat between her legs. Then he was with her again, and it felt as if her panties melted away.

Thunder rumbled deep inside her, and with a flip, her brain switched off, and her body took over. Their tongues twined, and her hands roamed, wanting to touch every part of his hulking body at once. She closed her eyes again, to better feel him: the supple skin of his back, his tight, dimpled buns, the taut cords of the back of his thighs. She was on sensory overload, trying to absorb this and her own body's input at the same time. He stroked her breasts, and rolled her nipples between his fingers. His cock pulsed against her sex, and she ached with hollowness.

She grasped him, wanting to guide him where they both wanted him to be.

His hands came around her arms and he lifted her until she straddled him. "It may work better this way."

Her hands looked so small on his chest.

He slipped his hands around the backs of her thighs, then paused. He was leaving this to her. She hesitated, wondering how she'd look back on this later. A beginning? Or another mistake? When her womb throbbed, she abandoned thought, took him in hand and led him to the edge of her. When he touched, she rocked against him.

She heard his teeth grind, and a trill of power coursed through her. To test them both, she rocked again, bringing him just inside. He moaned, but didn't move.

But then the lightning struck, and she was swept away in a flash flood of sensation. She sank onto his huge cock, burying him, filling her. Before he was even halfway in, a massive pulsing orgasm began and she cried out, frantic for him.

He clasped her to his chest, her arms caught between them, and thrust in a spasm, once, twice, burying himself to her pubic bone. They came together, pouring shouts of release into each other's mouth.

She lay her head on his chest and breathed, trying to fill her body's oxygen deficit as her muscles went liquid in the heat from them both. Bear was wrapped around her, in her. Cradled in his sheltering embrace, she sank into safety, light-years beyond where she'd ever been before. A purr-like sound rolled through her chest.

"Who was he?" he whispered.

"Who was who?"

"The man who made you stiffen when he touched you?"

CHAPTER THIRTEEN

"WAS IT AN old boyfriend who made you tense up?"

She tried to roll away, but he petted her, running his palms over her back until she relaxed again. This was less awkward if she didn't have to see him. "Both of them." Under her ear, the heavy thudding of his heart was soothing.

"You've only had two boyfriends? As beautiful as you are?"

This was embarrassing. But if he was going to let her into his past, she'd have to be willing to do the same. She rolled off, to lie beside him on her back. "You have to realize, my mother had exacting standards."

"But, didn't you tell me your mother passed away—"

"Over two years ago. I know. I'll get to that." She sighed. "The boyfriends my mother picked for me had money. More money than we did. Bright, up-and-comers, country-club kinda guys. You know the type—button-down shirts and loafers. Destined to learn the business from Dad. After Yale, of course."

"There's a 'but' coming." He stretched his arm out, and she lay her head on it.

"It was great. At first. They were polite and solicitous, taking me out to fancy restaurants, polo matches, parties... I was so dazzled that it took me a while to realize what was happening. He'd suggest that the dress I wore didn't suit my coloring. Or he'd make a passing mention that my purse wasn't a name brand, then the next time I saw him, he'd bring a present of a purse from a New York designer.

"My mother was thrilled, of course. But the demands progressed. What was I thinking, wanting to cut my hair? He wanted to vet my friends. He didn't want me to chime in on political or business discussions. But that wasn't the worst." She realized she was tapping her fingers on her thigh only when he took her hand to make her stop. "Of course the first boyfriend was my first. In bed, I mean. He was very happy to find I was a virgin, and very happy to relieve me of that burden. And the second wasn't very happy to learn that I had already been relieved."

Oh, God, was she really talking about this? How did she paint herself into this corner?

"Just say it, Hope. It's okay." He squeezed her hand.

"It's not horrible. They didn't beat me, or get kinky or anything." She bit her lip. "But that's how I figured it out, that no part of that relationship was about me. Not the places we went—they only cared about being seen, I guess with me as arm candy. Not the presents they bought me—they were just to make me look good enough to be with them. Certainly not the sex. That was *all* about them. What's that saying? Wham, bam…"

"Thank you ma'am. I get it."

"My part was to be the receptacle. I know that sounds awful, but that's what it felt like. My mother was mad when she found out I broke things off with the first guy, then harassed me until I told her why. She didn't even sound surprised, just informed me that was the way it was. If I wanted the good life, it came at a price. I told her the cost was too high." She turned her face away. "But when she brought guy number two, I still said yes."

"I don't think I'd have liked your mother much." He rolled onto his side, facing her.

Having admitted her shame, she rolled to face him. "She was only trying to—"

"I don't mean because of her mistaken beliefs. I'm sure that there were reasons in her past to explain those." He smoothed her bangs from her forehead. "I don't like her because she didn't trust her daughter was strong enough to handle whatever life threw at her."

In a tiny out-of-the way corner of her chest where pride lived, a warm spot expanded.

Dare she see herself as Bear saw her?

No.

But the warm spot was larger than it was before.

"Thank you."

The skin at the corners of his eyes crinkled. "You never owe someone thanks for telling the truth."

"I meant thank you for teaching me that not all men think only of themselves in bed."

His hand reached out to cup her breast. "I have lots more to teach you about that."

Oh, yes, please... His face filled her vision as he bent to kiss her.

"Bear!"

He woke with the rasping echo of a scream in his throat and his angel's voice in his ear.

Breathing hard, he lay in a sweaty bath of shame.

Overhead, the stars glittered. Not desert stars. *Hope.* He was in Hope's bed, and he was looking through a skylight. He touched her arm. "Thank God, you're real."

Her hands skimmed his chest. "Of course I'm real. What is it, Bear? You can tell me anything."

Anything? No way. He'd just found his angel. She'd be gone as fast as water in the sand if she knew what had gone on in the desert.

"Just nightmares about old shit, better left buried." He scrubbed his hands over his face. "Do you know what time it is?"

With a sigh, she rolled away to check the clock on the nightstand. "It's four."

He sat up, swung his feet to the floor, and reached for his shirt. "I've got to go."

She sat up. "Go? Why?"

He turned back and ran his hand down her cheek. "I don't want you to have to answer questions to your landlady, or any other neighbor who happens to look out the window."

"I'm a big girl. I can handle it." She twined her fingers in his. "Won't you stay?"

He wavered. He was an ex-con, in a good girl's bed. If anyone knew—

"Besides, I need more practice on the last lesson." She took his hand, and put it at the junction of her thighs. "How did that go, again?"

He groaned and pulled her into his arms.

AFTER WORK ON MONDAY, Hope ate dinner, straightened her already neat house, then looked around for something else to do. Her emotions were unsettled, her thoughts bouncing like balls in a Bingo hopper. Last night with Bear was more than she would have dared hope. Sex with him was much more than she'd known existed. God, those hands… She squeezed her thighs together.

But if she were naive enough to believe that a good meal, poetry and great sex was going to bridge the communication gap between them, Bear's nightmare had shattered it and scattered the pieces.

There were no easy answers. And what answers she had wouldn't matter anyway. Though she had a big stake in the outcome, this was Bear's issue to fix.

She stood in the middle of her sitting room, winding her hair around her finger.

Find something to do.

She looked out the window at the big lavender house.

Opaline. I'll go visit her.

On her way to the door, she snatched the vase of multicolored daisies from the antique table, as a gift.

She stepped onto the back porch of the big house, cupped one hand around her eye to see through the screen door into the shadowy kitchen. "Hello? Opaline?"

"Eeep!"

A flash of movement caught her eye. Opaline was on a stepladder beside the counter, arms pinwheeling. Hope ripped open the screen door, ran in and caught Opaline's arm to steady her. Bunnies scattered.

"Thank you, child." Opaline put a hand to her chest. "You startled me, and I lost my balance."

"What in the world are you doing on a ladder?" Hope's hands shook as she set the vase on the counter. It sloshed, splashing water onto both of them. "Ugh, sorry."

Opaline brushed drops off her flowered dress. "I'd much rather a bit of water than a nasty fall."

Hope held her landlady's arm as she stepped down to the linoleum. "What in the world were you doing?" She shuddered to think what a fall would do to those birdlike bones.

"I was putting up my china, after its annual washing."

Hope spied the yellow-and-gray chrysanthemum dishes through the glass fronted cabinets. "Why on earth are you doing that? I thought you had a housekeeper?"

"Are these for me?" Opaline turned on the tap and held the vase under it.

"Yes. And don't change the subject."

"Why thank you, child." She glanced to the hallway. "It's all right, babies. Come on back. I won't let her drop anything on you."

"Don't you try to distract me, Opaline. Why are you the one doing this?"

She fussed, arranging the flowers. "I have someone coming in once a week to do the floors, and the bathrooms, but I do the rest." She carried the vase to the table. "I was about to put on tea. Would you like some?"

"Sure. But you are way too...mature to be doing cleaning." She pulled out a chair and sat at the table. "Why?"

"Oh, I just don't like having strangers in my house. I had a maid service for a while, and several pieces of jewelry went missing. Thank goodness, nothing expensive, but I find it's easier to do it myself than to worry about it."

"I can understand that." So sad to be old, all alone and afraid. "We'll have tea, and then I'm your gofer for two hours."

"Oh, dear, no." She turned the gas on under the kettle.

"Opaline Settle. Are you saying you don't trust me?"

"No, of course not, but I couldn't impose—"

"You're not imposing one bit." She scanned the bunnies that hopped into the room. "Now, where's that little Buckwheat? I want to see how big he's gotten."

WEDNESDAY MORNING, THEY sat in the circle, waiting. All except Brenda. Hope shot a look at Bear. He winked back.

"We'll give her another minute, and if she's not here by then…" Bina looked up.

Brenda walked in, head down as usual, but even her hair couldn't cover the black eye.

"Oh, Brenda," Hope whispered, then patted the chair next to her.

Brenda fell into it.

Still, they waited.

Bina plucked the question that hung in the air. "Brenda, what happened?"

"I hit a kitchen cabinet door."

"Was his hand at the back of your head at the time?" Mark's face was crimson, except for the white around the jagged scar.

"Oh, honey, you do not have to live with this abuse," Bryan said, and double-crossed his long legs.

"Jesus, why would you?" Bear asked.

Brenda straightened, and looked to Bina. "Are you going to let them talk to me like that?"

"All I hear is concern for your safety, Brenda." Bina cocked her head. "Do you think you could tell us what happened?"

Brenda twisted her hands in her lap as she rocked back and forth in the chair.

Her unease was so palpable, Hope's stomach twisted in empathy. She reached for Brenda's hand, but she snatched it away.

"I told you I had to go!" It burst from her like

a stuck cork from a bottle. "You people don't understand. You make no effort to understand. You just judge me."

"I'm sorry, Brenda." Mark leaned his forearms on his knees and clasped his hands together. "But I'd think the one who gave you that shiner judged you harshest."

"Can you walk us through what happened, Brenda?" Bina's voice was soft, but there was iron underneath.

"He got mad, okay? I know the rules. I'm supposed to be home when he calls."

"You mean this happened because you wanted to be with me when Curtis…didn't you tell him where you were?"

"Phil calls the house during the day. He needs to know where I am."

"Why?" Mark asked.

She picked at her nails.

Hope tried not to judge. Sure, she'd put up with some manipulative behavior from her boyfriends in the past, but she'd never have put up with abuse.

Or had she? Instead of watching, concerned but detached, Brenda's squirming distress plucked a chord that echoed inside Hope. A familiar chord. Her mother had never raised a hand—but then, she hadn't had to, since her haranguing did the job. Sure, parents lectured their kids all the time.

But Hope's mother had gone further, not resting until Hope truly believed her mother was right. And sometimes that took hours. On rare occasions, days.

Wasn't that a kind of assault? She'd never thought of it that way before.

"That's just the way it is with Phil."

"I get that," Mark said. "What I don't get is why you think you don't deserve to be treated better."

Her lips thinned. "Phil loves me."

"Do you notice how everything you say is about how Phil feels?" Mark's voice increased in volume. "We don't give a shit about Phil."

"Oh, I do," Bear said. "I'd like to catch that dude—"

"Let's stay focused." Bina held out a hand. "Mark is onto something here."

"Do you love Phil?" Mark asked.

Brenda glared at him. "Of course I do."

He spread his hands. "Why?"

"Because he loves me." She nodded, as if that explained everything.

"You know, Mark's right," Hope said. "Everything you talk about ends up at Phil. We know a lot about him though we've never met him. But we know almost nothing about you."

"Why would you want to know anything?"

Bryan piped up. "Because you seem a sweet-hearted person, silly. Why wouldn't we want to get to know you?"

"Tell us something about yourself," Mark said.

"Like what?"

"Oh, I don't know. Like…where are you happiest? The beach? The mountains?"

She thought a moment. "No one thinks the desert is pretty. But I do."

"Why?" Bina asked.

She gazed unfocused at the wall over Bina's head. "Well, when you look at the landscape, it seems barren and unforgiving. But if you look close, beauty is everywhere. The cactus shelters the birds that nest in its protection. Night is like a photo negative; stark and cold, like the surface of the moon." She hesitated, searching for words.

Hope imagined Brenda's verbalization skills were rusty. Phil probably never asked for her opinion on anything.

She shrugged. "It's easy to love the ocean, or the mountains. But to love the desert…that takes paying attention."

"That's an interesting observation," Mark said.

Bina said, "Is that how you see yourself, Brenda?"

"I never thought of it that way." She ducked her head. "But yeah. Kind of."

"See? That's the first important thing we've

learned about you." Mark leaned back in his chair.

"We'll move on now, but, Brenda, I have some homework for you," Bina said. "I'd like you to practice seeing things from your point of view rather than Phil's. Or, if that's too hard, at least notice when you are doing it. Okay?"

"Okay."

"So, who else has something to share?"

"Bear and I are dating." Hope smiled and glanced to him.

Bear wasn't smiling.

"BUT I DON'T UNDERSTAND. We're supposed to share. And those are our friends." Hope trailed him as he pushed out the door of the hospital. "What did I do wrong?"

He needed to calm down before he answered. He shouldn't have been surprised; Hope was an open book. But her blurting out their private business in that room? It made him feel naked. And that made him mad.

"And don't you give me that grizzly bear look. It doesn't scare me anymore." She stopped in the middle of the crowded lane of the parking lot and crossed her arms. "Bear, talk to me."

He grabbed her elbow and led her between the rows of cars so she wasn't blocking traffic. "First. Those aren't my friends, and they're not yours. They're a bunch of strangers we're stuck with for a while. Second, what we do outside of that room is our private business."

Her brows scrunched. "What are you talking about? You sat in that room with Bryan, while his partner died. Why would you do that if he wasn't a friend?"

He threw his eyes heavenward, but the blue sky was no help. The answer wouldn't be beamed down. He sure couldn't tell her that he mostly did it to be with her. "It seemed like the thing to do at the time."

"I don't think so. I saw you. You cared about Bryan. And in that room a few minutes ago, you wanted to beat up Phil." Her eyes shifted from soft confusion to flint. "Why can't you admit it? Why should our dating be a secret?"

"It's private. Between you and me. It's—"

"It's bull." She crossed her arms again, and cocked her head.

She was peering through the cracks that had opened in him since he met her. They frightened him. What if she saw? What if everyone saw?

"Bear Steele, what happened to you? You live like a hermit outside of town. Though, I've never been invited. Most of your past is a black hole that you refuse to talk about and you're terrified to admit that anyone could mean anything to you."

She was getting too close. A squirrel of panic was loose in his brain, ripping through his carefully structured rooms, tearing stuff up. He had to do or say…something. He ran his fingers through his hair, hoping it would pull an answer out. "I'm just a private person. Why does everyone have to dig all the time? Why can't you just take me at face value, and go from there?"

"Then how do I get to know you? We talked about this, the night of the concert. Is this you trying? Really?" She spun on her heel and walked away.

Last night, holding Hope was the closest he'd felt to peace since before the army. He couldn't lose her. "Wait." He took two steps and put a hand on her arm. "Hope, just wait a second."

When she turned, her face was closed as a doorless maze.

"You're right, okay? I suck at this. But last night…last night was the best thing that's happened to me in a long time. I think maybe for you, too." He took a breath. "And I'm not talking about the sex."

"Shhhh." Her head whipped right, then left.

"Come out to my place on Saturday. We'll go for a motorcycle ride." He was making up shit as he went along. There was no way he was letting her in the house, but maybe he could…

The squirrel scurried. "I'll show you around my shop."

One eyebrow raised in a skeptical arch.

"*This* is me trying. Please, Hope?"

"Okay. But I can't on Saturday. I'm going camping. How about Sunday?"

He could breathe again. No clue how he'd explain not letting her in the house, but he had days to figure that out. "Sunday it is."

The squirrel in his head sniggered.

CHAPTER FOURTEEN

"WHY DID WE have to get up at the butt-crack of dawn?" The only way Hope could tell it wasn't still night was the slightly lighter shade of blackness in the east. She handed Lori her suitcase and a travel mug of coffee.

"You brought a suitcase? To go camping?" Lori lifted the back window of her Jeep. "Nevermind. Don't worry about it, just get in."

"What was I supposed to bring?"

"A backpack? A duffel? Something that can handle a little wear and tear?" Lori walked for the driver's door.

"I don't really own anything like that." Hope got in and buckled her seat belt.

"My fault. I should have brought you one."

Hope watched her neatly kept, civilized street recede into the dark. "Really. We have no tide to worry about, or wind. Why so early?"

"We've got a bit of a drive ahead of us. There are hiking trails around here, but they're all urban. To give you a real flavor of hiking and camping, I wanted to put the best face on it."

"Urban is pretty. Besides, it's got soft beds and fast food."

"Oh, quit whining, you're going to love it. We're going to one of my favorite places, Kennedy Meadows." She held up her mug in salute. "PCT, baby!"

"Am I supposed to know what that is?"

"Pacific Crest Trail. Man, you are not a morning person, huh?" She drove through downtown Widow's Grove. Deserted at this hour, it looked a bit like a darkened Hollywood movie set. "Tell you what. You take a nap, and I'll wake you when we get to the good part."

Hours later, a sharp bump jolted Hope awake. She squinted into the bright sunshine out the window. Just a wall of dirt and pebbles. She glanced across the car, past Lori, and squealed. The not even two-lane blacktop ended at an unobstructed drop-off, hundreds of feet down to a desert plain. Heart hammering her ribs. Hope slammed her eyes shut. "We are going to die."

"I was going to let you sleep through this part." Lori lounged, one arm draped across the steering wheel. "It's a bit disconcerting the first—"

"Both hands on the wheel! Ten and two!" Hope put her hands over her eyes and peered through her fingers.

"It's not as scary as it looks." Lori spun the

Jeep around a hairpin turn and downshifted through a scree of gravel that had washed across the road.

"Shut up. I'm praying."

Lori laughed. "Toss me a water out of the cooler, will you?"

"Are you kidding? You are not taking your attention off this goat track. Not for one second."

Lori pointed through the windshield. "See that up there? It's the last climb. Then it gets pretty. In the meantime, look down the valley. You can see all the way to Ridgecrest."

"Not on your life." Hope kept her eyes glued on the hill ahead, holding the Jeep on the road through sheer will alone.

They crested the hill, came around a corner, and it was as if the barren cliff never existed. Everything was green, with trees and wildflowers growing beside the much wider road. "Wow."

"This is nothing. Wait till you see the meadows."

They drove, it seemed forever, but that was okay with Hope, because it was beautiful. The road wound through the mountains like a lazy river of blacktop. Nature was only occasionally marred by man, with a log cabin or wood planked home.

"We're almost there," Lori said.

They topped a ridge, and before them spread a gentle valley with a river meandering through it.

"Now this was worth getting up for," Hope whispered.

"Told you. See that fork that goes across the river and up the other side of the valley? That leads to the primitive camping and eventually the pack mule station."

"We're not going there, though, right?" She swallowed. If Lori called it primitive, it must be *bad*.

"Not this time. I'm taking it easy on you. We're doing cush camping in the meadow."

"Oh, I can get behind the 'cush' part. Are we getting a cabin?"

"No cabins. But it's really nice, and we're close to the country store in case you've forgotten something."

They turned in at a narrow dirt road. Grass between the ruts brushed the bottom of the Jeep and Hope's expectations lifted, along with her spirits. It really was pretty.

A few vehicles and one RV were scattered through the meadow, but mostly the area was deserted. "Oh, good. We can get a spot next to the river." Lori turned off the dirt path and pulled under the trees. "It's great sleeping, listening to the river all night."

"The sound of water running makes me have

to pee." Hope looked around. There was a ring of stones that, from the blackening, must be for a fire. No other sign of civilization. "Where *do* we pee?"

"You saw those little buildings on the way in? They're restrooms."

"But the closest one is quite a ways back." Hope could barely see the roof from where she stood.

"There's always the bushes." Lori lifted the back window and lowered the tailgate. "Come help me unload."

"I'm not peeing in the bushes. Besides, I'll have to go there to get a shower." Hope grabbed her suitcase and a canvas bag full of rattley stuff and set them by the fire pit, where Lori had begun a pile.

"No showers."

"What?"

"The only water here you pump from spigots around the campground." Lori lugged two sleeping bags to the pile.

"Or from the bathroom, right? But that's a long way—"

"Bathrooms don't have water."

"But then how do you flush—oh, no. Do not tell me they're outhouses."

"Okay, I won't." Lori shrugged. "But they are."

"But I can't do those! I read a story once about

a crazy guy who lived in one, and when girls sat down…" Hope shuddered.

Lori's laugh was carefree, and way too amused. "That's an old wives' tale. Never happened."

"You may be right, but at night? Nuh uh. Not happening." Maybe she'd just hold it until tomorrow.

When the back of the Jeep was empty, Lori closed it up. "Now, I'll teach you how to put up a tent."

Hope slapped a mosquito. Bugs. Great. "Okay, what do I do?"

Lori lifted a long cylindrical bag from the pile, and dumped the contents on the ground. Sticks clattered and a roll of nylon unraveled. "I chose an easy-setup two-man tent. You put the braces together." She knelt, and spread the nylon into what turned out to be an octagon shape.

"You mean these?" Hope lifted some of the sticks. They were connected by elastic cords, and went together to become long poles. "Piece of cake."

"Good. Now those snap to the clips on the tent, see?" Lori demonstrated, and soon they had a little igloo-looking tent set up. "We'll put the fly on later. Too hot right now."

Hope thought a fly was a pesky bug, but whatever.

"Where is that foot pump?" Lori dug through

the pile, muttering. "Crap. I forgot it. No worries, we'll just have to blow up the air mattress the old-fashioned way." She looked at Hope. "If you'll do that, I'll get some lunch together. Okay?"

"Sure. I can do that."

She could. But not without getting sweaty, dirty and almost passing out from hyperventilating. When she was done, Lori handed her a peanut butter and jelly sandwich. "I burst a lung for that?"

"Nope, you did it so you don't have to sleep on the ground. You're going to be glad you did." Lori walked over to a pile of food in a canvas sheet. "Bring me your toothpaste, and any food you have on you, including gum, breath mints and mouthwash."

Hope dug through her stuff and handed over her stash. "Why?"

She held her hand out for Hope's crust-filled napkin and stuffed it in a Ziplock plastic bag. "I'll show you. Help me hoist this, will you?" A rope was threaded through metal grommets in the cavas sheet. Lori dropped the trash from "lunch" in the middle, took the other end of the rope and tossed it over a tree branch. Together, they hauled it up until it was fifteen feet or so in the air.

"Why are we doing this? Some new diet plan?"

"Bears."

"What?" Hope whipped her head right and left, but the scariest living thing she saw were the butterflies in the meadow.

"If I had a regular car, we could store our food in that, but a bear would rip right through the Jeep's fabric top to get to the food."

"You brought me where there are bears." Hope shook her head.

"They're just little black bears. They're not going to bother you if you don't have food on you." Lori dug in the pockets of her cargo shorts. "Most likely won't."

She could have taken orienteering as her last choice. Or fishing. Or...just about anything besides bears. "You brought me out here to die, didn't you? You can admit it. There's no one for me to tell."

"Quit whining." Lori pulled a bright yellow whistle from a deep pocket. "Here. Bears don't like the sound, so if you see one, blow this. It'll go away." She wiped her hands on the seat of her shorts. "Now, let's open the sleeping bags in the tent, then we can go for a hike."

An hour and miles later, Hope was done in. Her new hiking boots had rubbed a blister on her heel, she was covered in sweat, bug spray and scratches from brambles. "Slow down. Does this have to be the Bataan Death March?" She panted, but Lori was too far ahead to hear. "Screw it." She found a rock, checked for snakes, then sat. Lori would be back when she noticed her minion was no longer following.

When her heavy breathing calmed, she could hear the river beside the path, burbling over rocks. Birds called, and a blue-and-black one fluttered down from a tree to investigate her. It cocked its head, its bright eyes checking her out.

"I've got nothing to feed you. I'm not willing to be bear-bait, sorry."

The bird voiced its displeasure with a scratchy screech and took off.

The wind sloughed through the branches overhead. Hope pulled in the smell of sage, pine and hot dust. It smelled heavenly.

Something unwound in her, loosening like a watch spring. Her mind settled. She watched ants on the trail, scurrying in what appeared to be critical ant business. Wasn't that just a microcosm of what humans did, every day?

Peace settled over her like the golden dust filtering through the sunlight.

"Where the heck did you go?" Lori walked up, looking like a tanned amazon. "Scoot over." When Hope gave up half the flat rock, Lori settled on it.

"I needed to rest, so I sat down. Shhhh. Listen."

They sat a few minutes, just absorbing the beauty.

"Now this—" Hope sighed "—does not suck."

Lori threw an arm around Hope's shoulders. "Told ya."

LORI HAD PROMISED her a hot dinner, and Hope got the chance to sample more of The Adventure Outfitter's wares; MREs. Actually, the self-heating meal-in-a-bag lasagna tasted a lot better than it looked. It wasn't Luigi's, but it wasn't horrid, either. Before it got dark, they hauled the food stash into the tree and gathered wood for a fire. Hope found a secluded area to pee. It actually wasn't as bad as she'd feared…no snake reared up to bite her butt. Aside from the ewww factor, it was actually kind of peaceful.

Hope placed the lawn chairs around the fire ring while Lori got the fire started. They didn't need it for heat, but the flames were cheery and, Hope hoped, would keep the bears at bay.

They sat in silence a while, staring into the flames.

"Okay, so spill." Lori laid another stick on the fire. "I've been patient. I haven't asked once about your dinner with Bear, and I'm dying to hear." She did the Groucho Marx eyebrow thing. "Did you two do the horizontal bop?"

More than the fire made Hope's face heat. "Jeez, Lori. You have a way of making a romantic evening sound like an X-rated movie."

"Oh, my God, you did! Way to go, sista!" She held her hand up for a high five. "So? Tell me. Was he a bear in bed?"

"I'm not talking about this if you're going to be crass."

"You take all the fun out of it. But okay, I'll be good. How did the dinner go?"

Hope smiled. "He toasted me with poetry."

Lori clasped her hands in her lap, a look of longing on her face. "Awwww, I so like this guy. Tell me more."

"He's so wonderful." Hope frowned into the fire. "And so damaged. There's something in his past that's so painful that he won't discuss it. And he has nightmares about it."

"What could be worse than manslaughter?"

"I don't know. But he's so closed off that I'm kind of amazed he even asked me out. Whatever it is, if he'd just talk about it, I know it would help him."

"I don't know, Hope. Maybe you should back away. I mean, what if it was something bad he did, rather than something bad that happened to him? You don't really *know* this guy."

"I know him." She nodded, only partly to convince herself. "It's just going to take time. He's trying to open up. He agreed to show me around his place, and we're going for another motorcycle ride tomorrow."

"Just be careful. He could have killed people with his bare hands, for all you know."

She shot Lori a saucy grin. "Now that you mentioned his hands…" She fanned herself.

"Now *that's* what I'm talking about!" She leaned forward in her chair. "If you don't spill the deets, I'm going to go sic that guy that lives under the outhouse on you."

"Hold the airbrush like a pen." Bear handed down the high precision stylus to Nacho, where he knelt in front of the truck fender. "Now remember, you're working with something permanent, so don't spray until you're sure of what you want to do."

"I can paint anything I want?"

Bear chuckled, remembering back to the first time he'd held an airbrush. He'd felt as if his dad had just handed him the keys to the kingdom. And he had, kinda. "Sure, kid, have at it." He couldn't hurt anything. The past weeks they'd sanded his whole truck together. He was only using primer; if the kid messed up, they'd just paint over it.

Nacho practiced his strokes before shooting paint, just as Bear had taught him.

This thing had worked out better than he'd expected. Yeah, the kid spouted questions like a Gatling gun, and there were messes to clean up, and mistakes to fix, but there were benefits, too. Ones he hadn't expected. Nacho's constant chatter took Bear back in time to when the world was a place to be explored, rather than dreaded. His energy filled the barn to overflowing, and the hours when the kid was here flew by. Then there were times like this—when Bear could almost watch the kid mature—that he felt he was making a difference in his life.

It felt as if maybe Bear was making a dent in the massive pile of shit he had to atone for.

"Is this right?" Nacho frowned at the fender, tongue between his teeth.

"You're trying for flames, right? It's a start, but you have to make them flow, natural-like, to give the illusion of movement." He dropped to his knees, and covered Nacho's hand with his, to guide it. "See? Like this..."

"Hello?" His angel's voice came from the maze of boxes that shielded the bay from the world. Bear's heart skipped and his hand jerked, ruining Nacho's line.

"Dude!" Nacho looked up at Bear as if he'd just stepped on his puppy.

"Sorry, my bad. Move down a bit and try

again." He pushed himself to his feet. "Hope, we're back here." His breakfast bounced in his stomach like water in a hot skillet—half from excitement, half dread. Letting her visit even just the shop was taking a chance. She might judge. She might dump him as a loser.

But if he didn't let her closer, he was going to lose her anyway.

Well, he'd just have to walk that fine line, because the fall on either side was long and deadly.

Hope came around the last turn, and into the hot lights. "Oh, cool!" The look on her face told Bear that if she was judging, he'd not been found wanting. It had only been a few days since he'd left her in bed, rumpled and sated, her lips swollen from his kisses, her eyes reflecting only him. Heat shot to his face and his crotch as she crossed the floor to him. How had he gotten so lucky? He reached for her, wanting her skin under his hands. She was like a drug. If he'd missed her this bad after such a short time, he was hooked for sure.

He wrapped his arms around her, and when she looked up he kissed her, hard, trying to show her all he couldn't say.

"Gross, man. Get a room already."

That broke them apart. "Hey, squirt. You diss my lady, I'll take you out. This is Hope."

Hope blushed, but laughed as she finger-combed her hair back into place. "You've got to be Nacho. Bear told me all about you."

At Bear's glare, Nacho stood, and like an automaton, shook her hand. "Nice to meet you, ma'am."

"Oh, I'm not old enough to be a ma'am. How about just Hope?"

"'Kay." But Nacho's attention had already shifted. He dropped back to his knees and picked up the airbrush.

Bear tugged Hope's hand. "Come on. You can tell me all about camping while I show you around the shop."

"Yeah, but, Bear," Nacho said. "I don't know what I'm doing, and I'm gonna screw this up."

He couldn't look away from his angel. "You can't screw it up, kid. The whole thing needs to be primed anyway."

"Yeah, but." Nacho made that kid-tsk of irritation.

Hope smiled and shook her head. "I'll do the self-guided tour. You work with Nacho. We have all evening to talk."

"You sure?"

"Bear, is this right?" Nacho asked.

"You help him. I'll just wander."

"Okay, but stick to the barn, okay? And be careful. There's piles of crap everywhere."

"Really?" She gave him a Nacho-worthy eye roll, and walked away.

He squatted beside his apprentice. "That's better. Let's try it again."

AFTER WANDERING AROUND the mess downstairs, and drinking a cup of coffee at the card table, Hope climbed the ladder to the loft. She was surprised to find it very different from the ground floor. Supplies were stacked neatly on labeled shelves, and not a dust bunny marred the clean-swept floor.

Come to think of it, the work area of the barn was just as clean. So why the stacks of crap barring the doorway?

Was it one more gauntlet Bear had set up to keep people away?

What made him want to shut out the world so badly? Prison had to be a part of it, and his fear of losing his temper. That should have been enough. Could have been. But there was more. Something to do with his service. A sniper no doubt killed a lot of men; it could be guilt about that.

But she still felt something more, under the surface. Like an iceberg, the part Bear let others see was the smaller part.

She shouldn't have drunk that coffee. Now she had to pee, and she'd yet to wander across a bathroom anywhere in the barn.

She walked to a window and looked down onto the yard. The tired house with the sagging porch caught her eye. Though it looked abandoned, there was no evidence that Bear lived anywhere else.

What an odd study in opposites he was. He was big, intimidating, and had anger issues, but he was also an artist with a gentle touch and a sweet romantic streak. He appeared to be, by nature, neat and organized, but parts of the barn, and that house down there were a mess.

God, she had to find a bathroom. Soon.

Thanks to Lori, she could now pee in the woods she'd seen behind the barn. She hustled down the ladder. Bear and Nacho had their heads together, painting. She almost tiptoed past the card table and out the back door of the barn and stepped into the trees.

At least she had some tissues in her pocket. She unbuckled her belt, then froze at the sound of a Jake brake. The road must be…she peered through the trees. *There.* A Peterbuilt flashed by, zebra-striped by the shadows of the trees.

There was no way she was peeing within sight of a road. She rebuckled her belt. Bear told her only to wander the barn. She could go in and ask permission, or go find the bathroom she knew was in the house. A curl of curiosity like a wisp of smoke drew her to the house, whispering hints of answers to her questions.

Bear will tell you when he's ready. Hope Sanderson was no snoop.

She stepped to the barn door and glanced in. The tops of the guys' heads were bent beside the truck's fender. She stood poised, perfectly balanced between good girl...and what lay behind the door of that house.

Lori's warning echoed in her mind. *You don't really know this guy, Hope.*

She could run in, pee, glance around and be back here before anyone knew she was gone. Her bladder broke the tie. After a quick last glance, she jogged around the outside wall of the barn and into the dooryard.

The porch steps didn't look stable, so she vaulted them onto the worn boards. But she was going too fast; she skidded and slammed into the wall beside the door. "Ouch, dammit." She rubbed her shoulder and glanced around.

The yard was empty.

Grabbing the handle of the screen door that held only the tattered remnants of a screen, she pulled it open, then twisted the knob of the warped wooden door beyond it.

It turned.

Listening to the clock ticking in her head, she

took a breath, pushed the door open and stepped inside.

It appeared to be a living room, but stood empty of furniture. She saw only heavy dusty drapes at the window and an old plank floor. The air was heavy with trapped heat, and the smell of sawn wood and linseed oil. But it held an echo of sound; as if the house had been whispering, just before she stepped in.

A shiver danced across her skin, raising gooseflesh and the hair on her arms.

A threat from her bladder got her moving. She walked fast to the doorway ahead. An old door lying prone on sawhorses blocked her way. To the left, the kitchen, with new cabinets on the wall, but a counter of plywood. The kitchen ended at a closed door.

Hurry, said her bladder and the clock in her head. Seeing a hall to her right, she went that way. All the doors off the hall led to empty rooms, until the last. She barely glimpsed a single bed on her way to the bath she could see through an open door.

She had her jeans undone before she got halfway across the room, but still barely made it. While she took care of business, she looked around. This room had been redone. Mostly. A nice new slate floor. A shower stall with the sticker still on the glass. But the Sheetrock walls were bare of paint, and the mirror hung by a huge nail. She flushed, zipped her jeans, and washed her hands at the new vanity. The only towel was the one that hung on the shower door, and it was still damp. Bear must've showered earlier.

She decided to check out his bedroom on her way back out. It was Spartan, just a narrow bed covered by a blanket tight enough to bounce a quarter on and a battered dresser. She hesitated, hand on the closet doorknob, but the good girl won out. Well, that and the clock ticking in her head. Time to move. Retracing her steps to the kitchen, she paused, glancing at the door to what she guessed was the dining room. No reason to think there was anything behind it but another empty room.

But the house had yet to give up its secrets. And they were here…she felt them whispering across her exposed skin.

Hurry!

She jogged through the kitchen and pushed through the door. The afternoon light from the window threw a spotlight on the wall opposite. She stood frozen, staring at herself staring back at her.

It was her, or almost her, in a robe, hovering inches off a desert landscape. Her arms were spread from her sides, palms facing back in a protective gesture. Behind her a few feet, stood a boy of Middle-Eastern descent, with black hair and huge, liquid eyes.

Both of them had a lighter aura around their heads, and a look of utter peace on their faces. The image was so detailed—it must have taken weeks, or maybe even longer. "What in the *hell*..." she whispered.

Bang!

She jumped at the sound of the front door hitting the wall.

CHAPTER FIFTEEN

"SEE YOU TOMORROW, Bear." Nacho rolled his bike out the back door of the barn, threw his leg over and pedaled away.

"Yeah, see ya." Bear stood at the truck's fender, looking down at the amateurish attempt at ghost flames. The kid didn't know how to use an airbrush for spit, but it was clear he had the artistic talent he'd need for this job. Bear smiled, shook his head, and began disassembling and cleaning the equipment.

He felt bad, leaving Hope on her own, but— wait. He hadn't seen her since she climbed the ladder to the loft...a long time ago. Alarm jangled in his mind, then clattered down his nerves. His fingers spasmed and he dropped the sprayer.

"Hope?" The word echoed back, and like a bat, he sensed the emptiness of the barn. Still, he had to check. He jogged for the ladder and took the slats two at a time. His head came even with the floor of the loft. "Hope?"

The alarm in his head rose to a shriek. He shimmied down the ladder and jogged through the maze of boxes to the front of the barn. His heart lurched in a manic, syncopated beat and his intestines gurgled in a liquid rush. The dooryard was empty, except for Hope's little sedan.

She's in the house. You know she is. He crossed the yard at a full run. The mural. She'd freak, and he'd lose the trust he'd fought so hard to gain. *Goddammit, this is what happens when you let people in.* He jumped onto the porch and jerked the screen door. *You are so fucked.* He opened the wood door so fast it slammed against the wall. *You are so...* "Hope!" It came out an outraged roar as he stomped for the dining room. He felt naked; stripped of not only his clothes, but his skin, too, leaving all his nerves exposed.

She stood facing the mural, her mouth open in an O of shock, her expression slack with it. But her eyes...her eyes were swimming in tears and dawning distrust. Betrayal.

It scared him.

"Goddamn it, didn't I tell you to stay in the barn? This is none of your business, and—"

"None of my *business*?" She turned on him like a hissing cat. "That's *me* on that wall!" She pointed an accusing finger at his mural. "What the hell does that mean? Are you some kind of sicko?" Her head jerked with a realization, and she took a step back. "When did you start this... thing?" Her eyes narrowed. "Have you been stalking me all this time? Was I too stupid and naive to see it?"

Her fear went through him like a metal-jacketed sniper round, shattering his anger to shrapnel that ripped through his gut. "No."

"At least the bank robbers were up front about what they wanted from me." Shutters slammed over her expression, showing only a facade of wariness. "I'm leaving. But before I go, I need to know why. You *owe* me that much."

Air went out of him like a balloon with a tiny hole and he deflated in on himself, sliding down the wall to a crumpled ball. He'd been so absorbed with falling off either side of that fine line he'd been walking that when the line stopped, he hadn't noticed—he'd walked right off the edge. He'd lost her.

Even knowing there was no going back, he had to try. "It's not what you think." He hardly recognized his own voice through the listless defeat in it.

"Don't you tell me what I think." Hands on hips, she loomed over him. She may be small, but she held all the power. "You tell me what it *is*."

Here it was. The moment he'd dreaded so long. His sin, exposed. Of course it would come to that. He should have foreseen this. He *had* foreseen this. And yet, he'd still brought her here. Why had he done that?

He looked up at the mural. "It's my dream." His beatific angel looked down on him with a half smile, as if urging him on. "Remember having coffee, that first day we talked? This is what I couldn't tell you. You'd think I was crazy." He rubbed the heels of his palms over his eyes. "Hell, I think I'm crazy."

Hope's face held in a pained pinch. "Tell me."

He still had a choice. He could tell her to leave. But the worst had already happened—why not see what lay beyond that? Some quiet, sick part of him wanted to know.

He took a breath. "I was an army sniper, on my second tour overseas. Iraq, then Afghanistan. Snipers aren't chosen for their shooting skills alone. See, it takes a certain kind of person to lie in wait for hours, sometimes days, looking down the sights of a gun, watching a target. Because, after a time, they're not just a target. Sometime in the hours, they become human beings, with families, wants and fears. They become a lot like you, only in a different uniform, and on the other end of your sights. It takes a special kind of person to pull the trigger, knowing that." His lips pulled back from his teeth. "I was good at my job."

He heard her suck in a breath.

"I'm just stating a fact. I'm not proud of it." He glanced at the boy behind his angel. "I was assigned a target. A high-profile one. You'd know his name, if I was allowed to tell you. Twenty-four hundred yards—only two other guys could maybe make that shot. I was dropped in solo, and hiked miles to a rocky hill overlooking the compound. My orders were to lie in position and wait for the okay. I waited eighteen hours."

He heard a sliding sound. Hope was sitting on the floor at the opposite wall, watching him with dread etched on her features.

"He had a wife, who he treated with love and gentleness. He had two children, who meant a lot to him. How do I know that?" He moved his eyes to the window, for a change. "A sniper has to be observant; after all, his life depends on it. He'd give them a pat on the head as he walked by. A touch on a shoulder, when he spoke to them. His look of pride, watching them. Oh, yes, our scopes are that good. Nothing but the best for our troops." He rubbed his eyes again.

"Do you know what it's like to lie in the rocks in the desert for eighteen hours? I was dehydrated, and exhausted. But that's no excuse for what happened.

"The order finally came down to take out the target. I sighted and waited for the shot. But by then, he'd become more than a target. He'd become a human, and a father. Maybe someone I'd like to know, in another lifetime. Don't get me wrong; I could take the shot. But apparently, not without the slightest hesitation. In that millisecond, his oldest son stepped in the way." He gave up and covered his eyes. It made the photo in his mind sharper, but he deserved that. "The man looked up when I killed his son. He looked right at me. I know he couldn't actually see me. But I could see him—saw just when he began to comprehend what had just happened. My second shot didn't miss. And that one, I'm glad of. It put him out of the misery that he was about to feel. A mercy killing, that."

"Oh, Bear."

He looked back to his angel. The one on the wall. "She came to me in my dreams, when I was in prison."

"What?"

He nodded. "Just as she is there; her look soothes and her peace radiates, piercing the bunker I hide behind. I know I don't deserve her absolution. I killed an innocent. A child—" He stopped, waiting for the clot in his throat to recede. "But I'm weak enough to take it anyway. It's the only thing that gets me through the nights. She keeps me sane."

He swung his head, to look at the other angel he didn't deserve. "So you can see why I had to talk to you. It has to mean something, don't you think? Meeting someone who resembles so closely…" He couldn't read anything in her expression. He had no idea how this was affecting her, but it didn't matter. The words kept pouring out.

"How could I have told you? You would have thought I was crazy." He wheezed a deformed chuckle. "Shit, I'm not positive I'm not." He dug in his heels and pushed himself up the wall to stand. It was almost over. "So now you know. Why I'm a loner, why I hold apart from others. Why I don't have friends. I don't deserve to be a part of society." He looked down on her. "Why I certainly don't deserve a decent woman like you."

With one last bolstering glance at the mural, he walked away. "You can see yourself out."

WHAT DID IT MEAN? Hope tried to put the jigsaw pieces together, but it was as if every piece came from a different puzzle—none of them fit. How could he have seen someone, some*thing* that so closely resembled her in a dream, months before they met?

How could she, too, feel the connection to this odd man who was so different than anyone she'd ever known? How could she blame him for seeking her out, to discover why he'd seen her in his dreams? If she did, she'd have to blame herself, because she too wanted to know.

His pain clawed at her anger, shredding it. She may understand less than before about Bear, but one thing she knew. She had nothing to fear from him. He wasn't a stalker, or a bad person. He was lost in his memories and his misery, withdrawing from the world because he thought himself unworthy to live in it.

And he was so wrong.

She stood and hurried after him. "Bear." She caught up with him in the hallway outside his bedroom door. She laid a hand on his shoulder to stop him.

He didn't turn. "Please. Just leave." The words were dry as the dust in the desert she felt sure he was reliving in his head.

"I won't."

He turned on her, grabbed her upper arms and snatched her to him, his brown eyes cold, his features distorted with anger. "Aren't you afraid?"

"No." And she wasn't. A man who hid from the world in agony over a child's death held no danger to her. He was like a wounded animal, lashing out because he was in pain. "You wouldn't hurt me—or anyone."

His hands left her arms, falling to his sides. "Tell that to the guy I killed in that bar."

"Oh, Bear. You've been given such a heavy load to carry." She reached up, and ran her hand down his cheek.

He leaned into her touch, a grimace squeezing his eyes shut.

"You can put it down you know, anytime you want."

"You're offering absolution, too, then?"

"If you'll take it." She pulled his head down to her and kissed him. His lips were dry and slack. She backed up, but only a half inch. "Don't you see? My forgiveness won't matter. Or the angel's in your dream, if you don't forgive yourself."

"It's not that simple."

"Really, it is." This time, when she kissed him, his lips moved slowly under hers, as if waking from a dream. When she parted his lips with her tongue, he opened to her. She tried to tell him with her kiss that in spite of his past, and his mistakes, that she cared. Deeply.

Some of it must have gotten through, because he came alive, drinking her in as if she were water and he'd been wandering the desert for a long time. His arms came around her and he clung, taking what she offered…what he needed.

And she gave.

Without releasing her lips, he lifted and carried her to the bedroom. At the edge of the bed, he paused, waiting for permission she'd already granted with her first kiss.

And he wondered if he was a good person? "Please, love me. Not the Bear you show to the

world, but the man behind that. Doug Steele—
that's the man I want."

He clutched her to him so tightly that when a
groan came from deep in his chest, she felt it inside her. He laid her on the bed, and touched her
with shaking, reverent hands. "Even knowing
who I am, and what I've done…"

She touched a finger to his lips. "Shhhh. Come
to bed." She kicked out of her jeans and underwear as he stripped.

There was so little room in the single bed that
they lay on their sides, skin touching, from their
chests to their feet. Bear's back was against the
wall and afternoon light spilled over the bed,
bathing them in gold. She lay, head on Bear's
arm, tracing the whorls of hair on his chest. Until
he began tracing the whorls of hair between her
legs. She was wet, drenched with wanting him.
Her heart accelerated and she shivered in antici-
pation of him filling her aching hollowness.

He made love to her neck, nibbling behind her
ear, and following her throbbing veins down to
the hollow above her collarbone. Delicious trem-
ors shot though her. She mewled and rubbed
against his engorged cock, driving them both to
the edge.

With a smooth movement, he lifted her leg
over his hip, and slipped inside.

He lay still until she opened her eyes. Her

breath caught; his brown eyes drew her into their bottomless depths. There was need churning there, but also turmoil, regret and tenderness. A potent mixture that made her want—no *need*, to be closer. She pressed her heel into his butt as she tilted her pelvis, pulling him into her.

He moaned. "God help me. I don't want to, but I need you."

"Good," she purred.

He moved then, slow and smooth, in and out, never breaking eye contact. Hope watched, turned on even more by the lightning shifts of his expression, the tightening and loosening of the muscles of his face.

Her own emotion rose and fell, mirroring his.

They both spiraled up, coming together in a crescendo of their bodies, emotions and minds.

A half hour later, they still lay crushed together. Following the storm of emotion, peace had crept over them.

Bear played with her hair, studying it in the fading light. "So you never told me how you liked camping."

"It was intense. I worried about bears and the guy in the outhouse the whole time, but—"

"There was a guy in the outhouse?"

"It's a camping insider joke. You wouldn't get it. But you know what? I think I liked it. Hiking is sweaty and dirty, but also kind of wonderful.

You never know what nature is going to show you around the next corner. I saw a woodpecker, deer and a beaver fort."

"Dam."

"Don't you swear at me."

"No, it's called—"

"Gotcha." She tweaked his nose, eliciting a rare smile. The light was fast fading. She had to get home. But lying here with him, something relaxed in her chest that she hadn't realized was tight. *Safe.* That's what it felt like. She would never exchange her new life for her old, but safe was the one part she'd missed.

Who'd have guessed she'd find it with a man? Much less one like this—one her mother would have warned her about.

"Bear?" She backed up, just a few inches, to see his eyes. "Do you feel any better, now that I know?"

Warring emotions flashed in his eyes before he closed them and touched his forehead to hers. "I thought I'd lost you."

"I mean about what happened over there. Did talking about it help at all?"

He thought a moment. "No."

Telling her was only the beginning. She knew that to get past the guilt, he needed to talk about it. To others. *One step at a time. He'll see that all that stuff is better out than in.*

THEY WERE ALL sitting in the circle the next morning when Bina asked, "Okay, I think it's time we check in on our progress. Who'd like to start?"

It struck fear into Bear's heart. He shot a look at Hope and gave an infinitesimal shake of his head.

"Bryan? How are you doing?" Bina asked.

Bear breathed again.

Bryan double-crossed his skinny legs and twirled a strawberry blonde lock around his finger. "I work from home you know, and I go through the day listening for Curtis, moving around in the next room. I wait for his phone call." He sniffed. "But the nights are the worst…" He looked around the circle. "Does it ever get better?"

"You're asking the wrong people, dude," Mark said.

Bina shot him a look. "It will, Bryan. It's getting better already, just so slowly, you don't notice it. Someday, you'll realize it's been a few hours since it hurt. Then, a few more. That's the way grief works. It releases its grip very slowly. Are you doing anything to help yourself let go of it?"

He tucked his hands under his skinny thighs. "I should clean out his closet. I know I should. But it's totally beyond me. I just stand in front of it and cry." He ducked his head.

Mark cleared his throat. "I could come over and help, if you want."

He raised his blotched face. "Would you?"

"Like my social calendar is full?" He shrugged. "I'll pop for pizza and Chunky Monkey ice cream."

"I think that would be an excellent step, Bryan. I'm glad you're making progress." Bina looked to her next victim. "How are you feeling lately, Mark?"

"My next surgery is in three weeks. I'll have a nose after that, and I'm hoping that it'll get easier to go out." He rubbed his eyes. "But the nightmares are getting worse. I'm not sleeping much."

"The same dream about people running from you?" Bina asked.

"No, a different one. I'm driving at night and my old girlfriend is on the seat beside me. We're arguing. I mean full-out spit-flying yelling. I get so mad, I steer off the road, and into a tree. But only on her side. I'm fine. But I look over…"

Bear could see Mark's shudder. "Jesus." At least he had his angel, when his nightmares got really bad.

"Why do you think you're having those dreams, Mark?"

"Oh, hell, I don't know…trauma maybe?" He rolled his eyes. "I'm done. Can we move on?"

Bina hesitated a few moments, watching Mark

fidget. Then she shifted her gaze. "Bear? How are things with you?"

"Yeah, tell us about your and Hope's budding romance." Bryan perked up. "We want to live through you."

And he'd thought he only had to worry about nightmares at night. His face flamed. "Grow up, kid. What is this, high school?"

"You don't have to share that if you'd rather not, Bear," Bina said.

He kept his eyes lowered, to avoid Hope's disappointment. "I still get angry, but I'm *trying* not to take it out on other people." He hoped the emphasis would keep her from saying anything. He knew she wanted him to open up, but he'd been an introvert even before Afghanistan. And since…

"Are you getting more engaged with people in general?" Bina asked.

"Well, I'm working with a kid. An apprentice, I guess you'd call him."

"That's wonderful. How's that going?"

"He's learning. I showed him how to rough out flames the other day, and—"

"I wasn't talking about painting. How do you feel about working with this boy?"

Finally, something he could talk about that could be considered "sharing." "It's good, actually. He's a great kid, but he's got some problems. He's starting to open up."

"And how does that feel?"

"It feels good. Right."

"I'm glad." Bina moved on to her next prey. "Brenda, I like your blouse. It's a good color on you."

Brenda's hair was as limp as ever, but she had on a new blouse—a pastel-blue one, that actually almost fit her. "Phil bought it for me. To make up for…well, you know."

"How did you do with your homework? Did you notice when you were seeing things from Phil's point of view? Did you see any places your opinions weren't the same?"

"Yeah," she almost whispered.

"We can't hear you. Can you speak up?" Hope said.

"I didn't see anything, at first. But then, one night, we were watching a movie on TV. It had a cockfighting scene in it. It was horrible. I had to walk away. Phil, he told me I was a wimp, and why would I worry about a bunch of stupid birds. He said they're about the dumbest thing on the planet." She looked around the circle of faces. "But even if they are, isn't that more reason to see that they're treated well?"

"Of course it is, honey," Bryan said.

"Did you tell Phil that you didn't agree with him?"

"Oh, no. I wouldn't."

Couldn't, more like it. He'd probably beat the crap out of her for daring to have an opinion.

"But, it was weird. Once I noticed that, I noticed a bunch of things we don't agree on."

"Like what?" Mark asked.

"Big things and little things. Like, where the pillows go on the couch. Bigotry. Feminism. How the toilet paper roll goes on…you know, things."

"You did a great job this week, Brenda, I'm proud of you. Keep up the good work." Bina checked her watch. "We're almost out of time, but we've yet to hear from Hope. How's your new life turning out?"

"It's so much better than I could have imagined."

Her smile was a pure beam of happiness that smashed Bear's wall of worry.

"I just hope it can last." She looked right at him, her smile sliding away.

Shit. She wasn't going to quit pushing. He stood in the rubble of his wall, looking for a place to hide.

CHAPTER SIXTEEN

HOPE SAT WITH her coworkers in the break room, listening to her boss give tips to add-on sales.

"But, to be clear, you're not pushing a sale. You're helping them be prepared. Any questions?" When no one responded, Travis glanced around the room. "Hope, have you decided on your sport yet?"

"Yep." She smiled at Lori. "I want to be a camping and hiking specialist."

Lori raised a fist. "Yes!"

"When can I start?"

Travis chuckled. "Whoa there, Flicka. You're going to have to do more than one overnight before you know enough to work that department."

Hope's elation deflated a bit. She was ready for a new challenge, and looking forward to working with Lori.

"Road trip," Lori sang. "I checked the schedule, and neither of us is working this weekend. Want to go then?"

"Sounds good."

"I've got an idea," Lori said. "Hey, boss, can I borrow the loaner fly rod?"

"Sure. Maybe that'll be another department where Hope can help out." He clapped his hands. "Now, let's get out there and help people plan adventures."

Lori leaned over and whispered to Hope as they filed out of the room. "So? How's it going with Bear?"

"Okay." She regretted her unenthusiastic tone as soon as she heard it.

"Only okay?" Lori cocked her head like a bloodhound getting a whiff of a scent. "You were all moony-eyed last week. What happened?"

Hope didn't really understand the ice ball of doom in her stomach, but had no desire to explore it further. "Some of it I'm not at liberty to discuss."

"Well, we'll talk about what you can, at lunch." Lori strode away.

Hope's reprieve was only three hours long. Sooner than she'd have liked, she sat beside Lori at the drugstore soda fountain counter. "I like him. I mean I *really* like him."

"Then what's the problem?" Lori crunched a dill pickle slice.

"We're just so different."

"Hey, that can be a good thing. You know, gas and a lighter…" She splayed her fingers. "Boom."

"Yeah. That part works great, trust me." Hope ignored the blood pounding in her cheeks. "I've always heard that being different is okay, as long as you agree on core issues." She put a hand to her temple where a dull throb had taken up residence the past few hours. "There are some big ones we don't agree on."

"Like what?" Lori took a bite of her tuna sandwich.

Hope hesitated, not wanting to speak of it. As if saying the words out loud would make them real—make them true. She sighed. All she'd done since she'd left Bear's bed was think. The words were already true. "He's so closed off, he's almost a recluse. He uses his anger to push people away. I'm surprised he even asked me out." Though now that she'd seen the angel, she understood that better. Not that she would ever tell Lori.

"Yeah, that hardly fits you, or your new life."

"But everything else fits so well that all I want to do is spend time with him. He's not at all on the inside like he is on the outside. He's gentle and caring and kind. We can talk for hours and have the best time."

"There's that moony look again."

"Yeah, I know. See my dilemma?" She picked at her salad, moving it around her plate.

"Why don't you just let it be for now? Enjoy it, and not worry about getting serious?" She raised one eyebrow. "Get you some of those slow hands you told me about."

"I plan on it. But I'm worried. The more time I spend with him, the more time I want to spend. Then, if it doesn't work out, I'm going to be wrecked."

"You thought when you decided on this new life that the only risks you were taking were physical?" Lori gave her a sad smile. "Welcome to the real world, girlfriend."

"BEAR?" NACHO DIDN'T lift his head from the El Camino quarter panel he was sanding.

"Yeah, kid." Bear shut down the palm sander, pushed his safety glasses back on his head and ran his hand over the hood to be sure the transition between the Bondo and the metal was smooth.

"Could I bring my crew out someday after school to see what we're doing here?"

"Is this the same crew you got busted with, tagging the Bekins warehouse?"

Nacho keep sanding. "Course."

"What makes you think I want them on the property? How do I know they won't come back and steal my paint again?"

Nacho's brows scrunched over the hurt in his eyes. "That wouldn't happen."

"How do you know?"

"We went straight. We're not starting a gang until we're in junior high."

Bear bit his lips to hold back his smile. "How come?"

Nacho shrugged. "We figure by then, a bunch of kids will grow up from being pussies, and want to join. Safety in numbers, you know. We'll be so badass that no one'll dare mess with us."

"Is someone messing with you?" A red-tinted fierce protectiveness leeched into his bloodstream and when his knuckles whitened, he set down the sander. "They'd better not be."

"Nah, not now. When I was in the kid warehouse there were some guys—"

An acid hit bit his stomach lining. *Poor kid.*

"But my crew and me, we look out for each other now."

"That's good. But you let me know if somebody hassles you. I'll put 'em right."

"Thanks, Bear." The kid looked as if he just told him he loved him or something.

Damned bullies. They oughta be locked up. Better yet, lock up the parents who don't see that their darling untrained little puppies have grown to pit bulls.

"Hey, Bear?"

"Yeah."

"Who's in your crew?" He cocked his head. "I never see anybody out here, except that girl, Hope, that one time. You got biker buds?"

"I'm a grown up. I don't need a crew."

"You're kidding, right? Everybody needs friends, watching their backs."

Bear snorted. "Look at me, kid. Do I look like somebody's gonna mess with me?"

"Probably not. But buds are good for more than that. Joe and Diego an' me, we decided we could pick our own families. So we picked each other. You gotta have somebody to talk to. To bounce ideas off of. You know, so you're not all alone."

Nacho's downy innocent cheeks made it impossible to get irritated with him. "What's wrong with alone? I like alone."

The kid studied him as if he was a bug in a magnifying glass. Then he smiled. "Nah, you're just scared." He slid the too-big safety glasses back into place and studied the quarter panel. "Good to know that big guys get scared, too."

Scared? He opened his mouth. Then closed it. Then opened it. *He's a kid. He doesn't know shit.* He lowered his glasses and flipped the switch on the sander. "You wanna bring out your crew some afternoon, I guess that's okay."

THE NEXT MORNING, Hope sat in the bilious basement room of the hospital with her trauma group friends.

"So?" Bina asked. "Bryan and Mark, is the closet empty?"

"Mission accomplished." Bryan put a hand up, and Mark, sitting to his left, slapped it. "Tears were shed, beer and pizza were consumed. Thank God for Mark. I don't know if I'd ever have been able to face it without him."

"I'm so glad," Bina said. "And it got Mark out of his house. That's a win-win, right there. I'm proud of you two."

Bryan preened. Mark blushed. At least the nonscarred part did.

Hope half wished she'd been there.

Bina looked around the circle. "Bear? How are things with you?"

Hope had to bite her lip not to smile. The poor guy looked like a bear in the headlights. Even knowing his secret and his pain, she couldn't relate to his reticence. If only he'd force the words out, he'd find a receptive, supportive audience here. And it would help him forgive himself and move past the horrible experience—she just knew it would.

"I'm okay."

"I was looking for just a bit more detail. Isn't there anything you can share with us?"

He looked at his hands in his lap.

It was so odd…his greatest shame was what convinced Hope of his capacity for love. He acted as though he disliked people, but she knew he didn't, inside. Between that boy's death and the accident in the bar, Bear's faith in himself and his own humanity had been destroyed. Out of the rubble, he built a wall to hide behind.

When his eyes flicked to hers, she saw his panic. She wanted to jump into the conversation and save him. But even more, she wanted him whole. So she stayed silent. Pushing the corners of her mouth into a smile, she nodded. *Come on, babe, you can do this.*

"Okay. So, Hope and I are going out." He blew out a breath. "Dating."

"No shit." Mark rolled his eyes.

Bear's heavy brows came together and his lips whitened. "Hey, asshole. I don't give you crap when you can't go to the store, do I? Cut me some slack."

Mark raised his hands in a gesture of peace. "Sorry."

Bear glared his way around the circle, as if daring the others to comment. When he got to her, his expression softened like butter in the sun. "Hope gives me hope."

"Hope for what?" Bina asked.

"That maybe someday, I could become the man that she sees when she looks at me."

"Awwww," Bryan breathed. "That's beautiful."

A tide of crimson spread up Bear's face. He dropped his head to study his strangled, laced fingers.

Hope sat bathed in stupefied happiness. He'd revealed something in group that she *knew* he'd rather keep private. It was a beginning. A good beginning. She'd have crossed the circle to kiss him, if she didn't think he'd die of bashfulness on the spot.

"I think that's the most personal thing you've ever shared. Thank you, Bear," Bina said. "Brenda, how did you do with your homework? Any new revelations since we last talked?"

It was Brenda's turn to study her hands in her lap. "I guess."

"Phil's anger. Are you having any new thoughts about that?"

Hope could feel the tension in the room, pushing on her skin. Could hear the group breathing in the silence.

"I know ya'll are going to think I'm weird." Brenda chewed her bottom lip, but didn't look up. "Sometimes, when he hits me, it's a relief."

Someone sucked in a breath, but Hope didn't know who, because her attention was locked onto the hunched-over rag-doll woman.

"How so, Brenda?" Bina's voice made only soft ripples in the quiet.

"You know how it feels before a big storm? The light has a funny tint and the air goes still. You look at the sky, and the clouds are scary. You feel it coming. The hair on your arms stands up. You wait. And wait. Until you can hardly stand it. His anger builds like that. When he hits me, the storm breaks."

She was almost whispering, but in the silence, Hope heard her just fine.

"The waiting is the worst part."

"And the yelling, right?" Bina asked.

Brenda just nodded.

"I've heard this from many women I've counseled. Bruises show, but the worst scars are the ones that no one can see. Those are the ones that are the hardest to get over, because they destroy your self-esteem."

Brenda looked up, eyebrows raised in surprise. "That's just what it's like."

That gave Hope an idea. When the meeting broke up, she walked up to Bear, stood on tiptoe, and gave him a peck on the cheek. "You're my hero."

"Some hero." He shot a look to the people walking out of the room. "Want to go for coffee?"

"I can't." She wiped lipstick off his cheek with her thumb. "Want to go to dinner tonight?"

"Sure thing."

"Great, I have to go catch Brenda, but I'll call you later." She glanced around at the empty room, then stood on tiptoe and gave him a real kiss. She knew how hard it was for him, exposing his feelings in public—she was so proud of him. And...the kiss morphed. It was like stepping from a cool room into the sun. Warmth spread down her limbs and a thrill shot to her head. His arms came around her, pulling her tingling nipples against his chest. She felt him getting hard against her.

A higher part of her brain niggled. Something she had to... *Brenda!*

She broke the kiss. "Crap. Gotta go, but I'll see you later."

He chuckled. "You can count on that."

She caught up with Brenda on the sidewalk outside the hospital, under the bus stop sign. "Got a minute?"

She looked up, startled, then scanned up and down the street for the bus. "I've got to get home."

"I know you do, but I really need to talk to you. Can I drive you home?"

"I have to be—"

"Home in case Phil calls. I know." Hope dug in her purse for her keys. "We won't stop. You'll be home faster than if you were on the bus." She dangled the keys. "What do you say?"

"I guess." But her glance from under her hair was full of caution.

The drive was only ten minutes. On the way, Hope talked about her job, hoping to put Brenda at ease.

"Surfing, sailing, then you went camping? Weren't you afraid?"

"Unsure and a little uncomfortable, but afraid?" She pulled up at the tiny guard shack at the base. "Not much."

"Well, you're braver than me. I'd *never* have the guts to do that." Brenda leaned over and flashed a card to a soldier who looked way too young to be holding an automatic rifle. He waved them on.

"You'd be surprised what you can do. Six months ago, I'd have never thought I could do these things, either." She followed Brenda's point to a row of generic apartments with toddler-filled swing sets out front. "But almost dying somehow made me see things differently. I figured, if I can die at any time, why not live, right up to that second?" She pulled around the back and into a marked parking space.

Brenda's grimace told Hope a lot about her life…and her husband. "Maybe, but I don't want to do anything to bring that time one second closer, either."

She turned off the key. "Mind if I come in for a few?"

Brenda threw her head up "Why?"

"I wanted to talk to you about something, but I'd really rather not do it in a hot car."

Brenda chewed her lip.

God, this woman's life must be a minefield. "You'll be there if Phil calls. And he'll never know I was there. I promise."

"Okay. But my place is a mess. I'll tell you that right now."

The apartment was small, generic, and eat-off-the-floor immaculate. Hope stepped into lifeless, closed-up air.

"Hold on, I've got to go to the bathroom. I'll turn on the A/C." Brenda hung her purse on the edge of the wooden chair, tucked into a two-person dining table. She turned, and put her hands up, palms out. "Don't touch anything until I get back, okay?"

Hope didn't have to ask about the odd request. The panic in the young woman's eyes was answer enough. "Promise."

Brenda walked down the short hall and disappeared in a doorway on the right. Being careful not to move her feet, Hope craned her neck to look around. To her right was the small kitchen. Cabinets gleamed, linoleum shone. A small window looked over the playground she'd passed on the way in. Against the wall to her left was the dining table, and a tiny living room beyond it, dominated by a looming flat-screen TV, a recliner paying homage before it and an end table with a lamp beside the lounger. There was no other furniture she could see.

A toilet flushed, and Brenda appeared, fiddled with something on the wall, and a brush of tepid air washed over Hope. She walked back to the kitchen, her eyes darting. "Sorry it's hot in here. We can't waste electricity; it's expensive." She stepped to the counter and reached for the towel rack on the wall and infinitesimally adjusted a perfectly ironed linen tea towel. Then she turned, and clasped her hands. "You wanted to talk to me?"

The poor thing was so uncomfortable, Hope's skin twitched in sympathy. "You have a lovely home, Brenda. Do you mind if I sit down?"

Brenda glanced at the chair, then nodded. "I'm sorry. I'm not used to having company." She shot a glance at the clock over the sink. "Would you like some coffee? All I have is instant."

Hope pulled out the chair closest to her and sat. "If you'll make one for yourself, I'd love one."

She walked to the counter and opened the cabinet. Canned goods were stacked, label out, the exact same amount of space between them. Brenda reached for the jar of coffee, but paused to turn a can just a bit.

"You are a very neat person. You should see

my cupboards. I can't find what I need in there half the time." It wasn't true, but she'd say anything to try to relax the rigid line of the woman's back.

"Oh, it's not hard to do, if you put it away correctly to begin with." She spooned grounds into plain white cups she pulled from another cabinet. "How do you take it?"

"Just black, please."

"Same as me." A ghost of a smile lingered on her face as she carried the mugs to the sink and filled them with tap water, then settled them in the microwave on the counter.

When they were both seated, steaming cups in front of them, Hope said, "I wanted to tell you a story. About when I was growing up."

"Oookay." She sounded like a person who'd just discovered the person on the other end of the phone was an insurance salesman.

"My mom was the daughter of a banker. The biggest bigwig in a small Mideast town. She was Daddy's girl, and I suspect, very spoiled." Hope took a sip of coffee. "You know, I think everyone gets a great time in their lives, when everything is going their way. Did you ever see a guy who was a star football player in high school talk about it, years later?"

Brenda tipped her head, frowning.

"They get this faraway look, and they have

this tiny smile that you know they're not aware of, because they're really back there. You look at them, and you know, that was The Time of Their Life. When my mom talked about growing up, she was like that. She'd take out her dad's pocket watch and show it to me while she told me those stories." Her mom's memories were like that watch; shiny gold, and worn from years of polishing.

"But then the economy tanked in the '70s and the bank went under. My mom had just graduated from high school, and there was no money for her to go to college. Worse yet, though, for her, was the loss of her place in the world. See, she had this beautiful life all planned out, and it never occurred to her that anything could stop her from having it. It changed her, I think."

"That's sad, but why—"

"I'm getting there, I promise. Mom played the best hand she could. She married my dad; a young man on the fast track to a corner office. And I think they were happy, at least in the beginning." She made herself take another sip. "I was ten when my dad died. We had the kind of mortgage that got paid off in cases like that, and he had some insurance, so we weren't out in the street, but money was tight. My mom had never worked. Didn't even know how to drive a car. She was totally unprepared to make it on her own, much less with me to take care of."

Brenda's eyes flicked to the clock, then to her cell phone on the counter.

"Bottom line, my mom was *pissed*. This was not how her life was supposed to be. And if disaster struck twice in her life, who's to say it couldn't happen again? At any time." She took a sip, and the cup chattered in the saucer when she put it down. "All those little quirks of hers got worse. She went from pinching pennies to making them cry out. She sewed all my clothes, we had very little meat in our dinners. I never had seen a movie until a friend from school's family took me to one." When she realized she was bouncing her foot under the table, she made herself stop.

"But that wasn't the bad part. I suddenly couldn't do anything right. According to her, I was on the verge of disaster of one kind or another, every waking moment. She was determined to make sure I knew the right way to do things. Which, of course, was her way. Right down to the subtle nuances. She was afraid. She made me afraid."

She took a deep breath. Time to finish this... for herself, and for Brenda. "Were you rebellious, in junior high?"

Brenda nodded. "Sure"

"I guess everyone is, even if only a little bit."

She smiled, remembering. "We had a roller rink in town. It was a way to hang out, and giggle about the boys who went there to show off. Patty Schroeder was my best friend, and she was having her birthday party there. Of course she invited me. But I didn't skate. My mom wouldn't allow it—I could break a leg, or crack my skull, or...well, you see."

Brenda squinted. "You snuck out and went, didn't you?"

"Me? Heavens no." She put a hand on her chest and tried to look innocent. "Patty had a sleepover and we went from there."

Had Brenda just winked?

"I was a total klutz on skates, of course. But that was okay, because Jimmy Fielding would give me a hand up, every time. Eventually, he just held on to my hand, and put his arm around my waist, to steady me."

"Then your mom showed up."

"Yeah. I don't know what tipped her off. Maybe she had radar, I don't know. But she called Patty's parents, and yelled until they came and picked her up and brought her to the roller rink. My mom wasn't a yeller, but she walked in that rink yelling, and didn't quit until she'd marched out in the middle of the rink and snatched me away from Jimmy." She put a hand up and covered her eyes. "I was mortified. I felt every eye in the place on me as we walked out. Patty's parents took us home. I wanted to die."

Brenda winced. "Oh, man, that sucks."

"She kept me in my room for the weekend."

"Grounded?"

"Not your average grounding—she stayed with me the whole time. Telling me what a naive fool I was. I could have broken my neck. Ruined my reputation. Didn't I know what kind of people hung out in places like that? I was heading for high school pregnancy at this rate, and it would serve me right. Didn't I have any respect for how she worried?"

"Two *days* of that?"

"Forty-three hours, and twenty-six minutes of it."

"Jeez."

"I never disobeyed her again. And those lessons…over the years, I came to believe them as the truth. How could I not? That was the only side I was allowed to see. The world became a dangerous, unreliable place, and nothing was to be trusted. Least of all, my own judgment." She tipped her cup up, tasting the last cold dregs, then set it down.

"I just wanted you to know… I know how hard it is to trust your own opinion, when someone is hammering theirs into your head all the time. That you're stupid, inept…unable." When Brenda looked away, Hope put her fingers under her chin and lifted her head, to look her in the eye. "Don't you believe it."

The phone on the counter buzzed, and they both started.

Brenda jumped up and snatched it. She looked at the screen. "It's Phillip. I have to—"

Hope stood. The tension in the room had shot to DEFCON. "I'll let myself out, no problem. But, Brenda?"

She looked up, eyes wild.

"Remember what I said. If you ever need a place to stay, I have a blow-up mattress you're welcome to."

Brenda held a finger to her lips in a "Shhhh" motion, and slid her finger across the screen. "Hi, Phil. What? No, I'm home. Where else would I be?"

Hope lifted her purse, and tiptoed to the door, turned the knob and opened it slowly, hoping it wouldn't creak. It didn't.

"It was fine...They are not crazy losers. No, I didn't say anything..."

Hope didn't have to imagine the other side of the conversation—she'd heard it, many times. She stepped out and pulled the door softly closed.

CHAPTER SEVENTEEN

THREE WEEKS LATER, Hope sat alone in the hospital meeting room circle. She'd come early on purpose, to have a few minutes to think. Everything was different, yet mostly the same. She'd been promoted at work, to camping and hiking specialist, though she could fill in for the surfing and sailing departments in a pinch, too. Working with Lori all day was a blast, and last week, together they'd surpassed the skiing department in sales. With every day that went by, she felt more sure of herself; at work and in the rest of her life. She spent one evening a week with Opaline, helping out with the cleaning, and any job that required a ladder. Hope had made friends with many of the bunnies in the bunch, but her heart belonged to Buckwheat, who begged to be in her lap whenever she sat.

She and Bear were going out two or three nights a week, and on those nights, more often than not, sleeping over at her place or his. She shifted in her chair. *The nights...*

He'd taught her things she hadn't known about

her body—and his. He was a giving, loving teacher, and she'd let go of all her tentativeness in bed, following wherever he led. *His tongue...* She stood, and paced.

But their problem still remained. Well, it was *her* problem, since Bear didn't see that he had one. Instead of her drawing him out, it seemed that he'd brought her in to his insulated world, and it closed around her. She had her friends outside the relationship, but he showed no interest in meeting them, and he had none. Not that she wasn't happy to spend alone time with Bear, but she could see down that road, into the future. If they were invited out, he wouldn't want to go. She'd either go, and miss him, or stay home, and resent him. He'd come to dread her asking him to go.

She imagined them, years from now, sitting at a kitchen table staring at each other over coffee, everything they had to say to each other, said.

Is that all there is? Is that how lovers end up, when they are very different, and get set in their ways?

But there were more imminent problems. He refused to talk about anything important in group, much less what had happened in the desert. He still feared his own temper. Not that he'd discussed it, but she could feel it, like an electric current running just below the surface of his skin.

She'd been afraid almost all her life, of almost everything in the outside world, but after being around Bear, she'd take that over being afraid of the inside world. Not being able to trust yourself—that must be horrible.

He wouldn't discuss it though—not with her, and certainly not with the group.

"Well, good morning, Hope." Bina strode into the room. "You're early."

"I wanted to talk to you. Alone."

"Come, sit." Bina sat in a chair, and patted the one beside her. "You'll have to hurry though; we won't be alone for long."

The weight of dread pulled her into the chair. She still felt this could be a mistake, but after all, Bina was here to help. "I can't tell you specifics, because they're not mine to tell. But this group has taught me that fears grow bigger and bigger on the inside, and talking about them gives perspective. Once you say them out loud, you can see that they're much smaller than they first seemed." She sighed. "But how do you make someone else see that?"

Bina's hand covered Hope's. "You can't."

"But they'd be so much better—"

"I know that. You know it. But Bear needs to discover that for himself."

The frustration burst from her, louder than

she'd meant. "How is he ever going to discover it if he doesn't *do* it?"

At the sound of a shoe scuff, they looked up. Bear stood in the doorway, looking as if he'd just walked into the door frame. "I heard that." He didn't even sound angry. He sounded hurt.

No, deeply wounded.

Hope's heart plunged and her blood pounded in ears that threatened to burst into flame. She opened her mouth to say something, but his eyes stopped her. *He didn't trust anyone. No one but you. Now he's going to think...*

"Bear, come in." Bina waved him over, but he didn't move. "We were discussing you, but you know Hope wouldn't betray any of your confidences."

Thank you. He may not believe her, but he'd believe Bina.

"Hey, big guy. Want to let me in?" Bryan's voice came from the hallway.

Bear walked away.

She was up and out of her chair before she thought, and ran down the hall to catch up to his long, determined strides. When she pulled abreast, his face was hard and closed—the face of that angry stranger she'd seen that first day in the room behind them. He strode to the elevator, mashed the button as if wanting to cause it pain, and stood watching the floor indicator above the door.

"Wait, Bear," she said, though he'd already stopped. "I didn't tell her anything, I promise."

He didn't stop. He didn't even slow. He just waved her words away with an arm over his head, and kept going. When he slammed the stairwell door, it hit the wall with a hollow boom that made her jump.

He was *pissed*.

She stood in the middle of the hall, pulled by the stairwell ahead as well as the meeting room behind. The stairwell door clicked closed, but she could still feel the wave of anger and betrayal that Bear left in his wake. She shivered. Maybe she'd let him cool off first.

Yeah, that would be for the best. She'd run out to his place later, and explain.

Heart hurting, she turned and slowly walked back to the meeting room.

HOPE HAD TRIED to go home after the meeting. After all, Bear made it clear he didn't want to talk about this. But her car steered her to Bear's place like a GPS guided missile, so she seemed to have no choice. She tightened her fingers on the wheel, her stomach muscles and her resolve and made the turn into the rutted drive of the Gaudy Widow.

She pulled into the shadowed yard just as Bear stepped from the barn into the sunlight, blinking and wiping his hands on a rag he'd pulled from his back pocket.

She turned off the ignition, swallowed and opened the door.

Bear, head down, strode for the cabin.

"You can't just ignore me, you know," she raised her voice and slammed the car door. "I'm not going away until we talk."

"Why?" He turned and skewered her with a look. "Why did you feel the need to talk to that shrink about me? I trusted you."

Skewered by the hurt in his eyes, she hesitated, knowing she stood on a fine line between treason and truthfulness. If she put a foot wrong, she'd lose Bear. But she also knew that she couldn't live the life of a recluse, either. "Because." She strode to where he stood in the middle of the dusty dooryard. "Because, for the first time in my life, I feel like I'm starting to find my way in the world. I've somehow, somewhere, found the guts to do more than huddle and wait for bad things to happen." She shifted from foot to foot, antsy as one of Opaline's nervous bunnies.

"What's that got to do with—"

"I'm really afraid."

He cocked his head and looked down at her for the first time. "About what?"

"For a smart man, you're so damned dense."
She huffed out a breath.

He just stared her down, waiting.

"I really like you, you idiot."

A flash of joy shot across his face before his
brows pulled together again. "That doesn't really answer my question. Why did you talk to
Bina about me?"

She almost reached out to grasp the easy answer. But what good would it do to back her way
out of this, only to have to face it later? The problem wasn't going away. She toed the dirt, until
she realized she must look like a guilty kid, and
made herself stop. "Look, I may be getting ahead
of things here, but this is what women do. This
is how we think. We plan, and—"

He rolled his eyes. "Why don't you just say
whatever you're trying to tell me?"

She looked up at him, hoping it wouldn't be
the last time she saw that particular mix of caring and confusion in those brown eyes. "I just
came out of living where you are—afraid all the
time—hiding. I'm not going back."

He reared backward as if she'd just punched
him in the nose. "You saying I'm afraid?"

"Um." She scoured her mind for a less objec-
tionable word, but one didn't surface. "Yes."

His lips thinned to a straight seam. His face

reddened. He leaned over her. "You calling me a *coward*?"

Though she'd stepped over that thin line way back, something told her to push. She leaned in and crossed her arms under her breasts. "Yes."

His face edged toward purple. She heard the scree of teeth grinding.

"I'm afraid?"

Through his slitted eyelids, she could see his pain. "Bear. I'm not doing this to hurt you. Or to goad you into doing anything you don't believe is right. I'm just telling you the truth, for me. I made a vow, after I woke in the hospital—I can't prevent my death, but I'm going to *live*, right up until that last second." She uncrossed her arms, reached out and touched his forearm. The muscles beneath were like corded wire. If he could stand here and listen, what right did she have to chicken out now? "You see, I think I'm falling in love with you."

He looked dazed—as if someone had hit him over the head with a two-by-four.

"But I can't be the only one who loves you."

He tipped his head in a "go on" motion that his expression belied.

"You have to love yourself. And you can't do that until you forgive yourself. Without reservations, without fear." She held her hands out and shrugged. "The best way I know to do that is to

talk it out in group. But I know that for you, it's
the hardest way. And that's fine. You don't have
to do it my way." She shrugged, hands out. "But
you have to do it. Not for me, or us. For you."

Emotion flashed across his face like summer
lightning. "Is this some kind of ultimatum?"

"Of course not." She reached up to cup his
barely bearded cheek. "I'm telling you as hon-
estly as I'm capable, that someday it could come
to that. Not because I want it to…but because I
can't—no, I *won't* give up the freedom for anyone. It was too hard won."

He huffed out a breath and looked down at her
as if she was an insect. "How about you?"

"Me? We're not talking about me. We're—"

"Oh, yeah, I know. You're telling me. Now I'm
telling you." He poked a finger at her chest, but
didn't touch. "Yeah, you may have come a long
way. But you're not ready for a relationship."

Surprise drove her back a half step. "Me?"

"You. You're all big on what I have to do. How
about what you have to do? A relationship isn't
one person trying to save another. Trust me, lady.
I don't need saving." He glanced to the cabin.
"Not by you, anyway." He swung his heavy head
back, and his anger burned holes in her. "If you're
ready to commit to a relationship, it isn't con-
ditional. You don't get to say, 'I'll accept you,
if you will…fill in the blank.' I'm either good

enough for you, or I'm not. I may be an uncouth animal, but even I know that *saving someone* is not a solid basis for a relationship." He turned and stomped away.

Warring thoughts clashing in her ears, she let him go.

WEDNESDAY, BEAR LEANED against the cinder-block wall across from the elevator. He would've loved to walk away. But he wouldn't. *You have to change. I love you. But I may leave you. Jesus, this woman is tearing my guts out.*

The elevator door slid open. His angel and Bryan stepped out. Her eyes flicked to Bear, then away.

With just a glance, his heart sped up, hammering his chest. If loving her was so hard, why was walking away, harder?

You just answered that, idiot. You love her. Without his say-so, his feet followed her down the hall. The first night that his angel had appeared in his dream and absolved his sin with only the love in her eyes, he'd fallen for her. When she appeared in his waking hours, how could he do less?

No, Hope wasn't an angel—she was pushy, opinionated, sweet, caring, beautiful… Shit.

Admit it, man, you got it bad.

And, given what she wanted of him, it was going to get worse.

Talk? Admit out loud in a group of people his biggest sin? A shudder ripped down his spine, raising gooseflesh on his exposed skin. He wouldn't even have told Hope, if she hadn't been ready to walk out of his life.

But wasn't that pretty much what she'd just told him she'd do again?

You're a man. An army sniper and an ex-con. You're going to let a little thing like that lead you around by the nose?

No. Yes. Fuck.

He followed her into the room and took one of the two remaining chairs, next to Bryan. Hope took the other, across the circle, next to Bina.

"Lover's spat?" In the chair next to Bear, Bryan batted his eyelashes.

Bear flipped him the bird.

"All right, everyone, let's get started." Bina waited until the conversations died. "Let's begin with the mystery man under the bandages. How did the surgery go, Mark?"

The white bandage and clear plastic guard couldn't disguise the bulge on Mark's face that had to be a new nose.

"Dey say id went well. I habn't seen it yet."

He sounded as if he had a cold, but it was probably packing from the surgery. *Damn, that had to hurt.* Bear's gut burned with sympathy.

Bina uncrossed her legs, and took out her notebook and pen. "Mark, you said in our first meeting that you don't remember anything about the accident. Have any details come to you with time?"

He stared at the floor. "Not much."

"Why don't you tell us what has. It may help you to heal."

He sat fidgeting for long seconds.

"My fiancée had dumbed me two weeks before. I was sick of my abartment and my own combany, so I just went out for a drive. But it wasn't any better."

He pulled at his jeans and shifted in the chair. "I stobbed at a beach, and walked for a while. But the moonlight and being alone…it made it worse. So I got in my car and drove. All I could see was an embty life stretching ahead into the distance like the long straight highway."

"Damn, dude, that's a lot of remembering." The words were out before Bear realized he'd said them aloud.

Mark's face turned as red as a toddler holding his breath. It looked even worse, against the white bandage. "Fine!" His voice echoed off the cinder-block walls. He stood. "I was trying to kill myself. Is that what you want to hear?" He shot daggers at Bina. "You bunch of vultures, bick, bick, bicking at people until they come abart. Well fine then, I fully blanned to splatter my brains all over that overbass." His labored mouth-breathing was loud in the dead silent room. "You habby now?" He bent over, leaned his hands on his knees and a choked sob escaped. "I thought things couldn't be worse. I tried to kill myself, and I couldn't even do that right." Head hung, he whispered, "I only managed to turn myself into a monster."

Bear's gut tightened in sympathy. *At least my scars are on the inside, where no one can see.* Well, almost no one.

Brenda, oddly enough, was the first to move. She didn't say a word, just stood, walked over, stood shoulder to shoulder with Mark and took his hand.

Bryan was next. He stepped to Mark and took his other hand.

Bear glanced across the circle to Hope, willing her to stay in her seat. If she didn't get up, he wouldn't have to.

But her eyes were on Mark as she stood, walked over, leaned forward, and touched her forehead to his.

It wasn't that he didn't feel for the guy. Bear was squirming inside, imagining how awful

Mark's life must be. But how would it help Mark for all of them to get up and sing "Kumbaya"?

A shiver of guilt slipped between Bear's ribs, fileting his dispassion. After two months in group, he couldn't pretend not to know these people. He couldn't pretend he didn't feel sorry for them, either. But PDA? He shifted his ass in his chair, determined to hold out.

Across the circle, Bina watched. There was no judgment on her face—she just studied him. *Well, shit.*

He stood, reached out, and laid his hand on Mark's back, feeling the rise and fall of his tortured breathing.

Bear was grateful to be released from the "group hug" a minute later. God. Not only reveal his deepest secret, but *cry* in front of these people? And he thought his worst nightmares were at night. They weren't. With a last shudder, he returned to his seat.

Bina passed the ever-present box of tissues around the circle, and more than one person took one before it got to Mark. "I know that was hard, Mark. How do you feel, now that you've spoken of it?"

He dabbed his eyes. "I'b not sure."

"Maybe we can dive into that a little deeper next time. Great work, Mark." Bina checked the clock on the wall. "We have a few minutes left. Does anyone else want to talk?"

The brown mouse raised her hand.

"Yes, Brenda?"

"I know I can't go on like it's been. At home, I mean. I've been thinking. If Mark, Bryan, Hope and…" She nodded to each as she said their name. When she came to him, her voice faltered, and her eyes skittered away. "If they can be brave, I should be able to."

"What are you thinking of doing?" Bina asked.

"I'm going to talk to Phil." Brenda wriggled until she sat taller in her seat. "I'm going to tell him that he can't hit me anymore." She nodded, whether to convince herself, or the group, he couldn't tell.

"I mean, if he doesn't agree, I'll know he'll never change, and I'll leave him. But if he does…" Her expression slid to that of a naive teenager. "Maybe we can find our way to a good marriage."

Hope looked as if she'd pinched her finger in a door. "Oh, Brenda, I'm not sure—"

"I am. I've spent a lot of time thinking about this. See, I've never told him before. I just sit like a scared rabbit. I know if I can find the right words, to explain how it feels when he…gets mad, I can make him understand. He'll see. He loves me."

Bina's brows pulled together. "Brenda, I applaud your hard work, your conclusions and your progress. But you need to be careful. Do this in a public place, where you'll be safe if he doesn't react well."

"I could be there if you want. Not at the table, just in the background," Mark said.

"Oh, I'd love to be there." Bear scrubbed his palms on his jeans.

Bina raised an eyebrow at him.

Temper. You're going to have to keep that in check.

Brenda smiled. "Thanks guys. That means a lot. But I have to do this by myself. If he gets mad and hits me, I'll have my answer, right?" Brenda shrugged. "After all, I've lived through that before."

It wasn't her words that drove needles of ice into Bear's blood. It was the casual, day-to-day way she said it. It was more horrifying than any picture she could paint.

Bina said, "Please, Brenda, don't do this alone. You don't know how Phil will react. How about bringing the police into this?"

"I guess." She glanced over. Her eyes dropped to her lap, where she worried a hangnail. "Thank you for offering. I've never had anybody stand up for me before."

Good for her. Bear nodded.

HOPE SAT WHEN Bear pulled out a chair on the red-brick patio of Dougie's Place, a squat flamingo-pink building that sat at the edge of the ocean like a gaudy fat lady on a beach towel. The outside was ugly, but the patio was warm and welcoming. A window-wall blocked the wind, but red-and-white umbrellas flipped their skirts in the onshore breeze. "What a great place." She shrugged out of Jesse's suede jacket, and tugged down the cap she'd put on to cover her "helmet hair." "Nice end to the day."

They'd ridden the motorcycle north on the Pacific Coast Highway to the hippie-throwback village of Big Sur, then spent hours wandering the funky shops.

Bear pulled the chair from the opposite side of the table to sit beside her. He jostled her, bumping her elbow. "Sorry."

She scooted her chair away a few inches. "No problem."

"Great view, huh?"

She looked over the ocean that had gone sparkling gold in the light of the sun falling into it. "The best."

He reached for her hand, just as she raised it to tuck hair behind her ear.

She sighed in frustration and went to take his hand just as he lowered it to his lap.

They were saved by the waitress, who left menus, took their drink order and disappeared.

It had been like this all day. He'd lean into a turn, and she was late, making a curve that was usually smooth, an awkward series of overcompensations, by her, then him. She just couldn't seem to relax and fall into the rhythm of the ride. But that was only the outward manifestation of something deeper, something her mind had worried at. This felt more like a first date. He'd been polite and friendly, but distant. No, not distant, exactly, but…not close. As if the past weeks had been only a dream.

Bear ordered a double burger and fries. Since her stomach was jumpy, Hope ordered only soup. When the waitress walked away, a lumpy silence fell.

Someone was going to have to bring up the pachyderm on the patio. When she took Bear's hand in hers, his head came around. "Can we talk about this?"

He sighed. "I guess we have to."

"You've been distant all day. What's going on in your head? Are you mad at me?"

"Never mad." His fingers tightened on hers. "But I do feel a bit…manipulated."

She'd have taken her hand back, but he didn't release it. "Why?"

"Look at it from my side. I know, you're not

telling me how I have to go about changing, but if I don't, I'm going to lose you. I feel like I'm dancing on burning coals stretched between two cliffs. I've got no good choices."

The pain in his eyes tore something in her.

"I never asked you to change. I accept all of you. Isn't that how it's supposed to be?" Bear asked.

Salt poured in the wound, making her burn. It was true. He'd never asked a thing of her. Was she being unfair? Pushing where she had no right to push? Becoming one of those bitchy, bossy women she had no respect for? She thought a moment before answering. "What advice would you give Brenda?"

"That she should leave the bastard. What does that have to do—"

"When you see someone you care about making decisions that are hurting them, you have to tell them, right?"

His heavy brows drew together. The angry Bear was back. "It's not the same thing."

"But it *is*." She squeezed his hand. "Except instead of someone beating you up, you're doing it to yourself. That's harder to get away from."

"You don't know what you're talking about."

"I know you're still having bad dreams." She ran her thumb over the dark circle under his eye.

"You're not getting enough sleep. I'm worried about you."

He pulled away and looked out at the waves sliding over the sand.

"I don't want to change you, Bear. I want you to be who you are. But the scars, the damage, the nightmares that haunt you *aren't* who you are." She laid her hand over her heart. "I know that, in here. If you told me it was, I wouldn't believe you." The burning cooled, as if the words contained aloe. She hadn't realized until the words popped out, that they were true. Right. "I want more for you than you want for yourself, and that hurts me."

He didn't turn to her, but squeezed her hand. "So where does that leave us?"

"I don't know, but I'm not willing to give up. Are you?"

"No."

"Then I guess we just keep doing this awkward dance until we figure it out." She squeezed back.

CHAPTER EIGHTEEN

"BEAR! BEAR!"

The kid's yell from the stack of boxes brought Bear to his feet. "In here. You okay?"

Nacho rounded the last box and sprinted into the painting area. "Guess what I just heard?" From his panting, he must have torn up the road on his bike.

"Whoa there. Don't stir up dust. This is wet." Bear checked the primer coat on the hood of his truck to be sure he hadn't missed any spots. "What'd you hear?"

"There's gonna be a car show." He gulped air. "In Santa Maria. In September. Old cars, funny cars, hot rods— It's gonna be epic!"

"That's cool, kid." He pushed down his mask and pulled a rag from his back pocket.

"You don't get it. There's gonna be booths, with people selling stuff and everything."

"So?" Bear squatted to get a better angle on the hood.

"When we finish this—" he swept his arm

in an arc over the hood "—you can enter it in the show."

"Nah. Not for me." He wiped his hands on the rag.

"Dude." Nacho let out a stage-worthy sigh and looked at Bear as if he was brain damaged. "You can get a booth to show off your stuff. Hello, advertising?"

Bear scratched a trickle of sweat under the bandanna he'd tied on his head. "You're going to tell me about marketing?"

Nacho shrugged his tiny shoulders. "Somebody's got to."

"I've always had enough business just from word of mouth."

Nacho pulled a matching bandanna out of his back pocket and laid it over his knee to fold it. "Maybe. But when I finish high school, and I'm here full-time, we're gonna need more work." He wrapped the bandanna around his head. "So you have to start now, building up the business." He knotted the cloth and jerked the ends tight.

Bear missed his beard. It had been good for hiding smiles. "What're you, my agent?"

"Nah. More like a salesman."

He had enough business. Well, almost. Besides, the days he didn't have a job, he worked inside the house. The bathroom was done, and he only needed to install the garbage disposal for the kitchen to be complete. But the house didn't pay the bills. Quite the opposite, in fact.

But stand behind a booth and talk to people all day? It made him itch to think about it. Or, worse yet, sit there all day while people walked by, feeling like a snake oil salesman?

Yeah, that sounded like a good idea.

But entering his truck, and putting a sign in the windshield, advertising the business? That just might be a good idea. Maybe he'd even pay the kid to hand out business cards. He ran his hand over the scruff on his cheek. "You may have a point, kid. I'll think about it. In the meantime, grab a mask. We're gonna finish the primer coat today."

Nacho's narrow chest expanded his "delinquent in training" T-shirt. "I can do that part. That's easy."

Bear's phone rang in his back pocket. He pulled it out, but didn't recognize the number. "Gaudy Widow," he growled.

"B-Bear?"

A woman, but not Hope.

"This is Bear."

"It's Brenda. I just wanted you to know that I set up a date with Phil, for tonight. But if you have plans, it's okay to—"

"No. Wait." He strode to the card table where the coffeepot sat, along with a carpenter's pencil, and a small notebook. "I'll be there. Just tell me when and where."

"I THOUGHT YOU liked the camping department." Lori's hurt look across the top of the tent they were assembling wasn't less for the fact that Hope could only see the top half of her coworker's face. "Is it me?"

Hope sighed. Was she destined to disappoint everyone in her life? "No, I love working with you. You know that." She tucked the tent pole into the pocket on the corner of the tent.

"Then what is it?"

She shouldn't have said anything until she understood herself. Lately she'd begun to notice a growing ennui with regard to her job. She still liked helping people, and she and Lori were a good team. So what *was* the problem?

"I don't know, it's like… I changed my entire life to go find adventure, and now I'm only selling it to others."

"Oh, you're just out of sorts because you and Bear are having issues." Lori grabbed the fly and tossed it over the completed tent.

Hope snatched her side before it could slide off, and pulled one of the elastic bands to hook into the slot on the bottom of the tent. "No, I don't think that's it, either. This is about me."

"Look, you never had a normal life, so maybe

you don't know… This *is* a normal life." Lori moved around the circumference, clipping the fly in place. "Nobody without a huge trust fund runs off to climb Everest every month." She raised a finger in Hope's direction. "Not that I'd suggest you do that. You'd probably trip and fall into a crevasse…"

"Oh, thanks for the vote of confidence."

"You get what I'm saying. Life isn't like a reality show. You know they cut out the boring, do-your-hair, go-to-the-bathroom, grocery-shopping parts, right?"

Hope put her hands on her hips. "I've been on the planet a long time. I figured that part out."

"So? What's the problem?"

She didn't know. *That* was the problem. This job was starting to feel "just okay." And she hadn't thrown her old life away for "just okay." What the heck was wrong with her? Everyone around her knew what they wanted to do with their lives, and they were doing it. How long would she wander around, trying to find where she fit?

She forced a smile she didn't feel. "Oh, I don't know, maybe it's just hormones."

SEVEN O'CLOCK THAT EVENING, Bear stepped into the cool air and slammed his truck door. Bina may not like it, but he, Mark and Brenda had dis-

cussed it after group. He didn't want Hope anywhere near this. And Bryan...wouldn't be much
help if things went bad. Better they took care of
this themselves. From the looks of the crowded
gravel lot, The Farmhouse Café did a brisk business. The sun hadn't set, but the lights from inside were making faded yellow rectangles on the
sidewalk.

At the sound of a slamming door, he turned.

There was no mistaking that face. Mark walked
over, shooting glances to be sure there was no one
to gawk at him. "You ready to rumble?"

"That's exactly what I *don't* want to happen."

"Yeah, I know. But it's tempting, isn't it?"

Bear shook his head, "More than you know."
Phil's abuse of his wife was a hot coal, burning
in his chest. He lectured himself all the way over
about keeping his temper. He had full control.

But he had to admit that coal concerned him,
just a little.

He snatched at memories to douse it—Nacho
puffing his chest, his face lighting up when
Bear praised him. The pride in himself, when
he turned the keys of a job over to a customer
and saw their joy. The acceptance and tenderness
when Hope looked at him.

*Remember that, when you get mad. That's
what's at stake.*

He turned and walked to the door.

Mark followed. "Do you think they're here?"

"Only one way to find out." The cowbell tied to the door clanked when he opened it, and he was hit by the clamor of conversations and smell of bacon. He scanned the tables, booths and stools along the bar. Many couples, but no mouse.

"I don't see them," Mark whispered from behind Bear's shoulder. "I wonder what her asshole looks like."

"I don't think you meant that the way it sounded." Bear shot Mark a wink and a half smile.

Mark's scar and bandage were white against his blush.

"Let's find a place to sit before they show up." Bear pointed to a booth in the far corner that would afford them a view of the entire room. "Over there."

Mark led the way, but when he would have sat on the side with the best view, Bear steered him to the other side. "No offense, dude, but that mug of yours is going to attract attention."

"You have a point." Mark settled into the red vinyl booth. "God, I can't wait to be done with these surgeries. I'm never going to be mistaken for a movie star, but hopefully I won't look like Frankenstein's monster."

Bear sat. "In a year, you'll be getting on with life. This won't matter so much."

"Right," Mark mumbled, studiously sweeping crumbs from the table.

Bear was so not good at this small-talk thing. He cast about for something to fill the hole in the air where talking should be. "I think your talking in group the other day was a brave thing."

Mark snorted. "Oh, yeah, spilling your tears and your guts all over everybody is really brave."

"Hey, it's what I thought at the time." Bear grabbed a menu to have something to do with his hands. "Take it or leave it. I ain't Oprah."

God, how do people do this?

He let out a breath when a high school girl in jeans, a checkered shirt and a waitress apron wandered over. He'd worried that Jesse would be here and want to chat him up about Hope.

The girl was staring at Mark as if a zombie had just plopped down at her table and asked for a plate of human flesh.

"Hey." Bear snapped his fingers to break her concentration, and her rudeness. "I'll have an iced tea."

"Same for me," Mark said, eyes down.

When the waitress had gone, Mark's distress hung as thick in the air as the stench of a truck stop bathroom.

"Shit. No wonder you don't go out."

"Yeah, but in a year, this won't matter so much."

Sliced by the cutting edge of his own inane

comment, as well as the naked pain in Mark's eyes, Bear winced. "I admit, I suck at this, okay?"

"I know you meant well." Mark just shrugged. "So, why don't you ever talk in group?"

Bear lifted an eyebrow, the facial equivalent of "really?"

"It's not easy. But I gotta tell you, I felt better, after." Mark looked out the window at the approaching dusk. "I didn't realize it, but that secret was like an infection, deep down. Talking about it kind of cleaned it out. I'm not saying it's all better, but…"

The cowbell clanked, and the mouse walked in, followed by a tall thin blond guy with a mustache, thinning hair and a look-down-his-nose attitude. He herded her to a booth near the door.

"They're here." Bear sat up. "Don't look."

Brenda sat with her back to the room, the asshole sat facing Bear. Perfect. He'd be able to read the guy's facial expressions.

"If you don't want me to look, you'll have to tell me what's going on." Mark practically bounced in his seat.

"I will, keep your pants on."

The waitress took the couple's drink order, and left them alone.

Phil looked past his wife as though she wasn't there, looked around at the room, then out the window, as if bored with it all.

"What's happening?" Mark snuck a look over his shoulder, then back.

"Nothing, yet. Uh-oh." Bear couldn't hear the conversation of course, but Phil's expression sharpened. To a dagger point. He put his hands on the table and leaned over them, listening intently.

"What?" Mark whined.

Brenda sat, shoulders squared, back ruler-straight against the back of the booth.

"Rough water ahead," Bear whispered.

"You're killing me here, you know. Is she telling him?"

"That would be my guess… Hang on."

Phil's long face drained of color. His lips disappeared into the straight line of his mustache. His brows slammed together and his nostrils flared as red spread up his face like mercury rising in a thermometer.

"Be ready, this is about to—"

Quick as the strike of a snake, the man grabbed Brenda's forearm, and she flinched. He lunged out of the seat, stood and turned for the door, dragging his wife's arm behind him. Since it was still attached, Brenda had no choice but to follow. But she was slow, and awkward with surprise. She almost ended up on the floor.

Bear didn't have to explain. Mark had turned and was staring openmouthed.

"That's our cue. Let's go." Bear stood, threw a

ten on the table and followed the couple out the door, Mark on his heels.

He scanned the lot for movement, and caught it to his left. They strode over and looked down the aisle. Phil held a cowering Brenda against the car, stabbing a finger in her face. As he approached, Bear could already see the imprint of the man's fingers on his wife's arm. His face was purple with anger and spittle flew from his lips. Grabbing Brenda's jaw, he leaned in, his voice a growl, and scarier for it.

"Hey, dickhead," Mark's voice came from behind Bear, "What's your problem?"

"This," Phillip snapped, without looking, "is none of your business. Move on."

Bear put out an arm when Mark would've muscled his way past him. He tipped a chin at Phil. "We will, if the lady tells us she's okay." Muscles twitching, his fingers curled into fists he was itching to throw. Still, he held his voice calm. "Are you all right ma'am?"

Brenda's eyes held equal parts relief and fear. "N-no." Her jaws chattered over the word as if she were freezing. She tried to pull her arm away, but Phil's fingers dug deeper. Clearing her throat, she said louder, "No. I don't want to be with him."

Phil's mouth opened in shock. His eyes slitted. "*What* did you say?" His voice was a rattlesnake's warning.

Mark jostled, but Bear held him.

"I said, I want to leave." Brenda held her own, and his stare.

You go, Mouse.

Mark ducked under Bear's arm. "You heard her, asshole. Let her go."

"This is none of your business." Phil turned to them for the first time. "Jesus, what the hell happened to you?"

Mark surged forward. "The same thing that's about to happen to you."

Bear stepped between the two men. *How the hell did I end up the referee?* Mark was much smaller, but rage made him almost as strong as Bear.

"Better hold him back, before I hurt him worse." Phil jerked the car door open and tried to stuff his wife inside. The crack of Brenda's head hitting metal echoed between the cars.

"Nunh." Brenda stumbled but caught her balance in time.

Tucked behind, Mark didn't see it, but Bear did, through a pink-tinged haze of anger. He shoved Mark back, turned, and rabbit-punched Phil in the face.

Mark came around Bear, took Brenda's elbow and his arm went around her waist, supporting her.

"What the hell?" Phil touched his fingers to

his rapidly swelling lip. "Where do you get off?" He snatched for Brenda's hand. "This is *my* goddamned wife, and I'll handle her any way I—"

Bear's fist stopped whatever he was going to say next. "She doesn't—" he punched Phil in the stomach "—belong—" his fist cracked against Phil's cheek "—to you."

Phil staggered, fell against the car opposite them and dropped to his knees.

Bear stood over the weasel, willing him to get up. He'd held himself in so long...his fears, his nightmares, his shame. He was tired of hiding, and the target in front of him deserved every bit of the whup-ass he was dying to unload.

Just like that, his pent up junkyard-dog rage was loose, ripping and tearing through every one of his promises. His fist throbbed—not with pain—but the need to continue.

To finish this.

The son of a bitch stood right in front of them, and said he *owned* this woman. He must have a death wish. Well, Bear was just the guy to help him out with that. He drew back his steel-toed motorcycle boot and kicked Phil in the ribs. Twice.

"Bear!" Mark's voice was close. "That's enough."

But the anger was in his blood now, a high as quick and potent as a bolus of heroin. "Oh, I'm just getting started." He filled one fist with Phil's lapels and lifted. He jerked his other fist back—

His elbow hit something that gave way with a sickening crack.

Mark screamed.

When Bear let go, Phil fell to the ground, his head bouncing off the car's fender.

Mark lay crumpled in the gravel, unmoving, his face a blood-spattered mess of crimson.

"Mark!" Eyes wild, Brenda dropped to her knees beside him.

Ah shit. Bear knew a blow to the nose could drive splinters of bone into a man's brain. Why had he allowed Mark to come? He knew Mark was healing from a surgery. And in a situation like this, there was always the possibility for… what had just happened. The lights of the café dimmed, tiny stars against the blackness of night. The world spun. Reality spun out, worse than any nightmare.

Voices pinged around the inside of his skull. *You thought you could keep your temper. That you could be like everyone else.*

That you could change.

He put a hand to either side of his head to keep his skull from exploding. "I'm sorry." He panted in a sobbing breath, "I'm so sorry."

Brenda looked up, horror etched on her face, fear in her eyes.

It hit him like a bullet to the chest, driving him back a step.

Even people he tried to *save* felt in danger of his fury. The careful world he'd constructed fell from under his feet. He could shave, put on nice clothes and be loved by a beautiful woman, but it was only a persona, put on to disguise the animal beneath. He wasn't a better person now than the day he'd stepped from behind the razorwire prison gate. Or the day he killed an innocent child.

He took off running. He knew it was useless; he couldn't go fast enough to run out of his own skin, or turn back time.

Or outrun the truth.

The air rushed by his ears. The dark swallowed him whole. When he came to himself, he stopped under a streetlight on a dirt road. He put his hands on his knees and pulled air into his heaving lungs. He had no idea where he was, but it didn't matter.

He had nowhere to go.

CHAPTER NINETEEN

"I TOLD YOU, I like vacuuming, Opaline. Besides, the idea of you trying to lug that vacuum up and down those steep stairs is enough to—" Hope's phone vibrated its way across Opaline's kitchen table. She picked it up, frowning at the number she didn't recognize, before answering.

"You said to call if I needed help. I need help."

Hope stuck her finger in her ear, to better hear the breathless voice. "Brenda?"

"Oh, Hope, this is just awful. Please, will you come?"

In the background she heard "Code blue, to room 365. Code blue." Adrenaline punched Hope to her feet. "Where are you? What's happened?"

"I'm at the Santa Maria Hospital ER, and—" *She talked to Phil!* "Are you all right?"

"I'm all right, it isn't me. It's Mark." A damp sob came through the phone. "I tried, like I said… I'd rehearsed what to say and I really thought I had it just right. I didn't mean for this to happen. Bear and Mark… Can you just come? I'll explain it all when you get here."

"I'm on my way. Don't go anywhere, you hear me?" Hope already had her keys in her hand. "Wait, Brenda?" She closed her eyes. "Is Bear okay?"

"Yes." She hesitated several wobbly breaths. "No. Can you please come?"

"I'm in the wind. Don't you move." She pressed End.

"What can I do?" Opaline stood at the sink, wringing the dish towel in her hands, eyes full of worry.

"I don't know. That was a friend. She's been in a fight with her husband. I have to go." She lifted Jesse's jacket from the back of the chair and pulled it on.

Opaline's little sparrow eyes went hard. "If there's anything I can do, you bring her back here. I was a nurse in the Korean War, you know."

The words followed Hope out the screen door and down the stairs. She ran for her car, threw herself in and cranked the key.

What the hell happened? It sounded as if Mark was hurt. What did she mean that Bear was and wasn't okay? If he wasn't hurt, was he in trouble? *Oh, please, don't let it be his temper...*

She shouldn't have let Brenda off the phone until she knew. Backing out as fast as she could, she cut the wheel to the left at the bottom of the driveway. The car rocked on its springs as she threw it into Drive and floored it.

Calling back for more details was out; speeding and talking on the phone was a recipe for disaster. Luckily rush hour was over, and most of the tourists should be tucked in their hotel rooms for the night. She barely slowed at the turn onto King's Highway, not at all at the turn onto PCH. Wind rushed by her open window as fast as her thoughts. She picked up and discarded sickening scenarios one after another.

Bear... Please, let him be all right. I'll go back to being a bank manager—anything, just let him be all right.

Panic scrabbled in her chest like a crazed rat in a trap, trying to get out.

And Mark, too.

A record-breaking ten minutes later, she ran to the lights of the ER, a beacon in the dark. When the automatic door didn't open fast enough, she had to put a palm against it to stop her momentum, but it threw her off balance and she ended up staggering to the desk.

A young blonde woman looked up, startled. "Are you all right? Are you hurt?"

"No, it's not me." She took a breath. "Brenda…" *Shit, what's her last name?* "Mark…" *What the hell is his last name?*

"Let me see if I can help you." The woman consulted her computer screen.

A swinging door pushed open by a man in scrubs gave her a view of the treatment area beyond. She caught a glimpse of Brenda, sitting on a table, holding an ice bag to her head before the door closed again.

"Never mind, I see her." Hope jogged for the door.

"You can't go in there!"

Brenda's hair was disheveled, and the ice bag couldn't hide a bruise spreading along her cheek. But what frightened Hope more was the defeat in the line of her slumped shoulders, the way her hand hung lifeless, its pallor matching the paper sheet it rested on.

"Brenda."

When she looked up, Hope's heart stuttered. She'd seen those eyes in photos of crash survivors.

"It's all my fault."

The paper crinkled when Hope rested a hip on the table. She put a steadying arm around Brenda's shoulders. "Are you okay?"

"Yeah, the doctor released me. I'm just waiting for word on Mark."

"Tell me what happened."

The story gushed out almost faster than Hope could absorb it. When the last few words dribbled out, she sagged against Hope's shoulder, depleted. "Mark's in surgery. They're fixing his nose. Again." Bottom lip wobbling, Brenda lay the ice bag on the table. "I'm done with Phil." Her breath hitched. "Just so you know, no matter what happens, I'm never going back."

When Hope gathered her in her arms, Brenda sobbed as if her world was ending. And from Hope's experience, she knew that it was, in every way that mattered. She rubbed circles on Brenda's back, calming them both.

Bear. He'd lost it. Again. Dammit, when would he learn? Prison hadn't been enough? He'd ruined everything. Her emotions churned in a manic agitation cycle.

She understood now. It didn't matter that she knew he was capable of change. It didn't matter that she saw beneath the angry bear persona. It didn't matter that under all the damage, Douglas Steele was the best man she'd ever known.

He didn't believe in himself. He'd failed, because he never really tried. Bear would never forgive himself now, not after all he'd been through. Not after this.

Oh, yes, she was mad at him. Plenty mad. Mark had been through enough without this, and the fight had traumatized Brenda. But Hope's anger was only a layer of rancid fat over a deep vat of soul-sucking discouragement.

They were over. She knew Bear. There wouldn't be any tumultuous goodbye scene. He would slink back into his cave and roll a rock in front of it. She'd never hear from him again.

She could try to get in touch with him, but even if he answered the phone (which he most likely wouldn't), what would she say? All her logic, support and cajoling hadn't gotten him to budge before tonight's debacle. He sure wouldn't be listening now. She couldn't make him want to change enough to overcome his reticent personality, distorted tenfold by his guilt and fear.

She'd just have to learn to be okay with that. Somehow.

She grasped Brenda's shoulders and sat her up. "Come on, I'm taking you home."

Brenda shuddered under Hope's palms. "I'm not going back there—"

"No, I meant my place. You can stay with me tonight." A memory floated through her brain of a movie where a husband who stalked his wife… "Where's Phil?"

"I don't know. All I know is that he didn't come into the ER." Brenda slid off the table. "After Bear left, Phil rolled around on the ground for a while, moaning. Then he got up and hobbled away. He might have a couple of broken ribs. Serves him right."

"No argument here." Hope led her through the

swinging doors. "Why don't you check on Mark's condition? I've got to make a phone call."

When Brenda tottered away, Hope pulled out her phone. No call from Bear. Not that she'd expected one. She pushed his name on her favorites list and stared at the photo that came up of him, arms crossed, leaning against his Harley. She ran a fingernail along his jawline, down his chiseled biceps, while listening to the tinny ring. At the fourth, she put the phone to her ear.

"You've reached Bear Steele, of The Gaudy Widow Custom Paint Shop. Leave a message. I'll call you back."

She was so busy listening to that deep, barking voice that the beep startled her. "I'm not sure why I'm calling, since you probably won't even listen to this. I guess I just can't let this go without saying goodbye." She stepped to the window to get out of the flow of traffic, and try to channel the peace of the night outside. "I'm so mad at you, but for more than the reason you think." She took a breath in slow, to calm the jitters in her voice. "You have such a capacity for giving. I don't understand why you fight against it so hard. But that's not what I wanted to say." What the hell *did* she want to say? She put a finger in her ear to block the noise around her, but it didn't help, because only silence echoed up from inside. "I just wish I could take you inside my head, so you can see the Doug Steele that I know. He's pretty amazing. But I learned tonight that what I know doesn't matter. It only matters what you know." She saw Brenda's reflection coming toward her in the glass. "I guess I just wanted to tell you to have a good life."

How to end this? How do you say goodbye to the best thing you'd ever found? Brenda tapped her on the shoulder. She held up a finger, trying to think of something to say—a blinding spotlight of insight so brilliant that Bear would have to see the solution. It was so damned easy...

But wasn't this as impossible as Brenda trying to find the right words so Phil would never hit her again?

Yeah, it was. She was a fool. Time to end this. She sniffed, then breathed into the phone, "Bye. I love you."

She hit End.

"You know it's not Bear's fault, right?" Brenda looked worried, but also, changed. Maybe it was the way she carried herself. She'd always looked uncomfortable in her own skin. Now, as if she'd decided to inhabit it fully, it seemed to fit her better. "Bear saved me, you know. He was wonderful. I've seen Phil mad before, but not like this. I've never stood up to him before. He was out of control. I'm afraid to think of what would have happened if he and Mark hadn't been there." She shook her head, as if to dislodge the thought. "Mark knows what happened was an accident. He told me in his car, on the way over."

"I know." Hope longed to give in to the despondency that tugged at her. To fall into her bed and rail against the unfairness of it. To wallow for a time, and mourn her loss.

But she had miles to go, first. She sighed, and draped her arm over Brenda's shoulder. "Let's get you somewhere warm and safe."

Brenda put her arm around Hope's waist, and together they walked out of the hospital. "Like Scarlett O'Hara says, 'Tomorrow is another day.'"

HOPE STOOD IN the shower the next morning, attempting to get the water hot enough to ease the ache of her restless night. She'd stopped in at Opaline's when they got back from the hospital, to introduce Brenda, and ended up sitting at the kitchen table, drinking hot chocolate while Brenda told her story.

She and Brenda had lain on opposite sides of the bed, each to their own thoughts. Brenda's breathing had evened out into sleep hours before Hope had managed it. Her dreams had been dark and restless: of being ancient and alone in a run-down old folks' home; Brenda, spattered in blood; Bear, running in the dark, pursued by demons.

Bear. Her heart pinched. She missed him already. Maybe, just maybe, he'd hear her voice mail, and call. No. He wouldn't. She ran her hand down her soap-slicked side. Her skin tingled, missing him, too.

Stop it.

Thoughts like that weren't going to help. Besides, she had to look forward, not back. Sometime soon, she was going to have to decide on a new career. Work was getting to seem more like, well, work, every day.

Fifteen minutes later, she walked down the stairs, buttoning her khaki uniform blouse. Brenda sat at the small kitchen table, in underwear and Hope's borrowed T-shirt, hair in a ponytail, drinking coffee from one of the two mugs on the table. An inch-wide bruise ran from her hairline to her chin.

Brenda looked up from the pad of paper in front of her. "Good morning."

"What'cha doing?" she said in a cheery voice that sounded fake to her own ears. She slid into the chair, and picked up the steaming cup in front of her. "Thanks for making coffee."

"The least I can do." Brenda dropped her forehead into her palm and stared at the list. "I'm trying to assess and prioritize. It's not pretty."

"You're not rethinking your decision to leave Phil, are you?"

"Oh, hell, no." Her nose wrinkled. "It's just…
Here, let me read you the list. I have: no job, no
money, no credit, no car, nowhere to live, few
skills, and I need a divorce."

"And a restraining order," Hope said.

"Right." Brenda made a note, then dropped
her head onto her folded arms.

Hope patted her forearm "Buck up, hon. I'll
research how to get a restraining order at work
today over lunch, and I'll think about the other
items. I'll bet we can come up with some answers. And don't forget, tomorrow is Monday.
Bina will be able to help, too."

Brenda jumped at the timid knock at the door.

Hope glimpsed her landlady through the curtains. "Morning. The door's open."

Opaline stepped in, arms full of rabbit. "Buckwheat wanted to stop by and say hello." She
crossed the room and handed the bunny over.

Hope settled him in her lap. He took up much
more of it than he had a month ago. "Only for a
minute, dude, I've got to get to work."

"How are you feeling today?" Opaline patted
Brenda's shoulder.

Hope could see an agenda brewing. She may
have a bun of white hair, but Opaline's eyes didn't
miss a thing.

"I'm good."

"Why don't you come over and…how do you young people say… 'hang with me' today?"

"Thanks, but I'll be fine here. I've got a lot of thinking to do." Brenda stared down at her list.

"Well, to tell you the truth, I came over to ask a favor."

Did that old lady just bat her eyelashes? Hope petted Buckwheat and watched the master at work.

"The friends of the library are having a garage sale next weekend, and I promised them some things to sell. But the stairs to the attic are very steep, and my old hip…"

Brenda hopped up. "Oh, of course. I'd be more than happy to help."

Hope chuckled, "You might want to think about putting some pants on first. *Mi* closet *es tu* closet, *amiga*." She stood, gave Buckwheat a kiss on his soft head, and handed him to Opaline. "I've got to go. You two enjoy your day."

CRASH!

His bare feet slapped the floor and he was in the hallway by the time he realized he was awake. "What the fuck was that?" The sound had seemed to come from down the hall… Bear stepped into the sun-drenched kitchen.

A section of his new cabinets had fallen off the wall, hit the countertop and splintered. "Christ in a sidecar." He could only hope it hadn't cracked the granite countertop underneath. He tiptoed through the fragments to see what had caused his latest disaster.

He checked the time on the oven. Nine o'clock. He never slept late. Of course, he usually got to sleep before three, but it had taken hours to walk back to his truck last night.

Is Mark dead? Where did Brenda stay last night? Did she go back to Phil? The splinter lodged in his heart stabbed deep. *Does Hope know what happened?*

It didn't matter. On that long walk, he'd decided. He was giving up on civilization; he was obviously incapable of it.

He was going back to his cave, to hibernate forever.

That is, if the cops didn't show up. If they did, his cave would have bars on it.

He swept off the ledge by the sink with the side of his hand and hopped up to get a close-up view. The boards that had held the cabinet had broken away. He could see the dry rot that had caused the failure. He'd been in a hurry, and figured if the boards had held all these years, they'd hold for more. "Steele, you are an idiot." He slammed his fist against the wall, not caring that it went through the wallboard. The new cabinets he was going to have to buy would cover it. He pulled out his hand and shook it off.

That's what happens when you try to build without a good foundation. People still saw through the pretty paint to the beater underneath. Given enough Bondo and bullshit, it'd pass muster with most people. You can mask what's underneath for quite a while. But eventually...

He jumped from the counter and retraced his steps to the bedroom to put on jeans, a T-shirt and some shoes. Tying his last shoelace, he noticed his phone on the floor. He'd turned it off last night. He picked it up and ran his thumb over the on button.

No, that's over.

He crammed it in his back pocket and walked back to the kitchen. He opened the back door and heaved the broken cabinets down the back steps. He'd been lucky. There were scratches in the granite, but they could be buffed out. He got a broom from the pantry and started sweeping.

If anyone had left messages, he was deleting them without listening anyway. He was cutting ties with all those people. Except for the kid. The kid accepted Bear for who and what he was. And besides, there was still that atonement thing.

Through the doorway to the dining room, he glimpsed his angel on the wall. She looked disappointed.

You have truly and completely lost it now, Steele.

He turned away and swept the splinters out of the door. It was past time he got to work. After all, he was going to have to earn enough to buy new cabinets, goddammit. He opened the door and stepped out on the porch. Except for the birds tittering in the trees, and a squirrel that chattered at him from halfway up the maple, the yard was deserted.

"Just the way I like it." He pulled the door closed, then opened it again, turned the lock, and pulled it closed.

He never had been great at lying to himself.

Halfway to the barn he stopped, threw his head back, and yelled at the innocent blue sky. "Aaaargh!" He pulled his phone from his back pocket and turned it on. He'd listen, then be done with it.

Hell, probably nobody even—

Two voice mails.

He stood holding his phone as if it was the detonator to an IED. He pushed the button.

"Dude!"

Mark's nasal voice stopped his feet.

"Just wanted you to know I'b okay. Dey made me another new dose." Mark's mouth-breathing came heavy. "Don't worry about Phil. He crawled away like a cockroach. If he pressed charges he'd have to adbit to beating his wife." He paused, and said, quieter, "I just wanted to thank you. I neber got to star in a action bovie before. Neber got to be a hero before either.

"So I guess I'll see you at group huh? Later." *Click.*

A flush of relief hit, loosening muscles he hadn't realized were taut. Then he remembered. He didn't care anymore.

The next number, he knew by heart. Bracing for a blow, he pressed the button with a shaking finger.

Hope's voice flowed over him, calming his pain like butter on a burn. He soaked it in, savoring the sound of the voice, knowing it would be the last time he'd hear it.

Except for all the times he'd replay this message.

The second time through, he listened to the words, knowing he couldn't accept what they offered, but incredibly grateful for them, nonetheless. He hurt people, even when he didn't mean to. Hope was too good, too precious to suffer at his hands. He'd have the memories of his angel. It was more than he deserved.

Careful not to delete it, he turned off the phone and walked to the barn.

CHAPTER TWENTY

NERVOUS, BUT FOR different reasons, she and Brenda walked into the meeting room of the hospital the next day. Hope misjudged, and hit her shoulder on the door frame on the way through.

One chair stood vacant.

You knew he wouldn't be here.

Hope felt the edges of the hole where Bear used to be—in the room as well as inside her. The wrinkled balloon of hope in her chest wheezed out its last precious gasp, as reality settled in. Bear had retreated to a place where she couldn't follow. The empty balloon filled, this time with sadness. She wouldn't see him again. Oh, maybe someday, months from now, they'd pass on the street, or in a store. This was a small town, after all. His eyes would look past her, as if she didn't exist.

With a sigh, she sank onto his usual chair. The cold hard seat held no comfort.

Seeing Mark's and Brenda's bruises, Bina's mouth twisted. "From the looks of you, things did not go as planned. I think you better tell me what happened."

If Brenda looked as though she'd been in a tussle, Mark looked as if he'd fought for the heavyweight title—and lost. A clear plastic guard sheltered his new nose, but both eyes were black, swollen almost shut and white packing peeked from his nostrils. But he was smiling. "Bear was Jean-Claude Van Dabe, and I was Chuck Dorris. No, he was Rocky, and I was—"

Bina held up a hand. "Brenda, maybe you'd better tell me."

Brenda told the brutal story, with interjections from Mark that made it sound almost like an adventure. By the end, though her voice was shaky, her shoulders were back and for the first time, she didn't avoid people's eyes. "I'm so grateful to Bear, Mark and Hope." When she flipped her hair over her shoulder, the vertical bruise was dark on her white skin. "I'm grateful to you all, really. I'm not sure things ever would have changed if I hadn't come here. See, when you're cut off from other people, and the only person left gives you his opinion at the top of his lungs, your own opinion gets very small. You learn to back off, to let someone else be in charge of your life." She shrugged. "I'm still scared. I have to start a whole new life, and I'm not sure how. But I know one thing. No matter how many mistakes I make, I *can't* do as bad a job as Phil did."

Bryan clapped, and they all joined in. "You go, girl."

When it was quiet again Bina said, "I am so proud of you, Brenda. You did a very brave thing. Why don't you stay after, and you and I can talk a bit about what you want your new life to look like." She turned to Mark. "That was a harrowing tale, Mark, and you paid the price. Do you want to explain to us why you're smiling?"

"Are you kidding? I was on my way to agoraphobia, so wrapped up in by own bisery, I forgot there was a life out there. That fight bade be realize dat, awful as this is—" he pointed to his face "—it's temporary. I'll get through the surgeries, and hopefully end up halfway normal looking. And then I'll have a life ahead of me." He shook his head. "I forgot that, somewhere along the way. If you're looking back, you can't see where you're going. That's how you end up crashing into a bridge abutment." He looked over at Brenda. "Don't you ever look back. If we keep butting one foot in front of the other, we'll end up sobewhere, right?"

Something about Brenda's blush made Hope wonder if maybe, somewhere down the road, Brenda and Mark might—

"Does anyone know where Bear is? Hope?"

"He's gone," she whispered. "He won't be back."

"Because he lost his temper again?" Bryan asked.

"That, and other things. He has issues that he's just too afraid to face." Her voice sounded hollow to her own ears. "He's a proud man. A good man. But until he's willing to face the demons that are chasing him, it won't matter."

"I have an idea." Bina tapped her pen against her teeth. "No one can make Bear drink, but I can make sure he comes to the trough. Let me work on that. In the meantime, how are you doing, Hope?"

"You mean aside from my love life, right? Because I just can't go into that right now."

"I want to go into that," Bryan piped up.

Bina gave Hope a long considering look. "Okay, aside from that."

Great. She didn't really want to go into anything else, either. She pushed down her doubts and tightened her muscles, to hold the squirming little buggers. "I've thought about it, and I'm recommitting to my career."

Bina's eyebrows went up. "Why is recommitment required?"

"Well, my job has been getting kind of…boring." When the word she hadn't let herself name just popped out of her mouth, she wished she could take it back. "I mean, not that, but… I like learning about the sports. I do. It's just…"

"You feel unfulfilled?" Bina asked.

"Yes. No." *How do you explain something if you don't understand, yourself?* "Look. I was always the good little girl, with an overbearing mother. I was who she wanted me to be, even after she died. It took the robbery for me to pull my head out and see what *I* wanted. And I chose. I just need to calm down, live life and stop second-guessing myself. If you vacillate and jump around all your life, you'll never get anywhere."

"What?" Mark jumped in. "Your first career wadn't eben your choice. Dis one was. And it's not right. So whad? Go find what bakes you happy."

She ran a hand through her hair. "God, you sound like Bear."

"Dat bakes us both right."

Bina asked, "Hope, why is it so important that this job be the right one for you?"

"Because." She gritted her teeth. "I gave up a degreed position on the fast track for this. It was what I wanted. Now I'm going to make it work."

Bina shook her head. "But, Hope—"

She put a hand to her pounding temple. "Can we leave it at that for now? I don't feel well."

AFTER WORK ON FRIDAY, Hope walked into a quiet house.

"Brenda? Where are you?"

Funny how only a week ago, she hadn't noticed being alone. Now the rooms echoed with hollow emptiness that struck a familiar chord inside her.

All week, Brenda had been helping Opaline clean out her closets during the day, but she'd always been home by dinnertime. Some nights, she'd even cooked dinner.

Monday after work, she and Brenda had gone to the courthouse to get a restraining order. They walked out with a piece of paper that may physically cover Brenda's ass, but Hope had no illusions about its power to do so, if Phil discovered where she was living.

They also made a side trip on the way home. Brenda now had her own cell phone; one that Phil couldn't track her with.

Hope wanted to help. After all, she had money coming in, a stable job and a home. Brenda had nothing.

She crossed the room, got down a glass from the cupboard, pulled open the refrigerator door and poured herself a glass of iced tea. She sipped it with the door open, letting the cold air cool her sweaty legs. Summer had roared in the past week, sending temps into the low nineties.

I'll bet it's hot in that barn.

She was distracted at work to the point that Travis had asked her if everything was all right. She answered with a yes of a recent widow—the equivalent of "of course not, but what good does it do to talk about it?"

Was he suffering, too? Was he still working with Nacho, or had he cut *all* ties? She'd eaten lunch at the drugstore diner where Nacho's sister Priss worked, three times this week, hoping to run into her so she could ask about Bear. No luck.

She jumped when the phone buzzed. She closed her eyes while she fished it out of her pocket, *willing* Bear's photo to be displayed on the screen. When Brenda's photo came up instead, her galloping heartbeat didn't slow. "Where are you? Are you all right?"

"I'm fine, don't worry. Opaline, that's enough garlic already!" There was some rustling on the line. "Hey, your very sweet landlady has invited us to dinner. Change your clothes, and come on over."

She let out a breath filled with relief. "I'll be there in five."

The smell of spaghetti sauce and garlic bread hit Hope before she'd stepped onto the back porch. She tapped on the screen door. "Knock, knock."

Brenda said, "You'd better get in here, before Opaline feeds the salad to the rabbits."

They laughed through dinner. Opaline entertained them with stories of the old days in Widow's Grove, and her life with her husband, Virgil. It was past dark when Brenda stood and started stacking dirty dishes.

Opaline reached over and patted Brenda's hand. "Please, sit. That can wait. I need to talk to you girls."

Hope settled back in her chair. "That sounds serious."

Brenda sank onto her seat, looking as if her name had just been called in the dentist's office.

"I've been thinking." Opaline fingered the napkin in her lap. "You both know this big house is getting to be more than I can handle. And though it pains me to admit it, no one on my side of ninety should still have a driver's license." She sighed. "I need some help."

Brenda said, "I love helping you, Opaline. Once I get a job, I'll come over every night and help if you need it."

Hope jumped in. "And I can help, too. Between the two of us—"

"You don't understand. I'm looking for someone full-time, to clean, drive me to the grocery store, run errands, things like that." She glanced across the table to Brenda. "I'd be willing to pay you in room and board, as well as a small salary."

Her little eyes sparkled. "Enough to divorce that SOB you're married to."

"I couldn't." Brenda's brows scrunched and she looked to Hope for help. They both knew Opaline couldn't afford that.

Hope thought fast. "You don't need to worry; we'd both be happy to help."

"You girls don't think I can afford it." Opaline gave a little wind-chime laugh. "Hon, at one time Virgil owned most of the land that's now downtown Widow's Grove. He sold high, and invested wisely." She made dismissive waves with her tiny hands "I have no heirs. I have more money than I have things to spend it on."

Hope glanced around, at the 1960s Formica table they'd eaten on, at the dip in the worn linoleum in front of the sink, at the tired, sagging cabinets.

Opaline's wavery voice brought her attention back. "I don't keep the house like this because I don't have the money to fix it. I keep it like this because this is the way it was when Virgil was alive." She lifted her napkin to her nose and sniffed. "But maybe I'm ready to move on now." She gave Brenda a soft, shaky smile. "So what do you think? Will you take the job?"

"I don't know what to say." Brenda looked a bit weepy herself. "You really mean it? You're not doing this out of charity?"

Opaline patted her hand. "If a blessing goes both ways, doesn't that make it even better?"

"In that case—" Brenda held out her hand to shake "—I would be honored. And thank you, you are the answer to my prayers."

Hope ran a finger under her lower eyelashes. How could her heart be so full and ache so, all at the same time?

WHEN THE QUARTER panel of the 'vette blurred, Bear shut off the sander, shoved his safety glasses to the top of his head and palmed the sweat from his eyes.

Son of a bitch it's hot.

The small flakes of metal-flake gold paint stuck to the damp skin of his exposed forearms, sparkling in the spot lamps. His huge warehouse fan was set on high, but it was doing a better job blowing dust around than cooling him off. He'd have loved to take a break, go to the house and get a cool shower. But he knew within a half hour he'd be pacing, looking for something to do. He'd never been a couch potato to begin with, but lately if he didn't stay busy, his mind kicked into overdrive, tormenting him with film clip memories: riding the motorcycle; Hope's warm hands resting on his thighs, reclined on the blanket at the concert in the park, bestowing her enigmatic smile. Moonlight through the skylight, spilling over her bed, turning her hair to platinum.

He ripped the bandanna off his head. It was more than that, wasn't it? She was kind and caring, and giving…the hollow place in his chest ached all the time now like a bad tooth, rendering him incapable of ignoring it for more than a few minutes at a time.

She had loved him, even knowing what he was capable of. She loved him for the man she saw inside him. The man he'd *wanted* to be. He ran his hands through his damp hair. The man he could have been.

He walked to stand in front of the fan. It didn't help much. She'd ruined everything. The little part of the world he'd carved out for himself was no longer a cozy refuge from the world. Somehow when he wasn't looking it had morphed to a cold and lonely place that was beginning to have more in common with his last home—at the Men's Colony.

Shit, he was even starting to miss the people in that losers' group.

The plan had been to go back to his cave, but his cave was no longer there. He had nowhere to go—no way to move forward. He was stuck in a limbo of his own making.

This bear had made his own trap. Any moment his hands weren't busy he paced back and forth in front of the bars, wanting out…wanting in…wanting…

"Hello, Douglas? You in there?" A man's voice came from the front of the barn.

Even if Bear hadn't recognized the voice, there was only one man who called him by his given name. Sweat that had nothing to do with the heat popped on his upper lip. "Back here. Follow the path through the boxes."

Yeah, because I don't have enough shit in my life.

Bear's probation officer rounded the last corner and stepped into the work area. "Whew, it's hotter than the hubs of hell in here."

"Where else would the devil work?" Bear mumbled under his breath. "Look, if you're here about Phil…"

"Phil who?" He pulled a handkerchief from his back pocket and blotted his forehead.

Way to go, Steele, build yourself another trap. "He's nobody. Why are you here?" He made himself still. Only guilty men fidgeted.

"Believe me, I've got better things to do. I've tried calling you three times, I left messages. You didn't call back." The man trailed his fingers down the curve of the Corvette's fender as if it was a woman's thigh. "Damned fine hunk of metal. '74?"

"The body is fiberglass. And it's a '72."

"Regardless, toys like that are beyond this state's salary." He sighed.

Bear locked his knees to keep from pacing. "Did you come to talk cars?"

"No, I did not. I came out here to inform you that you've broken the condition of your probation." He took another swipe at his forehead with a handkerchief, then looked Bear square in the face. "We had a deal. You were to attend—"

"I did!" Bear threw up his hands. "I went to every damned meeting for more than two months. What more do you want out of me?"

"Hey, it isn't me. I got a phone call from the psychologist who runs it. She told me that you're not done." He shook his head. "Until she signs off that your anger issues don't pose a threat to society, your attendance there is mandatory."

Damn busybody, Bina. Frustration that had been simmering for a week boiled over. He reared back and kicked the 'vette's tire hard as he could.

"And from the looks of things—" the officer arched one brow "—I agree with her. You are to report to those meetings twice a week until further notice. If you don't show, I have no choice but to get a bench warrant for your arrest."

Bear putting himself in a cage was one thing. Having someone else force him in and lock the door made him want to punch something. He grumbled a few choice words under his breath.

"I mean it, Doug. Don't make me come back out here with a sheriff's deputy."

Maybe he could call Bina, talk to her one-on-one. It would avoid the hurt—his own, but more importantly, everyone else's.

"You hearing me?"

"Yeah, I hear you." Maybe if he—

"And turn on your goddamned phone. I don't have time for this shit." He turned and walked out.

BEAR SPENT THE entire weekend dreading Monday. Like a maze with no openings, it hadn't taken him long to squirm his way through every scenario and realize there was no way out. Unless he wanted to go back to prison. And deep in the night, after waking sweaty and panicked from another nightmare, that actually seemed a viable option.

But when the sun crept over the windowsill, he realized that, though he may not have much left, everything he did have was more precious for its scarcity. If he went back to jail, he would miss his house, his business, his land. But of the few things that still remained, he'd miss Nacho most. It turned out that atonement *was* good for the soul. The kid looked up to him for who he was, for what he knew. Nacho had potential as an artist, too. He didn't deserve what life had thrown at him already and if Bear abandoned him, it could be the straw that tipped the scales into delinquency.

Besides, how cool would it be to watch the kid grow up?

Screw it. He'd go, put in his time and go back to his original plan—keep his mouth shut and run through the doors that would lead him to freedom. The doors he'd really wanted, the ones that led to Hope, were already locked to him. The freedom to be alone was all that was left.

He rolled out of bed and padded to the bathroom, and a shower. After, he used the towel to clear the steam off the mirror, but no amount of wiping would remove the red, or the dread, from his eyes. He picked up the clippers and ran his fingers over his short stubbled beard. "What the hell." No need to shave any longer. A hairy face would give him more camouflage from the world. It was why he'd grown the heavy beard to begin with.

He put down the clippers and picked up his brush. A flash of silver stopped his hand. His gut clenched as a howling wind whipped around the hollow place in his chest.

He lifted a strand of white-blond hair from the bristles. It wasn't long, but when he lifted it to the light, it was almost iridescent. Lowering it to his nose, he inhaled, trying to catch the scent of her. Suddenly, he felt Hope's spirit, as if she were in the room with him—all around him. For the first time in weeks, his restlessness calmed, and the wind in his chest lay down. A relief so strong it weakened his knees, and he leaned into the counter to brace himself as he carefully wrapped the delicate hair around his huge finger and walked to the kitchen.

The past two weeks he'd spent in hell, missing her, trying to go back to before by stitching the huge hole in his life closed. It wasn't working—in truth, it had been doomed from the start.

The static had quieted, leaving his mind scoured clean. For the first time since his fight in the parking lot, he felt as if he could think. He stepped into the kitchen, and out of habit glanced through the door to the dining room. The morning sun formed a rectangle of gold that spotlighted his angel's gentle, Mona Lisa smile.

He stopped, stunned to stillness as an answer came crashing into him like a comet from the heavens. In all his maze wandering, he'd overlooked the simplest answer. *The* answer.

His old solitary life was in the past. He was no longer that man. All that remained to discover was what man was he going to be now.

When you've tried everything, the only thing left to try is the impossible.

The knots he'd tied himself into loosened, then

unraveled. What did a man who'd lost everything have to fear? He had nothing at risk.

Except maybe his pride. But like a lone falling tree in a forest, a solitary man had no need of pride.

He threw his head back and laughed. It was so simple. The walls in his mind came down, letting in the warmth of the sun. Hope found a footing in his scoured chest and unfurled, filling it.

He walked through the doorway and across the room, raised his fingers to his lips, and touched them to his angel's lips. "I don't know who sent you, or why. But thank you."

Then he strode to his bedroom to dress. He was going to find his future. Today, of all days, he couldn't be late.

CHAPTER TWENTY-ONE

NOTHING TO LOSE, nothing to lose, nothing to lose.

The words raced past in an endless loop, like the white lines ticking by the bike's front tire. Bear's muscles twitched when he upshifted and he missed a gear.

So what does a man who has nothing to lose got to be nervous about?

He pulled the clutch and slammed down a gear.

The answer was there, as if it had been locked in his brain waiting for him to ask the question.

Hope.

The emotion? Or the woman?

Both.

All the chances he'd wasted. All the times he'd turned away. All the opportunities he'd walked past.

All the fuckups.

He had no right to one more chance. He knew that.

Still, he hoped.

Slowing for the turn into the hospital's crowded parking lot, he cruised the rows and got lucky. He snagged an opening front and center.

Maybe it's an omen.

"If I'm to the point of depending on omens, I am in deep shit." Dropping the bike on the side stand, he shut it down, threw his leg over and unbuckled his helmet.

Who was he kidding? He'd been in deep shit since the day he'd seen that white-blond hair and followed it down to the beautiful face of his angel.

He dropped his helmet in the side bag and, stomach bouncing like a car with no shocks, forced his feet toward the door.

Thanks to having to stop at the restroom for one last nervous pee, the meeting had already started by the time he got there. He stood in the doorway, his heart banging hard enough to throw a rod. Before he could hesitate and potentially chicken out, he strode in.

Bryan said, "When friends invite me out now, I make myself go, as long as it's not anywhere that Curtis and I…"

Bear crossed the room and sat in the only open chair, beside Bina. Heat shot through him as the group's attention lasered in, burning his skin like the sun through a magnifying glass.

Bina ignored him, and nodded to Bryan. "Go on."

"My friends are sweet and supportive, and I'm very grateful for them, but…"

Bryan's words faded to white noise when

Bear's self-consciousness receded enough for him to focus—on Hope. He drank her in like an alkie on a bender as the odd peace he always felt in her presence stole over him, and his heart slowed. What a fool he'd been. How had he ever thought he could walk away from this woman?

She studiously avoided looking at him, but that was okay. He'd come here to have his say. At least that way, he could take away some peace of his own. He forced his eyes and his attention on to the next in the circle, and took a blunt force hit at the sight of Mark's face. The clear plastic guard didn't hide his purple-fading-to-green bruises, on his nose or under his eyes. Bear wanted to turn away, but he made himself look. To take responsibility.

"Thanks for sharing, Bryan." Bina's voice broke into his thoughts. "I think you're on the right track. I'm proud that you're going out, even if you have to make yourself do it in the beginning. Mark can relate to that."

"I'm not saying it gets easier, but you kinda get used to it after a while. Good work, dude," Mark said, and held up his hand for a high five.

Bryan's hand slap ended up in an over-the-head "bro-shake."

"So, Bear. Good to have you back." Bina's attention ambushed him. "How are you?"

No more fidgeting, no more nerves. It was

time. He closed his eyes, dropped his fear, his shields and his pride. He opened his heart, then his eyes—looking around the circle. "I'm pissed."

Bryan did that double-leg-cross thing. "Now there's a news flash." Sarcasm dripped onto the tile floor. "Could we take a break so I could alert the media?"

"You." Bear stabbed a finger at Bryan. "I've been pissed at you from the beginning." Bryan flinched.

"You thought it was because you're gay, but it wasn't. It was because I was jealous."

The kid's mouth dropped.

"You're secure and proud, and you don't give a crap what anybody thinks. You wear who you are on the outside of your clothes, and you paid the price for it—a price higher than anyone should have to pay."

An expectant silence hung as heavy as humidity in the air.

"You're flamboyant, irritating and very brave. *That's* why I was pissed at you. I sat here listening, week after week, wishing I had half the guts of a little redheaded gay dude." He stuck out a hand. "I've learned a lot from you about not hiding who and what you are, or apologizing for it."

Bryan wavered a moment, scanning Bear's face, looking for a trap. Then he shook Bear's hand.

"See? I told you. You are brave." Bear smiled, careful to keep his grip gentle.

One down, and you didn't die. Yet. He made himself ignore the internal magnet that pulled him to look at Hope. If he did, he'd remember that he had a ton to lose, and chicken out. He forced his eyes on the next in line, Brenda.

"You. I was pissed at you, too. I thought you didn't care enough about yourself to leave your husband. Turns out I was wrong about that, too."

Brenda looked like a spotlighted deer.

"They say the things that bother you the most about other people are things you need to fix in yourself. You were being battered by someone else—I was doing it to myself." For the first time since he'd known Brenda she held his stare. "I think my error was bigger than yours. After all, you didn't know for sure if Phil was going to hit you again. I knew very well what I was going to do to myself."

With every crumb of truth he spoke, tiny bit by tiny bit the weight on his soul lightened. But it didn't mean he felt good—his shoulders always could carry more than most. And the test still waited at the end. He had no idea if he was smart enough to pass it.

Mark was next.

"I was pissed at you because I thought you were weak. I was wrong there, too. You were just a normal, everyday guy who, in one moment of desperation, made a mistake and took the only way out that you could see. If *you* could do that, there's nothing to say I couldn't get to that point."

Keep talking. Keep talking. You stop now, and all this is for nothing.

"That scared the living crap out of me."

Mark's unscarred eyebrow disappeared into his bangs. "You? Scared?"

"Yeah. But now you're going out. I've witnessed some of the rude stares you get from ignorant people. Still, you continue to do it. I'm in awe of that kind of guts."

Mark smiled. It made him hideous and beautiful all at the same time.

Hope was next, but Bear forced his eyes past her, to settle on Bina, instead.

"I gave you so much shit. I didn't want to be here, and I took it out on you." He waved a hand, indicating the entire group. "I took it out on all of you. I walked in that first day, resentful." He leaned his forearms on his knees. "You were just losers—a messed up bunch of misfits." When he caught himself looking at the floor, he forced his head up. "I kept telling myself I didn't belong here, because then I didn't have to look at my own shit." Self-censure came out as a dusty dry chuckle. "Okay, I thought I was a loser, too. But at least I had the pride not to blurt it out in front of a bunch of strangers." He shook his head. "So I sat back and watched you all fall to pieces. But then, the strangest thing happened. You each picked up the shards, and put yourselves back together. It was like you chose carefully, and left out the faulty pieces, the weak links and the person you made was stronger than the one who fell apart."

"So that's why I came here today. Not because the state, or you, Bina, said I had to." He took a deep breath held it for a few heartbeats before letting it out slowly, in an attempt to calm the bugs that raced along his nerves. To ready himself. "I came here to tell you my story. I owe you all that. And I think… I might owe *me* that." This time when he realized he was staring at the floor he didn't look up; turned out he wasn't quite that brave. "I told you before, I was an army sniper in Afghanistan…"

Truth unwound from deep in his core and spun out through his mouth, like a spool of thread, freely, faultless, filterless.

HAVING HEARD THE story before, Hope was able to let the horror of the words flow around her, focusing instead on the man. She knew that for an experience to cause such damage, a person would have to have bone-deep integrity. To be able to face what he'd done took brutal honesty.

For an intensely private man like Bear to say it out loud, took incredible courage.

But then, she'd always known Bear was a good man. Bear didn't know. *That* was the problem.

When his words trailed off, the room sat in stunned silence, horror reflected in the faces of her friends around the circle. A silence she desperately wanted to fill with words. Words that would exonerate him and absolve him of guilt. But she'd already tried that. It didn't work. So she locked her jaw, sealed her lips to an impenetrable line and swallowed the words that crawled up her throat. She made herself hold stock-still with squirming unease.

No matter how this came out, no matter that he'd spoken to everyone in the room but her, she was so proud of this brave, beautiful man.

He finally looked up from his clasped hands, his eyes moist with pain. "My career cost many people their lives. I did my job. I can live with that. But my *mistakes* cost two people their lives. I'm owning that. Out loud." He straightened, his shoulders and chin rising to a crisp military line. "I learned a lot from you all, but I think the most important is, to be true to who you are—all of who you are—because that's the only shot you have to let go. To be free to become who you *want* to be." His chest rose with a deep breath. "At least, that's what I hope."

For the first time since he'd begun talking, his eyes found hers. Her heart took one heavy thud, then skittered in rushing rabbit beats that pounded the base of her neck.

"See, I know the man I want to be. I know him, because I've seen him, in your eyes." He stood, crossed the circle and she felt his shadow slide over her. But she looked away; the unease, impelled to panic, raced in the endless loop of her bloodstream. His gratitude wasn't what she wanted, but it would have to be enough. It wouldn't help to—

He lowered himself to his knees before her. She had to look up, to face him. His courage demanded no less.

"I hurt you. Wanting to keep us a secret, you must have thought I was ashamed of you, of us." He raised his hand and skimmed the backs of his fingers down her cheek, barely brushing the downy hairs there. "How could I be ashamed of an angel?"

A corner of his mouth lifted in a smile so sad, it tore something in her chest.

"I wasn't good enough. If anything, I was ashamed of taking what you offered, knowing I didn't deserve it—your forgiveness, your trust. Your love."

She gave in to the magnetic pull of his touch. Leaning her cheek against his fingers, she closed her eyes, taking in the essence of the man who'd made her realize how empty her life had been before he'd stepped into it.

"I don't know if I'll ever live up to be the man you've always seen. Maybe no man can be the man he sees in a good woman's eyes. But I want you to know that I'll spend the rest of my life trying."

The strong support in his hand was gone. She opened her eyes.

He squatted on the balls of his feet, forearms resting on his thighs. "I know I have no right to ask you for anything. But would you do me one favor?"

Confused and off balance, she could only nod.

"You had the guts to reject who your mother expected you to be. Don't fall into the same trap again, trying to be who you *think* you should be." A line appeared between his brows. "Hope Sanderson doesn't have to live up to anyone's expectations—even her own." His eyes caressed her face, as if memorizing it for when she was gone. "You're already...*everything.*"

At his last whispered word, she felt the *snick* of a lock's release deep in her chest. It loosed a blinding white light, exposing her mistake. Hope had chosen an opposite path, but when her mother was no longer there to browbeat her, Hope had picked up the stick and continued the lesson.

Bear was right. Her only limits had been those she'd put on herself. She could be anything she wanted. A warm, honeyed feeling of lightness—rightness spread through her, melting her tension and fear. She could choose any path she wanted.

And if it was her *true* path, she wouldn't stop to measure it with a stick—she'd run down it.

Her mouth stretched with a joy she couldn't hold in. "I'm not at adventurer." She spread her hands, palms up. "I'm a klutz who can't walk through a doorway without running into the frame. I only chose that because it was the opposite of what my mother wanted. I'm glad I tried it, but I've learned that just because you can get up the courage to do something, it doesn't mean that you should.

"I'm not sure what career I'll choose next, but I do know one thing." She reached over and took his hand, holding it in both of hers, grateful that he allowed it. "I choose you as my partner, Bear Steele."

The hope in his eyes gave her the courage to go on.

"Not the man you think I want you to be. Not for the man you aspire to be. Flawed, imperfect and afraid, introverted and reticent, I choose *you*." When her voice splintered, she stopped. Fully aware that her choice was only half of a whole, she refused to cheapen her offer with tears that could sway his decision.

Stripped naked, she waited.

His fingers twined with hers, and he stood, drawing her to her feet.

"I was wandering lost in a dark place. You are the angel I loved in my dreams, before I ever met you. You grabbed and shook me, making me see that I had a choice." He lowered his head until his breath whispered over her lips. "How could I not choose Hope?"

Then his lips were on hers, and everything else blew away.

EPILOGUE

Six months later

HOPE IN THE LEAD, the crowd streamed through the door of The Farmhouse Café, arms full of pink-and-blue wrapped boxes. By the time they all squeezed in, there wasn't a square inch of floor space.

A grizzled farmer rose from his chair beside the fire in the potbellied stove, walked to the window, and flipped the Open sign to Closed.

The door to the ladies' room opened, and Samantha Pinelli, the local builder and biker-chick, walked out, followed by Jesse.

"Happy Baby Party!" everyone yelled. The Farmhouse Café was the gathering place for the residents of Widow's Grove. Everyone in town knew Jesse, and she'd been a matchmaker to more than one wedding in town.

Jesse put a hand to her chest as her eyes got huge. Her chin wobbled. Her husband rushed over and took her elbow, putting an arm around her. "Do you need to sit down, Jess?"

"I'm fine, Carl. It's not like *I'm* pregnant."

The crowd laughed, and he led her to the counter and sat her on a barstool.

"I'm just flabbergasted." Her eyes narrowed. "Hope Sanderson, did you do this?"

Hope raised her hands in surrender. "Hey, wasn't my idea. Though I did help."

Jess's blond hair was piled high, her white waitress dress hugged her curves, and her dancer's calves were set off in strappy heels. She may not have been pregnant, but she was glowing. A high school girl in LA with big college plans was due to give birth any day, and the adoption agency had told the Jurgens the paperwork was a mere formality. Jesse would finally have a baby.

"I should have known." Jesse turned the glare on Sam. "This has Pinelli written all over it."

Sam, in her signature ratty jeans, tank top and leather jacket, sank onto the next stool and bumped shoulders with Jess. "Hey, I owe you one, after you did my Victorian Christmas party."

"Yeah, but the only surprise *then* was your engagement!"

"So sue me." She pulled Jesse into a one-armed hug.

Jesse stood. "Oh, ya'll sit down, you're making me fidgety. I'll get the coffee."

Hope stepped to the counter. "You sit. This is your baby party. We brought the cake, and we'll take turns pouring coffee." She turned to the crowd. "Everyone, if you'll put your gifts on the bar, we'll get started."

A decent portion of Widow's Grove's population filed past, leaving packages like gifts from the Magi.

Hope said, "Bear, would you mind pouring coffee?"

"On my way." He walked behind the counter, grabbed the coffeepot and a fistful of cups.

Jess watched him with a soft smile. "Who would've guessed that my little cousin would turn out to be a bear tamer?"

Hope's face heated. She rearranged packages to have something to do with her hands. "Oh, he's always been a teddy bear. He just had the world's best disguise."

A wavery voice came from behind her. "Well, if I were thirty years younger, I wouldn't mind hibernating the winter away with him. He's a hunk."

When Hope turned, Opaline thrust a package into her hands. "Jess, dear, I brought your baby a little tea set, but this one's for Hope. You don't mind, do you?"

"Of course not. Thank you, Opaline." Jess patted the barstool on the other side of her. "Hope, you sit right here and open it."

It was an old hatbox, pink-and-raspberry-striped silk, tied with a huge raspberry bow. "Opaline, what in the world?"

Brenda came alongside the old lady, taking her elbow and whispering in her ear. The makeover Hope and Jesse had given her transformed the former mouse. Brenda's feathery short cut framed her square face and the highlights showed off her light brown eyes.

Opaline nodded and shooed her away.

Brenda had a bit of a glow herself as she walked to the table where Mark had saved her a seat. His last surgery had made his scar much less noticeable. His face would always be flawed, but now the world saw a man with a scar, rather than a ruined face. Not that it seemed to matter to Brenda, or Mark; they had eyes only for each other.

"You need to open that sooner than later, Hope," Opaline said, drawing Hope's attention from the couple.

She fumbled with the bow.

Bear came back, handed the empty coffeepot to Sin, the soda jerk from Hollister Drugs who'd taken over counter duty. "What is it?"

"It's a moving present," Opaline said, then winked at Bear.

Hope finally untied the complicated bow and lifted off the lid. "Buckwheat!" She squealed, and lifted out the now full-grown beige bunny with a pink bow tied around his neck. "Are you saying…" She held him against her chest, and he snuggled in until his nose was burrowed into her neck.

"I want you to have him. He'd be so lonely without you."

"Hmm." She nuzzled his softness, then looked up at Bear. "Would you mind?"

"Hon, if you can handle my baggage, I can sure take on yours." He put out a finger and ran it down the bunny's soft flank. "If you want a whole herd of bunnies, love, it's fine with me, as long as you move in with them."

"Awwww. That's so sweet." Indigo DiCarlo, a local winery-owner, walked up, a bottle of the Tippling Widow's award-winning Twice in a Blue Moon Merlot on one slim hip, an envelope in the other hand. She handed the bottle to Jess. "Danovan had to work, but he sent this. For you, not the baby. And here—" she handed over the envelope "—is a gift certificate for free massages twice a month, for a year. I think you're going to need them."

"I think you're right." Jess hugged Indigo. "Thank you."

Bear took a full pot from Sin, and headed out on coffee patrol.

"Hey, Mrs. Settle—" Sin raised her voice to be heard over the babble of the crowd "—does this mean that sweet little cottage behind your house will be for rent?"

Opaline eyed the young girl's piercing-encrusted ears, eyebrows and nose, as well as the skimpy top that displayed her colorful full-sleeve tats. "Why, yes, it does. Are you interested in renting it, Cynthia?"

"Oh, hell—I mean, heck yeah. That place is epic."

"We'd have to talk. I don't allow sex, drugs *or* rock and roll, you know."

Sin put a hand on her hip and tried to look offended. "What would make you think I'm into any of that stuff?"

"Oh, Jesse, I'm so excited for you!" Priss Preston walked up and hugged Jesse's neck. Her husband, Adam, the owner of the town's pharmacy, stood behind her, hand on Nacho's shoulder. He reached around his wife and handed Jesse an envelope. "That's a year's supply of diapers from Hollister Drugs, and Nacho here has something for the baby, too."

Nacho handed Jesse a big-eyed stuffed pound puppy. "I hope you have a boy."

Jesse ruffled his stand-up hair. "We'll know soon enough. Either way, I know the baby will love this. Thank you."

Nacho ducked out from under Jesse's head rub, and looked around. "Hey, there's Bear. I'd better help him out." He wound his way through the crowd to his hero.

Priss's eyes followed him. "Working with Bear has made such a difference in him." She turned to Hope. "I'll never be able to thank him enough for taking Nacho under his wing."

Bear bent to hear what Nacho was saying, then nodded. Hope's heart pinched, seeing the two together. Bear would make such a great dad. Maybe someday... "No thanks are needed. Nacho has been very good for Bear, too. He loves that kid."

"I'm going to give Grandma a break. Looks like my daughter, Princess Olivia, is wearing her out." Priss ran a hand through her short hair. "By the way, Jess, the huge stack of books is from Olivia. Grandma, that is, not her namesake." She and Adam walked away.

"Jesse Jurgen, you're going to be the hottest new mother in town." Bina walked up, her barfly laugh overriding the crowd noise.

Jesse blew on her perfectly manicured fingers. "Well, a girl has to keep herself up you know."

Bina air-kissed both woman's cheeks, and not able to reach Hope, waggled her fingers at her.

"Hey, Bina," Sam said. "When do you want to start your attic remodel?"

"It depends. When can you get Beau to do some custom woodwork? Where is he, anyway? I haven't seen him in forever."

Sam leaned back and draped her elbows on the counter. "He's gotten so busy with his Raven's Rest Artist Colony, he's booked months in advance."

"I heard that Tim Raven left it to Beau in his will." Bina touched Sam's knee. "I know it was a blow to you and Travis, when you lost Tim last spring."

"I miss him every day. But it was a blessing that he and Ana passed within a week of each other. I can't imagine one without the other."

Hope shuffled packages.

"Hey, Jesse, you get to opening those presents." Bryan's red hair made him stand out, even from the far booth across the room. "I got her the most adorable dresses!"

"Fully half these presents are going to be inappropriate, when we find out the sex of the baby," Hope said, handing a package to Jesse. "This one is from Bear."

"Well, we'll just save them for your first." Jesse winked at her cousin.

"Let's not get ahead of ourselves here, Jess. Bear and I moving in together is a big enough step for now."

Jesse tore the paper off the box. "I know, I know. Just let me know when we can start planning the wedding… Oh, my God, how adorable!" She held up a tiny black motorcycle jacket.

The crowd ooh'd and aah'd.

Two hours later, all the presents were opened, gallons of coffee consumed and the sheet cake had been reduced to crumbs. The last of the guests were filing out, and Nacho was shoving the last of the wrapping paper into the garbage bag that Hope held.

Carl walked out of the swinging door to the kitchen, stepped behind his wife, wrapped his arms around her waist and whispered in her ear.

A sexy smile lit her face. "Leave that, Hope, I'll finish in the morning. You've got to be at the library tomorrow, and I've got a date with this hunky Norse god." She stepped out of Carl's embrace and walked over.

"We're done." Nacho took the bag from Hope and pulled the top closed. When he opened the door, the cowbell clanked and he dragged the bag behind him to the large garbage container.

Hope watched him, then turned to Jesse's frank stare. "What?"

"I'm just so proud of you. Who'd have figured you'd end up as a medical research librarian?"

"I'm not, yet. But my training is complete at the end of the month, and UC Santa Barbara tells me they have a position for me," Hope said. "All those career aptitude tests Bina gave me paid off. I can't wait to get to work every day."

"You may not have turned out just like your

mother would have chosen, but I think you're a pretty amazing lady."

"I'm a very happy one, Jess."

Jess hugged her. "Thank you so much for the party. It made me feel so loved."

"Well, in case you haven't noticed, you are, silly. I thought we were going to have to serve people in the parking lot!"

Bear stepped in, cradling Buckwheat in his arms. "Hope, are you ready to go? You've got to get up early, you know."

"You go. Carl and I are going to lock up, and we're out of here, too."

"On my way, big guy. Night, Jess. I love you."

"Love you back, sweetie."

Taking the rabbit from Bear, she bumped her shoulder on the door frame as they walked into the cool November night. When she shivered, Bear's warm, sheltering arm came around her. Following the cold white moonlight to the truck, she looked up. The stars were Swarovski crystals, scattered across the black velvet sky. "God, isn't it beautiful?"

He looked down at her. "Stunning."

"Not me, silly, the stars."

"I'd rather look at you."

Love for him radiated heat from her chest, banishing her shivers.

The overhead light came on when he unlocked the door to the truck, and helped her up. She put

Buckwheat down on the seat, and turned to find Bear looking at her, conflicting emotions flicking across his face.

A thread of worry laced into her warm mood. "What is it? Are you all right?"

"I'm not sure. I'll find out soon." He held out a fist, turned his hand over, and opened his fingers. There, in his big palm, was a small velvet box.

Her heart stumbled and her hand flew to her mouth. "Bear—"

His heavy brows scrunched, meeting over his worried eyes. "It doesn't have to be what you think it is. I wanted to somehow commemorate us moving in together." The box creaked when he opened it. "You can just think of it as a promise…for the future." Cradled in the velvet was an ornately worked open-weave silver band, with a large, pear-cut aquamarine gemstone.

"It's beautiful," she breathed, her hand shaking so hard she was afraid to touch it, for fear she'd drop it.

"Bryan designed it. He helped me pick out the stone. I wanted one to match your eyes." He reached up and touched her cheek. "Would you do me the honor of wearing it?"

"Oh, love—" her heart filled to bursting, she leaned down until her lips hovered over his "—the honor would be all mine."

* * * * *

LARGER-PRINT BOOKS!
GET 2 FREE LARGER-PRINT NOVELS PLUS
2 FREE GIFTS!

❖ HARLEQUIN®
Romance

From the Heart, For the Heart

YES! Please send me 2 FREE LARGER-PRINT Harlequin® Romance novels and my 2 FREE gifts (gifts are worth about $10). After receiving them, if I don't wish to receive any more books, I can return the shipping statement marked "cancel." If I don't cancel, I will receive 4 brand-new novels every month and be billed just $5.09 per book in the U.S. or $5.49 per book in Canada. That's a savings of at least 15% off the cover price! It's quite a bargain! Shipping and handling is just 50¢ per book in the U.S. and 75¢ per book in Canada.* I understand that accepting the 2 free books and gifts places me under no obligation to buy anything. I can always return a shipment and cancel at any time. Even if I never buy another book, the two free books and gifts are mine to keep forever.

119/319 HDN GHWC

Name _____ (PLEASE PRINT) _____

Address _____ Apt. # _____

City _____ State/Prov. _____ Zip/Postal Code _____

Signature (if under 18, a parent or guardian must sign)

Mail to the **Reader Service:**
IN U.S.A.: P.O. Box 1867, Buffalo, NY 14240-1867
IN CANADA: P.O. Box 609, Fort Erie, Ontario L2A 5X3
Want to try two free books from another line?
Call 1-800-873-8635 or visit www.ReaderService.com.

* Terms and prices subject to change without notice. Prices do not include applicable taxes. Sales tax applicable in N.Y. Canadian residents will be charged applicable taxes. Offer not valid in Quebec. This offer is limited to one order per household. Not valid for current subscribers to Harlequin Romance Larger-Print books. All orders subject to credit approval. Credit or debit balances in a customer's account(s) may be offset by any other outstanding balance owed by or to the customer. Please allow 4 to 6 weeks for delivery. Offer available while quantities last.

Your Privacy—The Reader Service is committed to protecting your privacy. Our Privacy Policy is available online at www.ReaderService.com or upon request from the Reader Service.

We make a portion of our mailing list available to reputable third parties that offer products we believe may interest you. If you prefer that we not exchange your name with third parties, or if you wish to clarify or modify your communication preferences, please visit us at www.ReaderService.com/consumerchoice or write to us at Reader Service Preference Service, P.O. Box 9062, Buffalo, NY 14240-9062. Include your complete name and address.

LARGER-PRINT BOOKS!

❖HARLEQUIN *Presents®*

GET 2 FREE LARGER-PRINT NOVELS PLUS 2 FREE GIFTS!

YES! Please send me 2 FREE LARGER-PRINT Harlequin Presents® novels and my 2 FREE gifts (gifts are worth about $10). After receiving them, if I don't wish to receive any more books, I can return the shipping statement marked "cancel." If I don't cancel, I will receive 6 brand-new novels every month and be billed just $5.30 per book in the U.S. or $5.74 per book in Canada. That's a saving of at least 12% off the cover price! It's quite a bargain! Shipping and handling is just 50¢ per book in the U.S. and 75¢ per book in Canada.* I understand that accepting the 2 free books and gifts places me under no obligation to buy anything. I can always return a shipment and cancel at any time. Even if I never buy another book, the two free books and gifts are mine to keep forever.

176/376 HDN GHVY

Name _____ (PLEASE PRINT) _____

Address _____ Apt. # _____

City _____ State/Prov. _____ Zip/Postal Code _____

Signature (if under 18, a parent or guardian must sign)

Mail to the **Reader Service:**
IN U.S.A.: P.O. Box 1867, Buffalo, NY 14240-1867
IN CANADA: P.O. Box 609, Fort Erie, Ontario L2A 5X3

**Are you a subscriber to Harlequin Presents® books
and want to receive the larger-print edition?
Call 1-800-873-8635 today or visit us at www.ReaderService.com.**

* Terms and prices subject to change without notice. Prices do not include applicable taxes. Sales tax applicable in N.Y. Canadian residents will be charged applicable taxes. Offer not valid in Quebec. This offer is limited to one order per household. Not valid for current subscribers to Harlequin Presents Larger-Print books. All orders subject to credit approval. Credit or debit balances in a customer's account(s) may be offset by any other outstanding balance owed by or to the customer. Please allow 4 to 6 weeks for delivery. Offer available while quantities last.

Your Privacy—The Reader Service is committed to protecting your privacy. Our Privacy Policy is available online at www.ReaderService.com or upon request from the Reader Service.

We make a portion of our mailing list available to reputable third parties that offer products we believe may interest you. If you prefer that we not exchange your name with third parties, or if you wish to clarify or modify your communication preferences, please visit us at www.ReaderService.com/consumerschoice or write to us at Reader Service Preference Service, P.O. Box 9062, Buffalo, NY 14240-9062. Include your complete name and address.

HPLP15

LARGER-PRINT BOOKS!
GET 2 FREE LARGER-PRINT NOVELS PLUS
2 FREE GIFTS!

HARLEQUIN®

INTRIGUE

BREATHTAKING ROMANTIC SUSPENSE

YES! Please send me 2 FREE LARGER-PRINT Harlequin® Intrigue novels and my 2 FREE gifts (gifts are worth about $10). After receiving them, if I don't wish to receive any more books, I can return the shipping statement marked "cancel." If I don't cancel, I will receive 6 brand-new novels every month and be billed just $5.49 per book in the U.S. or $6.24 per book in Canada. That's a saving of at least 11% off the cover price! It's quite a bargain! Shipping and handling is just 50¢ per book in the U.S. and 75¢ per book in Canada.* I understand that accepting the 2 free books and gifts places me under no obligation to buy anything. I can always return a shipment and cancel at any time. Even if I never buy another book, the two free books and gifts are mine to keep forever.

199/399 HDN GHWN

Name	(PLEASE PRINT)

Address	Apt. #

City	State/Prov.	Zip/Postal Code

Signature (if under 18, a parent or guardian must sign)

Mail to the **Reader Service:**
IN U.S.A.: P.O. Box 1867, Buffalo, NY 14240-1867
IN CANADA: P.O. Box 609, Fort Erie, Ontario L2A 5X3

Are you a subscriber to Harlequin® Intrigue books
and want to receive the larger-print edition?
Call 1-800-873-8635 today or visit www.ReaderService.com.

* Terms and prices subject to change without notice. Prices do not include applicable taxes. Sales tax applicable in N.Y. Canadian residents will be charged applicable taxes. Offer not valid in Quebec. This offer is limited to one order per household. Not valid for current subscribers to Harlequin Intrigue Larger-Print books. All orders subject to credit approval. Credit or debit balances in a customer's account(s) may be offset by any other outstanding balance owed by or to the customer. Please allow 4 to 6 weeks for delivery. Offer available while quantities last.

Your Privacy—The Reader Service is committed to protecting your privacy. Our Privacy Policy is available online at www.ReaderService.com or upon request from the Reader Service.

We make a portion of our mailing list available to reputable third parties that offer products we believe may interest you. If you prefer that we not exchange your name with third parties, or if you wish to clarify or modify your communication preferences, please visit us at www.ReaderService.com/consumerschoice or write to us at Reader Service Preference Service, P.O. Box 9062, Buffalo, NY 14240-9062. Include your complete name and address.

HILP15

WESTERN **WP** PROMISES

YES! Please send me **The Western Promises Collection** in Larger Print. This collection begins with 3 FREE books and 2 FREE gifts (gifts valued at approx. $14.00 retail) in the first shipment, along with the other first 4 books from the collection! If I do not cancel, I will receive 8 monthly shipments until I have the entire 51-book Western Promises collection. I will receive 2 or 3 FREE books in each shipment and I will pay just $4.99 US/ $5.89 CDN for each of the other four books in each shipment, plus $2.99 for shipping and handling per shipment. *If I decide to keep the entire collection, I'll have paid for only 32 books, because 19 books are FREE! I understand that accepting the 3 free books and gifts places me under no obligation to buy anything. I can always return a shipment and cancel at any time. My free books and gifts are mine to keep no matter what I decide.

272 HCN 3070 472 HCN 3070

Name	(PLEASE PRINT)

Address	Apt. #

City	State/Prov.	Zip/Postal Code

Signature (if under 18, a parent or guardian must sign)

Mail to the **Reader Service:**
IN U.S.A.: P.O. Box 1867, Buffalo, NY 14240-1867
IN CANADA: P.O. Box 609, Fort Erie, Ontario L2A 5X3